Foreign Wars

Foreign Wars

★ ★ ★

Keith Colquhoun

★

John Murray

© Keith Colquhoun 1985

First published 1985
by John Murray (Publishers) Ltd
50 Albemarle Street, London wix 4bd

Typeset by Inforum Ltd, Portsmouth
Printed and bound in Great Britain
by the Bath Press, Bath

British Library CIP Data
Colquhoun, Keith
Foreign wars.
I. Title
823'.914[F]   PR6053.0435
ISBN   0–7195–4210–3

We seemed to see our flag unfurled,
Our champion waiting in his place
For the last battle of the world,
The Armageddon of the race.

JOHN GREENLEAF WHITTIER

There is none so blind as
those that will not see.

MATHEW HENRY

★ 1 ★

James Palmer was English, and he had a fairly commonplace English name, although, like most names in widespread use, it had a history. The first Palmers were pilgrims to the Holy Land who embroidered their clothes with palm leaves, presumably to let anyone know where they were going. James Palmer did not look of pilgrim stock, tramping to places chosen by God for their awkward locations. He was in his sixties, when most people are going off. He would have liked to be thinner, but the body defends its weight. Nevertheless, he got about, as he put it.

For several years he and his wife Susie had taken two holidays, one to Greece, the other in winter to somewhere in England, usually Cornwall. This winter they had been tempted by a bargain holiday in Morocco. Now they were sitting in the sun on the beach at Agadir, and James was reading from an English newspaper, only one day old, the temperatures of English resorts.

'Penzance, fifty-five, raining.'

'We're very lucky,' Susie said. 'How clever you are.'

Susie was within a year of her husband's age. She looked neither younger nor older, but she looked fitter. There was long life in her. She was skinny almost to the point of emaciation, like a piece of wind-dried meat in a Chinese grocer's, and she was already charring in the North African sun. She was as perky and as constant as a dog. James was very fond of her, perhaps loved her.

Susie said she was wondering whether to remove her bikini top. It was a decision that had often occupied her mind on holiday; not in Cornwall where in winter it was too cold to sunbathe, but certainly in Greece where many women discarded their tops, although many did not. Susie had thought vaguely that Morocco, being a Muslim country, might have forbidden sunbathing of any sort, and during the journey from the airport

7

to their hotel she had noticed several women wearing veils. But here on the beach there were numerous women without clothes, or nearly so. None of them, Susie supposed, was Moroccan. She had heard German and French accents and one that James had told her was Swedish. Visitors, it seemed, were exempt from proprieties.

'I think you should,' James said.

'Oh, you would,' Susie said, smiling.

He watched her unfasten the harness. The gesture still gave him a spark, although what was underneath was no more than loose skin. His own breasts were fatter than Susie's.

'Ah, that's much better,' she said, stretching out on her sunbed. She opened a book. 'Very much better.' Susie could read while totally prone, using her stick-like arms like a music stand. It was a trick, James thought, like suspending by your teeth from a rope in a circus. He found it difficult to read unless he was sitting up. He found it difficult to read on the beach at all. He picked up the book he had allocated for his holiday reading. It was *War and Peace*. He was up to page twenty-five, and was beginning to suspect that he wouldn't get much further. On a previous holiday he had read almost one chapter of *The Way of all Flesh*. On nearly all his holidays he had tasted, but regrettably not swallowed, great literature. Susie was more accomplished with her holiday reading. She read at least a book a day. But she brought books she knew she would like rather than the ones James chose, which he suspected he would find tedious but which might contain extraordinary and entirely fresh experiences.

Before he had read more than a few words he was distracted by a couple who were throwing a ball to each other. They were old, a lot older than James and Susie, and were German, or at least spoke to each other in German. James had observed them the previous day. They had arrived on the beach, secured their sunbeds and their parasol, had oiled each other, had conversed for a while and then, at about the same time as today, had taken their ball, a large ball, to a patch of sand away from the sunbathers and played their gentle game. Afterwards, if they kept to the same routine as the previous day, they would have a short swim, dry off in the sun, eat a tangerine each and then leave the beach. James had composed a brief life for them. They would have been young adults in the Second World War, the man presumably in the Wehrmacht, sending her home the spoils of the conqueror, the woman a patriotic activist in some home front activity. There was still something forcefully appealing about her: James imagined that it was she who had bought the ball and ensured that it was not forgotten when they set out for the beach each day. She had probably looked rather fetching in whatever uniform she wore. James wondered if her hair had been blonde. It was now grey and withered.

'What are we going to do about it today?' Susie said.

James's reverie dissolved. Susie was asking about her luggage, which had been lost by the airline.

'I'll phone them again. At lunchtime.'

'Should we have phoned them this morning?'

'They said about one. The next flight's due at noon. So I'll try at one.'

'I think it's gone; don't you, James?'

'It'll turn up. They're pretty sure it will turn up.'

'But can you believe them?'

'I believe it must be somewhere. Unless it's been stolen. It might have been stolen.'

'Am I moaning, James? Shut me up if I'm moaning.'

'You've been very brave. Not moaning at all.'

Susie resumed reading.

Perhaps brave was too strong a word. Fortitude might be more accurate. Even that might be an exaggeration if one was referring to a normal hazard. But holidays were not normal. On holiday you bought a morsel of unreality. The sun shone, meals appeared and all the messes of living were disposed of by invisible means. The lost luggage was an intrusion by the normal world. Someone had been normally careless and stupid. Susie's suitcase, which should have arrived with all the other dreamy holiday luggage on the carousel at Agadir airport but didn't was now in the thrall of the bureaucracy of the normal world. It was that, James thought, rather than the value of the missing garments, that had cast a shadow over the holiday.

'It's an intrusion,' James said. 'That's what I resent.'

'And my clothes. I do miss them.'

'Of course you do.'

The German couple had finished their game and were eating

9

their tangerines. The man looked up before James could look away. James called across, 'No swim today?'

The German either did not hear or did not understand. He looked away. But his wife, assuming it was his wife, looked up and waved, a dainty wave, with her fingers. The gesture modified James's judgement of her past; it was not the wave of a former member of the Hitler youth.

'Who's that?' Susie said.

'Just the courtesies of the beach.'

Susie looked in the direction of the Germans. 'I'd love a tangerine,' she said.

James walked to the edge of the beach where the tangerine seller squatted. He asked for two tangerines, holding up two fingers. The merchant put five in a plastic bag and asked for a dirham.

'I had to get five,' he said when he returned to Susie.

'You're so extravagant.'

James smiled but he did feel a trace of anxiety about what to do with three tangerines. He could take them back to the hotel room, but there was a bowl of them there. Morocco seemed abundant with tangerines. He wondered if the Germans had a tangerine problem. Probably they insisted on two and no more and beat the merchant down to half a dirham.

'That was good,' Susie said.

'Have another.'

'Not for me.'

'We have three over.'

'Sling them,' Susie said. She was not wasteful, but she was practical. 'Shall we go up? The Germans have gone.'

James and Susie walked from the beach to the road, past a row of gift shops where they declined urgent invitations from the owners to look inside, had their first drink of the day at the Djellaba Bar, and then moved on to their hotel. Already they had a routine.

Before lunch James phoned the airport about Susie's luggage. This was the fourth call he had made since the luggage had been lost, so a routine had been established about that, too. He knew the airport number and had a name to ask for when he got through.

'Mr Yussef, please.'

'Good afternoon, Mr Palmer.' The man who specialised in lost luggage spoke recognisable English. The missing suitcase was not on the flight that had just arrived. Another flight was due that evening. This, James realised, was all the hard information that the call was going to yield, but it gave him some tiny comfort to spin out the call as long as possible, and Susie would expect it. So he said that it was important that the case should be found as soon as possible; it contained his wife's entire holiday wardrobe, and its loss had cast a shadow over the holiday; and it seemed extraordinary that this one case, checked in at London at the same moment as his own case, had gone missing; and could it have been stolen, and where could it have gone, and was this exceptional or did it happen frequently? All this had been said by James during previous calls, but Mr Yussef listened, seemingly intently and with occasional murmurs of sympathy, as though each thought was new. In reply he said that he had sent telex messages to Casablanca, Marrakech and London, that, yes, luggage was sometimes lost, but it always turned up, sometimes sooner, sometimes later. All this had also been said before, but James listened to it in the hope that there might be some phrase, some illumination, that would help to recover the luggage.

'So what's the next move?'

'Move?'

'What happens next?'

'I shall send another telex, Mr Palmer. To Casablanca. All flights come through Casa.'

He waited for James to open up a new line of thought on the subject of lost luggage, but his repertoire was exhausted. They said goodbye and James had the momentary feeling that Mr Yussef was sorry that they had nothing more to talk about. He gave the impression of enjoying his work.

James found Susie by the pool. She was talking to a woman who was very carefully packing her neatly waved hair into a bathing hat.

'Merle, this is my husband James.'

'James: what a good, solid name.' She had an American accent. She took his hand and squeezed it firmly. She was about Susie's age but did not have Susie's mummified simplicity. Perhaps she had been preserved in an American way with lotions and pills.

'Merle is going south,' Susie said.

11

'I'm hot enough here,' James said.

Merle nodded, as though she agreed with James. Perhaps she couldn't hear properly under the bathing hat. She stood and did a neat shallow dive into the pool, surfaced, turned, gave them a smile through her waterproof makeup, then struck out strongly for the far side. The pool looked only barely adequate to contain her.

'Has she got a husband?' James said.

'Don't say you fancy her.'

'I just wondered what her husband is like. Whether all the strength has gone to her.'

'Ah, appearances. Merle has a nervous disposition. Someone has just told her that Agadir has earthquakes.'

'It had one.'

'One is enough. She's off south tomorrow.'

'There's a civil war in the south.'

'Oh dear. Merle won't like that.'

'What won't I like?'

Merle was back on the bank of the pool, beached, an amazon grandmother. She seemed to have remarkably good hearing.

'James says there's a civil war in the south.'

'Tell me something else. Africa is so dangerous.'

James was about to ask why she had come, but did not want to sound impolite. He didn't think of Morocco as being Africa: Africa was the returning heart of darkness where western-educated cannibal chiefs ate each other.

'Morocco is safe,' he said. 'You shouldn't worry, and spoil your holiday.'

'Safe! With earthquakes and wars. You English are so cool.'

'The earthquake was quite a time ago. There is a war, but you won't be allowed to go near it.'

Merle said nothing. She was occupied removing her bathing hat without disturbing her hair. James looked at Susie, who received his silent message and stood up.

'I'm famished,' she said. 'Merle?'

'You go ahead. I'll dry off. *Ciao.*'

'*Ciao,*' James mimicked as he and Susie walked up the hotel terrace for lunch.

'Don't make snap judgements. She's quite pleasant. Would I like her if she wasn't nice?'

When they were eating Susie said, 'And how is Mr Yussef today?'

'Nothing doing yet.'

'So you said.'

'Did I say that?'

'Didn't you, darling? But I guessed there·wouldn't be.'

'It could be anywhere in the world.'

'I won't see it again, I know that.'

'I'm doing my best.'

Susie saw the warning signal and touched him on the arm. 'Of course you are, darling. You've been marvellous.'

'You'll need more things?'

Susie smiled. 'I shan't break the bank. You don't need too many furs in Agadir.'

'Shall we have a look round later?'

'I'm letting you off that punishment. Merle's coming with me. She knows some good shops. So you can thank her for that.'

James felt relieved that he would not be going shopping, although he did not feel that he should thereby warm towards Merle. The random thought that had come to him was a reckoning of the time he had taken to make his phone call to the airport, waiting for the hotel operator to make the connnection, waiting for Mr Yussef to answer, talking to Mr Yussef, and then the minute or two he had spent looking for Susie. The whole exercise had taken perhaps a quarter of an hour, to be generous. During that time Susie had met Merle and they had exchanged a series of confidences: Merle's anxiety about earthquakes and her plan to go south, and Susie's lost luggage and where she could buy some more clothes. In a quarter of an hour they had come to know each other, or thought they had.

'What are you thinking?'

James was about to tell her, but decided that his thoughts would sound critical, when they were no more than an observation. He suddenly felt warm and benign, at this table on this pleasant terrace, with the sun out and looking at flowers that belonged to the summer, and with the sea in the distance, and nibbling at the light summery meal, which wasn't at all bad, and sipping the local wine, which was surprisingly smooth.

'I was thinking that I loved you,' he said, 'and that I hope this luggage business hasn't spoiled your holiday.'

13

Susie looked momentarily questioning but a firm statement will usually dismiss a suspicion. 'I love you, too,' she said abstractly. 'You don't think there's anything in this earthquake thing, do you?'

'Nothing,' James said, but searching his mind for some convincing reason, some expert titbit that would convince Susie, he merely turned over a dunghill of barely understood information accumulated from sleepily watched television programmes, of seismic waves and bits of the earth's crust that moved under the sea. All he knew for certain was that there had been an earthquake in Agadir, but that was not particulary reassuring, as presumably another could happen in the same spot.

'Nothing.' He smiled broadly. 'But I shall save you. Merle will have to look after herself.'

After lunch when Susie went shopping with Merle, James sat by the pool resolved to persevere with *War and Peace*. After half an hour of diligence he rewarded himself with a swim. It seemed cold entering the pool, colder than the sea. But he immersed himself, did two strokes and drifted on to his back and felt the warmth returning to his body. How pleasant it was here, the perfect destination in the still centre of the day, better even than sleep. He felt indifferent to anything in the world. He had arrived safely after a journey of what seemed a huge number of years to lie in a pool at Agadir. That is how he should have answered Susie's question about earthquakes. He felt the same about the bomb, and the discourtesies of the superpowers and threats to the environment. They were problems for the young. Serve them right. He was old enough not to be selfish about death. He swam slowly for two lengths, got out of the pool, lay on a sun chair and allowed himself to drain.

But something had happened to disturb his reverie. During his second length of the pool he thought he had seen a face that was familiar to him. He scanned the pool but it was now empty. On the opposite side of the pool there was a man briskly towelling himself, but he had his face turned away from James's view. James waited but the man settled down without offering his face for identification. James considered wandering around to the other side of the pool to get a better look, but rational thought argued against curiosity. He wasn't sure that this was the man he had seen in the pool; and if it were he could not remember who the man was. He was surprised that he was still thinking about the incident; it was just that the glimpse in the pool had been strong, a face he should have recognised, but which was offered with subliminal speed. Perhaps it was the face of a showbiz personality or a politician, someone whose face had been in the papers too often recently, or someone who looked like him. It did not matter. It no longer irritated him. James went to sleep. He awoke knowing whom he had seen, or thought he had seen. After a few moments he put a name to him. Watney. James looked around the pool. The man who might have been Watney was gone. The pool was almost deserted. It was now mid-afternoon, when even in Agadir the winter sun begins to expire.

James put on his shirt. He was content that he had retrieved the ghost from his memory: it was like winning a little prize. But he wasn't proposing to go in search of him, even if he were still in the hotel. He had known Watney more than twenty years previously; and not really known him then, not as a friend. If he happened to see him again he might say hallo, if Watney also showed some sign of recognising him, or he might not. It was pleasant to know that people from the past were still alive, but that was all. He would tell Susie about it. She would be interested.

James went upstairs to his room and changed. When he came down again he found Susie and Merle in the bar. Susie's shopping seemed to have been successful.

'Don't look so anxious, darling. Some of this stuff is Merle's. And you're lucky we didn't come back with a carpet. We were practically importuned by this awful man.'

'We were kidnapped,' Merle said.

They shared their story, telling it in bursts. Susie's manner often mirrored the person she happened to be with, and now she chose to be girlish. It was a form of physical exercise, James thought, as she told of the adventure in jerky sentences that sometimes strained the syllables, part of the practice of trying to stay youthful. Susie believed in exercise. James didn't disbelieve in it, but he didn't practise it.

'Aren't they super, darling?'

Susie was holding up for his inspection a pair of rather fully-cut trousers made of blue silk, or a silky material, flecked with glitter, gathered sharply at the ankles. They could have been

15

long bloomers but the phrase harem pants came into James's mind.

They looked awful but James said, 'An Arabian night. You spoil me.'

'They're not for me, silly. You haven't been listening.'

Merle smiled at James, a trifle coyly, he thought. 'The truth is,' she said, 'this trip means something special for George and me. A kind of romantic thing.'

George was presumably Merle's husband, soon to be offered his amazon gift-wrapped in an Agadir souk.

'A second honeymoon?' Susie said. She approved of second honeymoons. Most of their holidays were second honeymoons.

'That sort of thing. Now this is a secret. George has been playing around. Nothing serious. We still adore each other. But I was hurt. So . . .'

Susie touched Merle on the hand. 'Very hurt. Isn't that dreadful, James?'

It did sound dreadful. Merle and George did seem quite a dreadful pair. 'Dreadful,' he said, murmuring the word, but with such an intensity that Susie said quickly, 'Well, things are all right now. I expect that's why you came to Morocco, for the romance.'

'It did seem to have a romance, before we heard about the earthquakes and all.' She gave a small laugh. 'So now you know our secret, our little fairy tale.'

If it were a fairy tale, James thought, it would resemble one of the sombre stories collected by the Grimm brothers, a compact human tragedy composed of rejection, suspicion and perhaps physical violence when the infidelity had been discovered. A slap from Merle could stun a man. Perhaps George would have stunned her back, although, for some reason, James imagined him to be a small man. But now Merle had regained possession of her man, who was contrite, and had brought her to Morocco where he was now being forced to act the role of ardent lover. Merle had won and was happily advertising her victory over her wayward husband, even to casual acquaintances in a hotel bar. Or she could be telling a lie to cover her humiliation. James no longer saw her as a silly matron of unusual build. She was a person, but he still felt antipathy towards her. It was not necessarily true that you liked people once you got to know them.

16

James signalled to the barman.

'No more for me,' Merle said. 'I've been very naughty, sitting here. A quick packing job and then we're off.' She got up, offered a hand to James. Susie she gave a peck on the cheek. 'You've been so supportive, darling.'

Susie didn't want another drink either. James ordered a beer for himself. It now seemed very quiet. Merely to make sounds, he said, 'Merle's leaving soon, then?'

'It seems. She's quite vague about it.'

'She sounded quite positive.'

'George will decide. I think she's really under his thumb.'

George in James's imagination grew physically taller.

'What does he do?'

'Dunno. Retired, I think. All Americans abroad seem to be retired.' Susie got up. 'I feel quite weary. I think I'll stretch out on the bed for an hour. Would you like to see the things I bought? I promise you there are no harem pants.'

James signed the bill for the drinks and they went up to their room. Susie had bought two dresses, some underwear and a pair of shoes. The previous day she had bought one dress and a swimsuit. She thought she now had enough to last her, provided it stayed warm.

'But I suppose I'll need a case.'

'Unless yours turns up.'

'It was already full.'

'There's some room in mine, I think.'

'Well, we'll see, darling James.' She put her arms around his neck and kissed him. 'Do you love me, devotedly?'

It was an embrace of affection rather than passion, a ritual of close companionship that had suddenly become due.

'Devotedly.'

'That's good.'

Susie lay on her bed and seemingly immediately went to sleep.

James lay on his bed and read *War and Peace*. He had now entered the book, was past the introduction, past the list of characters, and had committed himself to the chapters. He thought that this time he might make it to the other side.

'I'd like to get to the end of it,' he said to Susie at dinner.

'But are you enjoying it?'

'I think I am.'

'Like jogging: you feel it must be doing you good?'

'Would I be so silly?'

'Quite silly: you are a lovely silly man.'

The dining room was very full. Susie perused it in case Merle had arrived since her previous perusal.

'I expect she's still doing her quick packing job,' James said. Less expectantly, he wondered if Watney might be there.

'Would you recognise him?' Susie said.

'I did in the pool. I think I did.'

'People look quite different in their clothes.'

'He was a lean chap. What you expect a soldier to be.'

'That was centuries ago. In the war?'

'Not that long ago. But a long time ago. Years. Decades, I suppose.'

'Did I ever meet him?'

'Possibly.' James did a pantomime calculation on his fingers. 'We'd have been courting.'

'Is that him?' Susie directed James to a man eating at a table on the far side of the room. He had two women with him, of an age when one might be his wife and the other a grown-up daughter.

'No. I don't think so.'

'He looks soldierly. About your age.'

That was true. If James had provided a description, say, to the police, of someone they wanted to question, and said that he was middle aged and of soldierly appearance, this man eating his dinner would be a likely suspect. But he wasn't the man James had seen in the pool that afternoon, or if he was, he wasn't Watney.

'I'm beginning to think it was an illusion,' James said. 'I was feeling a bit sleepy.'

Before they went to bed Susie phoned Merle's room to invite her for a nightcap, but there was no reply. They did not see her next morning either, and for the rest of the day they were away from the hotel on a coach trip to another town, called Taroudant. On the day after that they returned to their routine of the morning on the beach, where the German couple's ball rolled towards James and he returned it amid smiles and gestures, and they had their drink at the Djellaba Bar and lunch on the hotel terrace, and James phoned Mr Yussef at the airport and confirmed that Susie's luggage was still lost. In the afternoon they sat by the pool. They had a routine there, too, sitting in, or near, the same place, which they had decided was sheltered from the afternoon wind. Nearby there was a noticeboard headed *Programme d'Animation*, with a list of promised events. The morning's attractions had been volley-ball and water-polo, and now, according to the schedule, there should be jelly games. However, no one was playing games. James suspected that there had been no games that morning either. On their first day at the hotel they had spent the morning by the pool and there had been no games, although games had, as now, been advertised on the board, carefully written in chalk and apparently renewed each day, for on some days the jelly games were in the morning rather than in the afternoon.

'Thank God for a civilised face.' Merle gave each of them an embrace and squatted down between their chairs. She looked full of news.

'But where have you been?' she said.

'Here, all the time,' Susie said. 'Well, yesterday we had an outing, but otherwise here. All the time. We thought you'd gone.'

Merle looked from one to another, smiling broadly. 'It's good to see you both again. Susie, I've got so much to tell you.' She placed a hand on Susie's arm.

James by now was standing. 'Would you like a drink or something, Merle? Celebrate our reunion.'

Merle bequeathed an even broader smile. 'You're so courteous. But nothing alcoholic right now. I thought I'd have tea here in the sunshine, and my wayward husband has promised to pour out. Why don't we make it a party?'

'I'd love a cup of tea,' Susie said.

Merle waved a hand that could not be ignored. A waiter appeared, and was given an order. 'We'll have sticky cakes and everything,' she said. 'A real English high tea.'

'Lovely,' Susie said, 'but that's not really what we call high tea.'

James sat down again, and withdrew into introspection as Susie explained the intricacies of high tea to Merle who listened with the sort of attention that Margaret Mead gave to Polynesian storytellers when she was coming of age in Samoa. He would quite liked to have had a drink, perhaps the first whisky of the day. But he seemed to have assented to tea. Merle was an

19

intrusion, but only to him, and he was becoming used to her. Susie seemed to be delighted at her reappearance.

Watney was standing about twenty yards away. This was not the man Susie had pointed out in the hotel dining room. This was the man James had seen in the pool. He wondered if he should go up to say hallo. It would be quite pleasant to do that. They might have a drink together.

Merle had her arm raised again, partly to interrupt Susie, partly to signal to her husband.

'There he is, the naughty man.'

Watney came towards them.

'George, I want you to meet two very good English friends of mine.'

He shook hands with Susie and then with James. 'I'm very glad to know you, Susie. But I think James and I have already met.'

'In the pool?'

George Watney looked puzzled.

'It doesn't matter. I thought I caught a glimpse of you in the pool the other day.'

George shook his head slightly and smiled, showing a set of very regular teeth. James remembered the teeth. They were beautifully cared-for American teeth. The rest of him looked cared for, too. A Dorian Gray. James felt worn.

'I remember exactly,' George Watney said. 'Norfolk, England, 1958. I ran the American base. You were in publishing? We got on perfectly.'

It wasn't exact, but it was still a remarkable recollection to be summoned seemingly instantly from his memory. It was so spontaneous that for a moment James hardly believed it could be produced without the sort of fumbling through the memory that James himself would have to do. But it went with the body. George Watney's mind had presumably been kept in similar condition.

'How are things going?' Watney asked, as though they had last met only a month ago.

'I'm still in Norfolk,' said James, hating his apologetic tone.

'Still in media?'

'Printing. My father's dead now, of course. I think you dealt with him more than me.'

'So you own it all now? I'm impressed.'

20

'And you?'

'Just a soldier still. And not that for much longer.'

'Hey, you two,' Merle called. 'You having a party on your own?' She stage-whispered to Susie, 'Such gossips, men. Why can't they be like us?' It wasn't a very sharp joke, but everyone laughed amiably. Tea had arrived, and a table had been found to put it on. There were no sticky cakes, but there were some biscuits. George poured out, first lifting the lid from the pot and stirring the tea. 'You see,' he said, talking 'perhaps to James, perhaps to Merle, 'I haven't forgotten my English lessons.'

James now remembered Watney's wife and she hadn't been Merle. That wasn't surprising, not surprising at all that a man should remarry; for all he knew Watney had had several wives as well as being, according to Merle, unfaithful. What was her name? His memory again. Neither could he recall what she looked like physically, but he recalled her, what?, her tone, and it wasn't Merle's tone, although she, too, had had a strong personality. Perhaps the only difference was that he had liked her, and he didn't particularly like Merle.

'Have you been to this part before?' Watney was continuing to make polite conversation and James answered him politely, exchanging commonplace for commonplace and taking his turn to ask similarly undemanding questions. Watney, it seemed, had had an army career in numerous places that James had only vaguely heard of and had now retired or was about to retire, it was not exactly clear: but he had plans. James asked what plans and Watney said that he was interested in films. 'Perhaps something in your line. The British are very good at films.'

James could think of no way in which he, a provincial printer, could in Watney's mind be connected with films. Perhaps Watney's memory wasn't so good after all.

After tea, when James and Susie were alone again, sitting on the balcony of their room, and James was looking at, but not reading, *Le Monde*, which was the only newspaper he had been able to buy at the hotel bookstall, he suddenly said, 'Frances!'

Susie looked up from her book and James said, 'George Watney's first wife. I've been trying to think of her name.'

'Couldn't you have asked him?'

'I suppose so. I didn't want to get too personal.'

'You'd never be that, James.'

21

'Merle was there. Wives don't always like to be reminded about their predecessors.'

'There's nothing reticent about Merle. Fancy her turning out to be your friend's wife. Isn't that extraordinary!'

It wasn't really extraordinary, James thought. A coincidence certainly, but coincidences were normal. Two Americans were staying in the hotel and they turned out to be husband and wife. That was not extraordinary. They were the only Americans he had come across in the hotel, so it was perfectly probable that they should be a couple. He might have connected them earlier had not Merle given him the impression, somehow, that her husband was a small man.

James meeting Watney after many years; that was not ordinary, but it was not really extraordinary. People you hadn't seen for ages did sometimes turn up suddenly. But Watney's immediate recollection of James, the date they had known each other: that was extraordinary, almost as though Watney had been expecting to meet him, which was absurd.

'Little puzzles,' James said.

'Sorry?' Susie looked up from her book again.

'I was thinking that so many things are puzzling: how Watney recognised me so quickly, where Merle disappeared to and why she hasn't gone away to escape the earthquakes.'

'Oh, mysteries. You think they are mysterious?'

'Not a bit. Mysteries are things that are explained eventually. These are tiny disturbances that may be explained but probably won't. You get a dozen of them every day.'

'I don't.'

'You don't notice them any more.'

'Merle is going to ask George about our luggage.'

'I didn't mean that sort of puzzle.'

'He knows the King of Morocco.'

James laughed.

'Don't you believe him?'

'I'm laughing because I do believe him. He's just the sort of person Watney would know, or would have met. What's he going to do, phone him up and blast him off?'

Susie did not smile. 'He could talk to a courtier or someone. We don't seem to be getting anywhere.'

By 'we' she meant James. The remark was meant to wound, but

22

James found it did not wound him. He was still smiling over Watney's offer, or Merle's offer on behalf of her husband. It had grandeur.

'I'm sorry,' Susie said quickly.

That evening the hotel receptionist handed a note to James which said that the missing luggage was at the airport.

'You see,' he said, showing the note to Susie, 'the King has intervened.'

'This is most marvellous, James. How do we get it?'

'Lacking a royal delivery service, I suppose we'll have to take a taxi.'

At the airport Susie's lost luggage stood alone in the arrival area, seemingly undamaged but presumably weary after its unmapped journey. James had the feeling that for a moment Susie was about to embrace it, but instead she planted a kiss on Mr Yussef's cheek. He shook hands warmly with them both and shook hands again with James before they stepped into the taxi that took them back to the hotel.

'I distinctly got the impression that he'll miss our daily talk,' James said to Susie. 'But no doubt others will take my place.'

Susie telephoned Merle's room to tell her the luggage had been found. 'She was so glad,' Susie reported to James. 'But she hadn't said anything to George yet.'

'I expect the King guessed what was up. A little puzzle, or is this a mystery?'

'Now you are being beastly. But I probably deserve it. Thank you, darling James, for all you did.'

The following day Merle accompanied James and Susie to the beach. George, for some reason, could not come or did not want to come: Merle's explanation was not clear. James wondered if Merle would remove her top, and prepared himself not to notice if she did. A great number of breasts of the pale northern nations were being heated slowly in gentle winter sun, although, equally, a sizeable minority of women had retained their tops, among them the elderly German woman with the beachball, with whom James was now on nodding and waving terms. Her top, James observed, was of a substantial manufacture, more a bodice than a top. Susie had discarded her top with a naturalness that belied her hesitation a few days before. Merle, though, still had her top on. She was on her sunbed, but not yet lying down. She

23

was scanning the beach like, like what, a voyeur? Hardly. But like someone hesitating before entering a very exclusive shop for the first time and wondering how she looked. She saw Susie watching her.

'It's easy for you Europeans,' Merle said. 'But Americans aren't used to this sort of thing.'

She said it lightly but, James thought, it had a strand of distress, of American uncertainty under its bullet-proof exterior. Subsequently Merle would tell her friends of this beach, giving it an atmosphere of naughtiness, of decadence even, certainly of foreign liberalism. James could hear her words as she told it. Her top came away. She fumbled with a button and then her American breasts came into full public view. James felt a twitch of response. He found it vaguely erotic to see her naked, partly because she was a friend, at least of Susie, and partly because of the suspense created as Merle had fretted over her decision. She looked at James, a trifle defiantly he thought.

He smiled at her. 'Very nice,' he said. It was a remark that came out of nowhere and was, he thought, utterly out of character. But he was glad he had made it, and had said it without embarrassment. It sounded European.

He picked up his book. He had become absorbed by the lives of the Rostov and the Bolkonsky families, and found it easy to progress by way of Tolstoy's short chapters and his way of quickly changing the scene if things looked like getting boring. James thought it an easy read for a masterpiece, more like following a radio serial. Tolstoy offered his readers the politeness of clarity. However, on a beach even Tolstoy has competition. James watched a Moroccan who was seemingly trying to sell blankets. He went from group to group and at each place was turned away by shakes of the head before he could begin his spiel, almost before he could offer his smile. But occasionally, say every dozen times, a woman allowed him to approach, or did not have the determination of turn him away, and he knelt before her and she was induced to hold one end of a blanket, which he then spread out. But the result, although delayed, was the same: he was dismissed without the blanket being bought. On previous days when James had been on the beach he had observed the blanket man going through the same routine, and had not once seen him make a sale. Yet he did not seem perturbed. He proceeded on his destiny of failure. He had now paused and was talking to another Moroccan who looked after a number of sailboards in an enclosure near the sea. Each morning he dragged the boards from their hut, rigged their sails and set up a notice offering them for hire. Not once had James seen a sailboard taken out to sea. He wondered how the blanket man and the sailboard man lived, and what they were discussing now. He felt, as he had sometimes felt in Greece, that he was missing a sense. He had a passport, air ticket, money and a phrase-book but none of these enabled him to know how these two men survived. He stood.

'It's time to swim,' he said.

Susie said she was too comfortable where she was. Merle looked uncertain.

'Isn't the Med polluted?'

James contemplated the lacy border of the Atlantic.

'I believe it is.'

'That's enough for me.'

The beach was broad and composed of sand that started dry and became moist and then slappily wet. As James marched to the sea, he thought momentarily of Margate when the tide was out. Then in the shallows he saw a dead jellyfish. It was huge, not a Margate jellyfish. James swam a few strokes, then turned on his back, his favourite swimming position. There were a few dozen people in the sea, most of them women. All wore tops. One dressed up to go swimming. He stretched out his arms, lowered his head and became a piece of flotsam. A wave broke over his face and salt entered his eyes. He returned to the beach.

Merle looked at him with curiosity.

'Lovely,' James said.

'You Europeans.'

James and Susie stopped for their beer at the Djellaba Bar, but Merle said she would go on to the hotel, because George would be looking for her.

'She probably thought the glasses would be polluted,' James said.

'Poor Merle. You're unkind.'

'Rather decent, I thought.'

'That business about the Med.'

'I didn't want to show up her ignorance. Frances would have known where the Med was.'

'Frances? Oh, yes.' A pause. 'You're sure there was a Frances?'

'Of course. A lovely woman.'

'You're sure George Watney was married before?'

'He was married to Frances, I'm sure of that. Is Merle saying he wasn't?'

'She just gives the impression she's known Watney all her life, all his career. She's not particularly reticent about what she says about him. But she's never mentioned a Frances.'

'They had two children, Frank and Pretty, short for Prettiford. How's that for remembering?'

'Merle's never mentioned them either. She said they have no children.'

'These were Frances's, not hers.'

'A little puzzle?'

'Something banal, I expect.'

'I shall ask her, right out. I must know before she goes.'

'She's going again?'

'Tomorrow. She wants us to have a farewell drink tonight.' James looked unenthusiastic.

'We needn't go if you don't want to. She left it open. She just wants to say goodbye to her pals.'

'A party?'

'Just a few friends, I think. Nothing formal. These things happen on holiday, James.'

★ 2 ★

The party was not the informal affair that Susie had promised.
James had assumed that they would have a drink or two in
the Watneys' room, or in a corner of the bar; and Susie, it seemed,
had assumed this, too. But during the afternoon a note was
pushed under their door which told them to come to an address a
mile or two outside Agadir. James had shown it to the taxi driver,
who had charged an extortionate fare: Moroccan taximen, at
least, did not believe in the philosophy of failure. The building
was not a hotel, but neither did it look like a private house. A
doorkeeper showed them into a large room where there were
perhaps eighty people, all of whom seemed to belong to each
other: they were an entity. A number of men were in military
uniform and their women were dressed for parade. James was
glad that Susie had persuaded him to wear a suit. She had taken
great care over her own dress.

'I suppose this is the place?' James said.

'Of course it is. There's Merle now.' Susie gave a small wave in
the direction of the middle of the crowd.

'I love these informal gatherings.'

'Don't be awkward. You know what Americans are like. Any
excuse to put on a show.'

Merle detached herself from whoever she was talking to and
came towards Susie with her arms outstretched. They embraced
like two staunch friends long separated since this morning.

'Merle, this is lovely.'

'People are so kind. I love your emerald. James, you're so
well-pressed.'

She moved them into the room and introduced them to a
couple whose names James knew he would not remember.
'That's the way to the drinks,' she said, pointing to a corner of the
room. 'I'm real sorry it's a paid bar, but you can use anything,
cash, plastic, beads if you like, or sign for it. The food is free.'

27

James was surprised but not dismayed that he had to pay for their drinks. At least he wouldn't have to drink party plonk. He bought a whisky for himself and a gin for Susie. When he got back to the couple they had been introduced to, Susie had moved on. He stayed there, sipping his own drink and holding Susie's in a stand-by position.

'This always seems to happen to me.' How quickly one slipped into the party vernacular expected of one's tribe.

'So you're one of George's old English comrades?'

'I knew him in England long ago. Not a comrade, perhaps, but a friend. And you?'

The American looked as though he might well be a comrade. He looked a bit younger than Watney, though of his generation.

'You could say I'd come a long way to raise a glass to George. But I can't match your journey. When did you get in?'

'We've been here five days, no, six.'

'Making a holiday of it?'

'We are on holiday.'

The two men stared at each other for a moment, seeking to clarify the ambiguities in their conversation without being impolite. Susie appeared at James's side and took her gin.

'James, you must come and meet this splendid person. She wants to know about printing.'

James smiled to disconnect himself from the comrade and his wife and followed Susie through the crowd. The splendid person was thinking of starting her own newspaper. She looked as though she had money to waste, James thought. Her wardrobe was probably full of the skins of endangered species.

'I know very little about newspapers,' he said.

'That's not what Susie says. I think you're a reticent Englishman.'

'We have much to be reticent about these days.'

'Oh, God, that's wonderful.' She reached out to a man nearby. 'Cliff, listen to this wonderful Englishman.'

Cliff made paper which, he said, was man's most important raw material. 'As you will know, being in print.'

James nodded. In print: it was a useful, all-purpose, meaningless phrase. He must tell it to Susie, who seemed to give the impression that he was either a press baron or a journalist. James bought himself another drink and one for Cliff, who seemed to be easy to be with: he talked readily and undemandingly and only required an occasional nod from James without sliding in questions to test his comprehension.

'You were having a very deep conversation with that man,' Susie said when he found himself next to her a little while later.

'You know me. Good mixer.'

'What were you talking about?'

'Paper, I think. Paper and business.'

'You having fun?'

'No.'

But James did now feel within the maw of the party, still not an insider, but not an outsider either. He looked at Susie's glowing face as she prepared to make her next foray into the crowd. He did it all for her, he told himself.

'That's Gerard,' Susie said, 'the one over there who looks like a boy.'

'Is he not a boy?'

'He's a film director. He's making a film with your George Watney.'

'About what?'

'Some film or other. He's not very forthcoming. Clever, though.'

James supposed he would have to be clever to be a film director so young. He could have passed for a teenager, although he was probably in his mid-twenties, perhaps older. James had known one film director: not a celebrity, he had made advertising films that lasted a minute or two. But he had carried with him a touch of Hollywood confidence with his corduroy jacket, his baseball cap and his taste for Perrier water. But brilliance presumably had a different look today. Gerard had short hair and, like every man in the room, wore a tie, although the knot was very loose, half-way down his shirt front, as though he did not wish to be wholly associated with it. He had metal-framed spectacles that appeared unusually clean, as though they had just been bought.

'Is Gerard his first name or his surname?'

'Dunno. Want to meet him?'

'Perhaps later. I see the free food has arrived. I feel hungry after all this socialising.'

The food was rich and tantalising. Someone with imagination

had selected it with the insight that novelty is as much appreciated by adults as it is at children's parties. James was eating his
third quail's egg when someone, one of the men in uniform,
called for silence. He said he wasn't going to make a long speech
because George Watney had told him not to, and George thought
he could still give orders. Laughter.

'But this is the main feature and I'm in charge.' Laughter,
cheers and a whistle. Then a raised hand for silence. James
thought he looked a very American American, relaxed and
confident, as sure of his audience as the compère of a television
show. He told a joke that James did not understand, but everyone
else did, or at least laughed at, some to the point of hysteria.

'But to be serious for a moment, for just a moment (a woman's
giggle from somewhere), George Watney brought command to a
new state of the art. This is classified, but let me run it by you. If it
gets out I'll be belly up.'

James had a memory of the last time he had been to the cinema,
and an American film had been showing and he had suddenly
realised that he didn't fully understand much of the conversation. It was partly the fault of the sound, which was too loud, and
some of the vocabulary was unfamiliar, but it was the phrasing
that was peculiar. His ears could not immediately decode it. If he
shut his eyes, cutting out the context, it was as unintelligible
as German or Italian, a passage of sound in which he could
occasionally recognise an English word. On the way home he had
remarked to Susie that American would eventually have to be
taught in English schools as a foreign language, but she had
laughed and said that she had enjoyed the film.

The American spoke for about ten minutes, then he handed
over a number of parcels to Watney who said that ever since he
was a child he had always delayed opening presents until the
last moment (laughter), and he wasn't going to change his childhood habits now (more laughter); they would have to be satisfied
with his thanks and his conviction that the parcels contained
just what he wanted (scattered laughter). He would always
remember the airplane folks of Morocco, which was a free
country because the Americans had been prepared to kick ass
when freedom was threatened (subdued murmurs of concord). 'I
sometimes think that we don't kick ass enough, if the ladies will
excuse the expression.' (Applause.) 'But I have been just a

30

soldier taking orders.' He thanked Merle for putting up with a soldier's life, for being ready to follow him from camp to camp, but he hoped that did not make her sound like a camp follower (shriek of delight from Merle). He mentioned several other people whose names meant nothing to James and he ended with an Eisenhower salute of gripped hands, a gesture that was applauded with claps and whistles. It was a good speech of its kind, seemingly sincere, sentimental and with some scatological spice, and delivered with articulation. James understood it all.

It was now half past ten. James had been at the party for nearly two hours. He was always impressed by the speed at which time was consumed at parties. He still hadn't spoken to Watney, but now the little crowd of arrivals that had continuously formed around him was being replaced by people who were leaving. James got himself another whisky, and was not charged, and found himself in conversation with a woman who said, 'I admire George for talking about kicking arse.' She used the vernacular, although Watney had used the polite form. 'Why should it be a forbidden subject?'

'Why indeed?'

'What's the use of living in a free country if we censor ourselves?'

James tried to think of a sensible response that wouldn't be another question. He said, lamely, 'Well, that's George Watney for you.'

'You know him well?'

'In his English period.'

'You're the printer?'

James now had a status, a credential for being there. He smiled amiably.

'Something to do with computers?' She was trying to be helpful.

'Just ordinary printing. My father was a printer, too. It's in the family. A family firm.'

'Oh, I see.' Vaguely.

'When I knew Watney I was helping him out on, what shall I say?' What would he say to keep things simple, when no relationships were simple? 'On the information side.'

'Hush-hush, I expect.'

'It was a long time ago.'

31

The woman was now looking at him with a new curiosity. Probably she now thought he was some sort of spy. Printers. Information. English. It didn't matter. Further clarification would not make his acquaintance with Watney the prosaic encounter it had been, but would only make it sound more mysterious. It was curious, he thought through the haze of perhaps, in total, a quarter of a bottle of whisky, it was curious that suddenly he had become an authority on Watney, a man who had hardly crossed his mind for umpteen years.

'How was that?' the woman said.

'I don't think I said anything. But you, you obviously know him well.'

'I love him.'

The woman had also drunk her party quota, of what? It looked like vodka. James wondered where Susie was. If there was going to be a confession he would like to have her there to share, or preferably assume, the burden.

'Don't misunderstand me. George has never screwed me, much to my regret. Have you ever loved someone, even though you may not have touched them physically?'

James could think of no one who fitted this exacting specification. There had been many women for whom he had felt desire, but whom he had not pursued. This, though, was not presumably what his companion had in mind. He wondered if he was being propositioned. The woman was, he judged, in her mid-forties, no longer a siren by the conventions of television or the movies, but not unappealing to James, nearly twenty years her senior. In a microsecond he had responded to the proposition, had taken her to bed, considered the impossible complications and cancelled the idea.

'There is more unrequited love in the world than the other sort,' he said, and as he heard himself saying it he thought it wasn't a bad reply. The woman seemed to think so, too, and touched his arm with approval, but James never heard her response because Susie arrived and said, 'You two have met at last.' Susie, James thought, must now know everyone in the room, and could throw her own party with them as her guests.

'Time for us to go, I suppose,' he said.

'Merle and I are sneaking off for a nightcap. I won't be long. Don't be naughty.' She beamed at them both and was gone.

James's companion was now talking to someone else. James looked around for Watney to say goodbye and found he was standing behind him.

'James, we haven't seen each other all evening.'

'I feel a bit of an intruder.'

'You're my oldest friend.' He looked around at what was left of the party. 'My very oldest.'

'It was a long time ago.'

'It was. And what does freedom mean if you can't drink with your oldest friend? How did you like the speech?'

A couple came up to Watney to say goodbye and were joined by another couple. James had a great desire to slide away but felt, in a curiously childlike way, that he had not been given permission to leave. He would wait a few minutes until Watney was free again, and then say goodbye and go. He didn't want any more to drink, and he didn't much want to talk any more. He sat down for the first time since he had entered the room and felt the bones in his back creak with relief. But parties never seem completely to empty. The last couples were getting their second wind and fresh drinks were being poured. James got up.

'I'll see you, George,' he said, softly gripping his arm. 'Thanks.'

'In the bar. Give me fifteen minutes.'

Watney had a sticky tenacity that James was starting to find tiresome. What bar? There was a bar here. But he asked the doorman if there was another and he was directed down some stairs into a quiet, softly lit room that was definitely a bar. He thought he might see Susie and Merle there having their nightcap but it was empty except for a barman who was watching television with the sound turned low. James sat on a stool. He would give Watney fifteen minutes and no more. He ordered coffee. The television was showing an American football game. The picture was very fuzzy. The barman fiddled with a knob, but it remained fuzzy.

'Best I can do, sir.'

'I'm not worried. I don't understand it anyway.'

'It's a great game, sir.',

'Not if you're English.',

The barman smiled.

'But you are English,' James said.

33

'I was born in Peckham.'

'I'd assumed you were American.'

'Thank you, sir. Anything with your coffee, sir?'

'Nothing thanks. You want to be American?'

'If they'll have me.'

'What are you doing in Morocco?'

'It's a way in, working for Americans. We have our own life, even our own fuzzy television.' He touched a knob and the picture suddenly became sharp. 'It's been on the blink all the week. Something to do with the satellite.'

'This comes direct?'

'It's a home comfort.'

James was impressed, but he tried not to look impressed.

'Your usual, General?'

Watney had arrived and been saluted.

'Some coffee for me, like my sensible friend here.'

'I'll brew some fresh, General.'

'These parties, James: I'd not have retired if I'd known what was ahead.'

'I thought it went well.'

'But too many, James, too many, and all the same.' Watney gave the impression that he was marking his retirement by making some kind of world tour of places where he had served. It sounded grand, however casually he spoke of it. 'Even the gifts are the same. A video-recorder: more a gift for an old man, and I'm not that old. A digital wristwatch, just a novelty. A typewriter. Neat, but I can't type. Kindly gestures, James, representing much canvassing for contributions and it is never easy to choose presents successfully. Gifts of their times, consumer toys. I probably won't keep them.'

'You'll give them away?'

'Mislaid, let's say. Could you use a video, James?'

It seemed an extraordinarily generous gesture, but James's instinct was to say no, even though Susie had been agitating for one for months.

'I don't blame you,' Watney said. 'Now this is something I shall keep.' He had under his arm a thick book like a photographic album, fastened by a large metal catch. Watney was about to place it on the bar, but saw that the bar top had splashes of damp. He looked around the room.

'Let's sit over there.' He led the way to a table in the corner. 'That's better.' He placed the book carefully in front of James. On the cover had been affixed a photograph of Watney getting out of a helicopter. Whoever had mounted the picture had done so with skill, cutting away a slot in the leather binding, fitting a plastic window and trimming it with gold leaf.

Watney fingered it. 'A very soldierly job. The picture's good, too, better than a dummy in a dress uniform, stern and wooden.'

Watney was in fatigues in what looked like a hot country. The sun made a silhouette of the helicopter and picked out the General's star on his cap. James thought the photograph did not look much like Watney, but Watney obviously recognised himself.

'Where was this?'

'Probably Libya, when Americans were welcome there.'

'Your coffee, General. Anything to go with it?'

'Bring us a couple of large brandies. You can use a drink, James?'

James did not dissent. He need not drink the brandy if he didn't want to. He said, 'Looks like some kind of lock. You have a key?'

Watney produced from his pocket an envelope with an inscription, 'The key to our regard'.

'Someone has gone to a little trouble. I'm touched. Now let's see what's inside my remembrance book. Is that the word? Remembrance is for the dead. Souvenir book doesn't sound right either. Farewell book, perhaps. There may be a snap of you in here, James, if it goes back that far.'

James wondered if he would recognise himself. Presumably, although he probably wouldn't remember where it had been taken. He couldn't remember being on snapshot terms with George Watney. Whatever Watney may say now, whatever cosy memory he had discovered, James's recollection was that their relationship had been distant, deferential even. The base that Watney had run in Norfolk all those years ago had had some pamphlets printed at the family firm. It was one of the admired features of the Americans that they gave work to local firms. James had delivered the pamphlets to the base. He remembered doing that. He had done the job of messenger boy, among many other jobs, until quite late in life. Until his father died he had felt that he was an employee. To his surprise, on one occasion, he had found himself in Watney's office. Watney himself had opened the parcel of pamphlets, and had received the contents with extravagant praise. Had James printed them himself? Yes, mostly. Chosen the type and everything? It was part of the job. And had changed the American words into English spelling? He hoped that was how they wanted it. Watney had meditated over the pamphlets for some minutes, then asked if he would do another job for them. Of course. A very important job. Some demonstrators were going to march on the base. He might have heard of it? James had. Did he have any feelings about it, one way or another? Not especially. Would he write a pamphlet which could be handed out to the demonstrators? Watney would tell him what should go in it, and James would give it Englishness. Watney could, of course, ask his own information officer to write the pamphlet, but it wouldn't have Englishness. What did he say? James said yes. He was flattered. There had been several trips to the base before the words were finally approved. By then Palmer had become James and Watney had insisted on being called George. He had gone to lunch with the Watneys, more than once. That was how he had come to know Frances and their children. It was possible that he had had his photo taken with them. But if one had been taken, it wasn't in Watney's farewell book.

He opened the book carefully. The first page contained signatures, so did the second page. Watney flicked through the rest of the book. Nothing but signatures, pages of them, with no sense of order, half a dozen on one page, twenty or thirty on another.

'Not very soldierly,' he said and closed the book. 'You donate a dollar and write your name.' He drank some coffee and took a sip of the brandy that had arrived silently during his moments of expectation. James was not sure what to say. A disappointment is the mildest form of grief, but a grief nevertheless. He said nothing.

Eventually Watney said, 'My grandfather was presented with a sword when he left the army. Presented with it, or simply didn't give it back. It was kept with the umbrellas and walking sticks in a stand in the hall, and was the subject of numerous unbelievable tales: grandfather was a terrible show-off. I'd like to have had a weapon as a souvenir. But what? I guess the equivalent of my grandfather's sword would be a nuclear weapon. Perhaps I could get hold of one, a small one, battlefield size. It could be polished up and stand in my hall. Over drinks I could tell neighbours what the markings meant, and how the timing device was designed to operate. You mean this is an actual nuke, live? In theory, yes, but it's quite harmless: there are six quite separate safeguards. They would be scared to death. I would come to sound as tiresome as my old grandfather. Daydreams.'

James was smiling, but only out of politeness. Watney's mood was sad rather than funny.

'I forget: were you ever in the army, James?'

'In the war. The usual thing.'

'Dunkirk, El Alamein, Normandy?'

'I never got to the desert.'

'Any souvenirs?'

'My discharge papers. They were enough for me.'

'Plus your memories?'

'I prefer not to think about it. It's long over.'

'Did you ever kill anyone, James?'

'Most of us did, in some way.'

'Many people?'

'I don't know. Didn't keep count.'

'I'd like to have killed a few people before I died.'

'That sounds like John Wayne, not George Watney.'

'I am John Wayne, a make-believe tough who never took part in a real fight in the whole of his life.'

Watney held up his hand as though to silence any protest that James could make. 'It's true. I'm a bit pissed, and you're a bit pissed, too.' He signalled to the barman and pointed to the brandy glasses. 'But what I am saying is not pissed. It's true. On my desk I had a homily. "If we have to use force, we have failed." But I didn't entirely believe that. I became a soldier prepared to fight, and I've never been tested. You talk, James, of the war, *the* war. But there's always been a war going on. I've missed them all. The final shot in the Second World War in Europe was fired the day before I arrived there. By the time I was sent to the east the war with Japan was over. I stayed out in the east too long: I missed the Cold War and the Berlin airlift. I came back to Europe just before the outbreak of the Korean War. So I missed that.

I missed Vietnam. I must have been one of the few regular American officers not to have seen service there.' He laughed, a great laugh of self-derision. 'God, what a mess. I'm a curious creature of the twentieth century. I'm an expensively made weapon discarded without being used. I'm an old soldier of nuclear warfare.'

It was bizarre. James allowed himself a small smile. His memory of soldiering was that one tried to avoid action. Yet Watney had never been able to find it, or so he said.

'You don't look homicidal to me, George,' he said lightly.

'I think I was homicidal, if you want to use the word. I'd have liked a little rapine, a little pillage, to be high on blood. And, afterwards, remorseful and world-weary.'

James was embarrassed. To avoid saying nothing he told a story of a friend of his, an officer in the British army who had been retired because the government wanted to save money.

'Couldn't afford him any more?'

'Him and others.'

Watney nodded in sympathy, thoughtful for a moment that there were soldiers with a grievance even greater than his, to be sacked because there was no money left, to be thrown out like an employee from a bankrupt firm.

'What an undignifed end for a soldier. At least the States isn't poverty stricken.'

James felt that perhaps he had overstated his friend's plight. 'He's got a pension, of course. Inflation proof.'

Watney nodded. 'Did he, poor guy?'

He leaned toward James and touched him on the shoulder. 'I like you, James. This isn't the brandy talking, or if it is, it's telling the truth. I don't like many Brits, and that's another truth. Do you remember Fairbanks? Hated him.'

James did not immediately recall the name, but Fairbanks had presumably been connected with the British side of the base in Norfolk.

'Something to do with the march on the base?'

'Fairbanks wouldn't support me. I suspect he was on the side of the marchers.'

'There are all kinds of English people.'

'Certainly there are. Yet when I think of England I think of Fairbanks, distant, mocking, superior. But what did he have to be superior about, with his white cliff teeth, thatched hair and rainy eyes?'

James smiled at the portrait. He remembered Fairbanks now. 'He was distant to everyone, not just Americans. I wonder what happened to him.'

'Dead now, I hope. Or gone to Russia. Some people you never stop hating. Most things you can forget in an hour, treacheries never. You're the England I like, James. No treachery. You were an ally, a collaborator.'

The word was clearly meant to be a friendly one. James had collaborated on the production of the pamphlet as, for instance, two people might collaborate on a book. Yet the word gave him a twinge of unease. Treachery on the one hand, collaboration on the other. Watney was hurling around heavy words. James told himself that Watney was not talking of collaboration in the sense that the French used it during the occupation. French usage was not, he supposed, Watney's strong subject. It was silly to feel uneasy. All the same . . . The Americans were the first intruders on British soil since the Normans, and the most innovative since the Romans. Intruders? Protectors, rather, although that was no doubt what the collaborators said when the Romans and the Normans came. Watney certainly didn't think of himself as an intruder and had been hurt by Fairbanks' obvious antagonism to Americans. Fairbanks hadn't been a collaborator. He probably thought of himself as a member of the resistance. It came as a shock to realise that Fairbanks, if he had thought about James Palmer at all, had regarded him as a collaborator, in the French sense. The fact that the hostility was a quarter of a century old did not diminish it. It seemed curiously fresh. He remembered that his very first transistor radio had been a gift from Watney. Presumably Fairbanks would have considered that a collaborationist gift. James looked at his watch. It was the following day. Watney said, 'You're right. One more and that's it.' James said, 'No more for me, George,' but Watney had already made signals to the barman and the brandy was on its way. When it arrived Watney said, 'To the grand alliance.'

'A safe journey south.'

'Who told you?'

'Merle. To escape the earthquakers.'

'Ah, good old Merle.'

'What about the civil war?'

'Nothing civil about it. A lot of bastards trying to undermine the Moroccans.'

'Dangerous, nevertheless.'

'Wait till they see Merle. They'll surrender on the spot.' Watney laughed loudly, and James laughed too. It wasn't unfunny. 'Just a loving joke.' A pause. 'I'm taking a couple of film folks down there.'

'Gerard?'

'You've met?'

'Susie has.'

'Ah, women, no wonder they make the best spies,' Watney said, although he didn't offer any more information about the man Susie had spied out. Probably there was nothing more to say except that Watney had decided he needed some company for his expedition south and Gerard was available. During his career in the army Watney had had an entourage, and it would have grown with each promotion, a retinue of retainers that moved around with him, and now he would find difficulty in moving around without one. It was hard to imagine Watney alone: on a solitary walk, say. He might jog but only as one of a group with him at the centre determining the route and pace. Gerard and his film folks were the retinue now. Not much of a retinue, although there might be others. James wondered how Watney would fare when they had done their business and gone. There would be old army pals, of course, but they would hardly be a retinue and would probably soon become bored with hearing Watney's stories of people he had never killed.

'Do you have a card, James?'

He did not, but he wrote down his address in Norfolk, and gave it to Watney. 'And you?'

'Not sure where I'll be presently. There's a few more goodbyes to make, a party in Charleston, although I don't see myself as a returning Eisenhower, brushing confetti from my hair. But I'll have to settle somewhere. Perhaps in London for a time. I fancy the memoirs bit. London would be quiet. But you can always get me care of the army.'

It didn't seem a very precise address, but James had asked for it only out of politeness. London and memoirs sounded vague. But Watney must have been asked a hundred times what he was going to do when he retired and that would have been a non-committal answer.

James drank the tiny puddle of brandy left in the glass.

'Well?'

'Yes.' Watney nodded in the direction of the barman for the bill. When it arrived there was a formal dispute over who should pay, and Watney insisted on signing it. As they left the bar Watney put an arm around James's shoulder. 'I've enjoyed our chat. Best bit of the evening. You're not at all bad for a Brit, James. James and George: how old-fashioned those names sound in these times. How very Anglo-Saxon. How different from the Karls and the Nikis, the Kurts and the Als who are taking over our jobs.'

James could think of no one in Norfolk with such names. The names that perplexed him were of an ambiguous character. Chris, Marti, Alex, Pat, Bev, Val, Les. They were genderless, perhaps deliberately so.

The two men went back to the hotel together in a limousine that had apparently been waiting for Watney. James assumed that Susie would be in bed and asleep, but her bed was empty. It was now after one. The word mugging came into his mind. He rang Watney's room. Merle had not returned either. That was some sort of relief.

'Does Merle often stay out this late?'

'You're not to worry, James. Go to bed. They're still talking somewhere. We're lucky to be out of it, hey?'

James did go to bed, telling himself that he would read until Susie returned, however late. But he went to sleep. When he awoke she was back: sleeping in the next bed. He got up quietly and kissed her lightly on the head. He felt a sense of happiness, compounded of affection for Susie and a return to normality. He showered and shaved and dressed in the elementary clothes of a warm climate and went down to the restaurant and had a pot of tea and bought the *Herald Tribune*. There was a story on the front page about an attack by Polisario guerrillas on a Moroccan base in the Sahara. James turned to the back page and read Art Buchwald. He went outside to sniff the air. Agadir was already bright with another vulgarly sunny day. He obtained another pot of tea and took it back to the room for Susie. She was up and dressing.

'I've got to tell you something, James. I hate to hurt you, if it does hurt you. But I'm too old to be coy. I've been what is known as unfaithful. I don't regret it. I enjoyed it. If you want to know about it, I'll tell you. If you don't, I won't. I love you today no less than I did yesterday. If you feel sick and disgusted, I'll understand.'

'Who was it?'

'A casual encounter, I think the phrase is. Merle and I went to a bar in another hotel, and got talking to a couple of chaps. The talk went well. One of them said he fancied me. I thought, why not? We went to his room, and that was that. Not bad for an old hag, eh?'

'You're not an old hag.'

'He said he liked skinny women. What are you going to do, throw me out?'

She gave James a radiant smile, and then suddenly, and to James inexplicably, started to cry.

'Oh golly,' she said. 'Nervous tension. I wasn't sure what to say. Didn't know how to get it out. Well, that's it. You've had your confession. Now it's your turn.'

James felt he had been demoted from judge to defendant. He was uncertain what to say in either role. He was surprised, of course, but astonished? Not quite. But very surprised. But surprised about what? That Susie should have been attractive to another man, or that she should have betrayed him? She was attractive to him, but after a long marriage who can separate attractiveness into its parts, familiarity, friendship and what remains of physical appeal? He still had sex with Susie and it was very pleasant, but he was still possibly making love to the image of the woman he first fell in love with. And betrayal? It was a technical betrayal, and she had already sought benediction. He was not disgusted; perhaps intrigued was the word that fitted his thoughts. He would say nothing of this to Susie. Honesty is always misinterpreted. She had probably not been wholly honest with him. He would react in a conventional way. To react otherwise would hurt her.

'Well, I'm hurt,' he said. 'That's about all I can say.'

'Oh, my darling.' Susie put down her tea, came over to James and put her arms around his neck. 'But I had to tell you. I don't want there to be an awful secret between us.'

But she had said that she had enjoyed it. It had been an adventure, a holiday snapshot to contemplate long after every other detail of Morocco had been forgotten. But this wasn't the moment for James to say it; never, unless they had a catastrophic row.

'I blame Merle,' James said.

'Please don't say anything to her.'

'She probably does this all the time. And all that stuff about George.'

'Let Merle and George sort out their own problems. Promise me?'

'Well, I probably won't see her again.'

'Promise me, James.'

'All right.'

'Promise?'

'Yes.'

'Say "I promise".'

'I promise.'

'I love you, James. I do really.'

Susie ate a large breakfast, unusually large for her: bacon and egg, fruit and toast. James watched her gollop it down and ventured a little joke. 'You'll lose your skinny appeal.'

She leaned across the table and kissed him. 'Darling, you're being wonderful. Did you have a wonderful gossip with George?'

'Two old bores reminiscing.'

'Sounds cosy. Dear old pals.'

James considered the word. 'Pals are equals. Watney doesn't consider any Brit, as he calls us, to be his equal.'

'Well, he's a General. That's important.'

James smiled. 'Self-important. But it's not just that.' He told Susie about Fairbanks. 'He was his equal at the base.'

'Well, if Fairbanks was uppity, I don't blame George for not liking him.'

'Fairbanks wasn't a bad chap. He used his pride against Watney's American wealth. Watney offered him courtesy, and Fairbanks spurned it. If you are poor and weak all the courtesy in the world cannot make you feel rich and strong.'

'Fairbanks was poor and weak?' Susie was trying to follow James's line of argument.

'Not Fairbanks himself. The British.'

'Oh, I see. Well, I don't feel poor and weak.'

You have just been fucked, and that is all you are thinking about, James said, but he did not say it aloud. He said, 'These are deep thoughts for breakfast time. I think I'll steal some of your coffee.'

As they were leaving the hotel for their morning on the beach they saw Merle and George Watney standing in the car park watching their luggage being loaded into a vehicle.

Merle gave a little cry of delight when she saw Susie. 'Oh, thank God. I thought we'd missed you.'

'You're really going?'

James watched the two women moving swiftly into an eager conversation, slightly lowering their voices to limit their range. He nodded at George who nodded back.

'Quite a tank you've got there,' James said. George contemplated the vehicle, as though James's remark had drawn his attention to it for the first time. It did have a tank-like confidence, with extravagant wheels and front seats that reminded James of lookout posts. The back seemed to be filled with luggage. Gerard was presumably not travelling with the Watneys. Perhaps he had his own tank.

'I'm wondering whether we should show the flag.' Watney had in his hand a small Stars and Stripes, the size of a pennant. 'I'd value your advice, James.'

James thought of this big, showy vehicle travelling to an area that was instinctively hostile to strangers. To put a flag on it would be to invite a brick through the windscreen, if nothing nastier. That seemed self-evident to James, but then he wouldn't have chosen such an ostentatious means of travel, and he wouldn't have gone there anyway. George Watney must have guessed that he would counsel caution.

'Why not?' James said. 'Nothing to be afraid of.'

'You really think so?' Watney examined James's face for an English joke.

'Certainly.'

'You're right.' Watney climbed on to the running board of the vehicle and fixed the flag on the aerial wire.

'Is that wise, George?' Merle broke off her conversation with Susie.

'Sure. Show the flag. Why not?' Watney stuck to a decision once it had been taken.

'What do you think, James?'

'I agree with George.'

Merle returned to her conversation with Susie, but George was now in the driver's seat and called her to join him. The two women embraced. The two men shook hands. James shook hands with Merle, and George leaned down from his seat and kissed Susie on the cheek. Merle climbed up into her seat with easy agility. James noticed for the first time that she was wearing fawn dungarees. She looked soldierly. If a brick came through the window she could probably throw it back.

'Wagons roll,' George Watney said.

Everyone waved, including a small crowd of hotel staff who had gathered in the car park.

'To the shores of Tripoli,' James murmured to Susie.

'Is that where they're going?'

'If it is, they're going in the wrong direction. God bless America.'

'I'll miss them.' Susie had tears in her eyes.

Susie said little on the way to the beach. It was less crowded than usual. The German couple were not there, and James felt curiously disappointed. Over their drinks at the Djellaba Bar he said that they would do something special. Most evenings they had eaten at the hotel. Tonight they would go out.

'Where?'

'I'll find somewhere.'

'I wouldn't mind trying that American place again. They have a restaurant.'

'Better than that.'

James's plan was to take Susie to a restaurant where they would be served with the very finest Moroccan food. Susie's skinny body concealed a well-fed stomach. He consulted a waiter at the hotel whom he had found to have a friendly manner. The waiter considered James's project and discussed it with one of his colleagues, but their consensus was that there were no great restaurants in Agadir, although there were several pleasant ones. For a great restaurant one would have to go to Marrakech or Fez. There the tradition of *fasi* cooking survived in certain establishments which he would be happy to recommend. Were those towns not far away? The waiter considered. Not if one flew, he said.

James settled for a restaurant in Agadir that was merely pleasant. He and Susie sat on divans and ate *tajine* and *b'stila* from low tables and there was background music softly played on a gramophone. Susie spoke to a man and a woman at the next table who said they were probation officers and lived in Rochdale. Susie said it was the loveliest evening of the holiday, and she loved James for planning it.

'I enjoyed it, too,' James said, but he wished they had flown to Marrakech or Fez. Watney, he suspected, would have done. He ended the day feeling ordinary, although he did not speak of his feeling to Susie. He would have been irritated by her fervent denials.

Next day on the beach the German woman was there, but not her husband or her ball. She exchanged smiles with James who asked her in English where her husband was. She seemed to understand but had no English for a reply. Instead she made a pillow of her hands and closed her eyes, which could have meant either that her husband was asleep or dead. James nodded in what he hoped was an understanding way.

In the afternoon Susie went shopping with the woman probation officer. She was friendly, Susie said later, but not a patch on Merle.

'Much nicer, I expect.'

Susie was about to reply crossly, but she saw James smiling. 'Don't you miss them, a bit?' she said.

'A bit.' That was true. They had been given two unexpected holiday playthings, and now they had been taken away. But James did not say that. 'I suppose we don't like change,' he said.

On the last day of their holiday it rained, the first rain for seven months, someone said, or it may have been seven years. In Norfolk it was bright and dry, a splendid winter's day. They told themselves that they had been lucky and clever. Normality resumed its grip on their lives. However, after they had been back for about a week Susie had a letter from Merle which said that George Watney had been wounded.

★ 3 ★

Merle's letter was long but it assumed knowledge of Morocco that neither Susie nor James possessed. A look at a map helped, so did a chat with a young woman at the local library who, it turned out, had hiked across north-west Africa with her boyfriend. Putting together these sources of information, James and Susie surmised what had happened to the Watneys.

After leaving Agadir they had had an easy drive to Goulimine. There the Sahara desert starts and the road had become slummy, to use Merle's word, although still drivable. They had stayed the night at Tan Tan at a hotel improbably known as the Royal. Merle had been bitten by a dog but as far as she knew did not have rabies. The following day the road was Endsville. The map marked hamlets as having *eau potable* or *eau salée*, or, more rarely, *eau douce*. Merle wanted to turn back. George Watney would not, and gave her a talk on being a good American. They drove on and crossed into what used to be Spanish Sahara.

When the Spanish left the territory in 1975, about a quarter of a million Moroccans, holding aloft copies of the Koran, walked in and claimed it for Morocco, an episode that is now known as the Green March. Morocco said it was simply occupying land it had owned before the Spanish took it. Easy, and seemingly fair. Even the communists in Morocco supported the government. However, the people who were already living in the territory thought differently and they set up their own state, the Sahrawi Republic, which Morocco did not recognise and said that its soldiers were terrorists. Troops from Morocco and terrorists from the Sahrawi Republic regularly fought small, swift but brutal battles. Merle could not fathom why anyone would want to live there, let alone fight over it. However, the desert contained phosphate, a valuable mineral used to make fertilisers and detergents, among other things. The town of Bu Craa had the richest phosphate mine in the world. The Moroccans had taken

47

over a large slab of desert, including Bu Craa, by enclosing it in a wall, more than 300 miles long. Although it had none of the fame of, say, the Berlin wall or the Belfast wall, it was just as workman-like, not merely because of its sandy impregnability, its barbed wire and its minefield but also because it was watched over by a radar system supplied by America. Within this enclave, the wall on one side, the sea on the other, life was safe and prosperous. Its centre was the town of Layoun where George and Merle Watney arrived three days after leaving Agadir.

After Endsville, Layoun must have had an oasis-like charm, with its well-lit streets, new houses, mosques and schools, and shops stocked with tax-free goods. However, as a garrison town it was populated largely by soldiers, with tanks among the traffic and a curfew at night. Merle rapidly came to hate it. She longed to be back at Agadir to go shopping with Susie and where the only danger was from earthquakes. It wasn't at all her idea of a second honeymoon. However, George promised her a third honeymoon if she was good and patient until he had finished his filming work there, the nature of which Merle did not elaborate. George Watney liked Layoun. He was received as an honoured guest and shown the elaborate fortifications and met the Americans who serviced them. Everyone likes to be appreciated, and here was a place where Americans were given proper credit for what they were doing. In addition, the Americans found themselves for once indisputably on the right side in a post-colonial war, supporting the legal government in a fight for what was clearly their own territory. The enemy might call themselves Sahrawi, but the Moroccans said that no such nation existed. They were a rabble of Mauritanians, Chadians, Malians, Nigerians with some renegade Moroccans and even a few Europeans. Their main support came from Algeria, which was like saying Russia.

However, after a few days of touring the enclave, George Watney became restless. Why were the Moroccans allowing the rest of the territory to go by default? The Moroccans smiled in answer to a question they had answered many times before. They had what they wanted. In time they would have the whole of the territory. Historically it was theirs. Whenever the terrorists attacked the enclave, which they did with singular regularity every ten weeks, they were driven off after a day or two with great losses. That suited the Moroccans. The enclave was as safe as a castle or, in American terms, a fort.

Castles were besieged and forts were overrun, Watney said. Not this one, the Moroccans said. It was indestructible. Did the Moroccans send out patrols from time to time to see what the enemy was up to? Oh, certainly. Could Watney go on one? They considered, and thought not. He would be perfectly safe, of course; Moroccan soldiers were more than a match for the terrorist rabble. But accidents happened in the desert, and the heat was bad. An American General was too precious to risk. However, Watney persisted, and finally it was agreed that he could make a reconnaissance of the area beyond the enclave, but only in a helicopter. He set out at dawn one day in a helicopter with a crew of two. For half an hour or so nothing much happened. The sun rising over the desert did not fill Watney with excitement. Then he spotted something on a track ahead. The pilot said it was a Pol, that is a Polisario, or terrorist. How did he know? That was their vehicle, a Land-Rover with the windows filled in. Watney asked to go lower. The pilot was reluctant but did not want to refuse an American General. The Land-Rover stopped, two men got out and fired at the helicopter with sub-machine-guns. The helicopter climbed swiftly away, but a bullet had hit something and fuel was draining away. The pilot called up Layoun and was told to land at Guelta Zemmur and check the damage. Guelta was a former outpost of the Spanish Foreign Legion that the Moroccans and the Pols fought over from time to time. At the moment it was in Moroccan hands.

On a reasonably detailed map Guelta looks a haven of sorts, with the promise of *eau potable*. This is an exaggeration. The tiny Moroccan garrison had just been attacked by the Pols and the Moroccans were loading their wounded on to a truck for a precarious journey back to the enclave behind the wall. They were short of nearly everything, including food, water, ammunition and nerve. When Watney's helicopter landed they at first assumed that it was bringing succour and were not pleased when they discovered that it wanted a service station. The pilot and his observer inspected the damage to the helicopter. It seemed slight, and they decided they could mend it themselves. The garrison drove away back to the enclave. Time passed. The helicopter crew discovered that a tool they needed to make the repair was missing. They called Layoun which said it would send another helicopter to pick up Watney. Time passed. No relief helicopter arrived; but, no problem, a tool was found and the repair could be carried out after all. In late afternoon the helicopter took off again. On the way to Layoun they passed the truck that had left Guelta that morning. It had stopped and was under attack from three or four Pol Land-Rovers. The helicopter pilot was for carrying on to Layoun, but Watney insisted on going down and buzzing the Pols, which then made off. At Layoun Watney was a hero. He was now in hospital recovering from his wound.

Merle's letter did not say at what stage of Watney's adventurous day he had been wounded: whether it had been in the morning when the Pols had opened fire on the helicopter, or in the afternoon when he had gone to the rescue of the besieged truck. Neither did it say where he had been wounded, or how serious the wound was. James and Susie were puzzled about what they should do. Merle had put no address on her letter and the postmark on the envelope simply said Morocco. They felt that some expression of sympathy was necessary. James phoned the American embassy in London and explained the problem. He was given an army number to phone. The American there consulted a directory but said there was no reference for Layoun. The only place in the area where the Americans had an office was Aaiun. It turned out to be the same place. Yes, sir, he'd be glad to send a telex there for the attention of General Watney. What did he want to say? This needed some thought. James said he would phone back. He consulted Susie. She had now written a letter to Merle and wanted to send that, but James said it was much too long for a telex. The message they agreed on was: 'Distressed to hear of your injury, but relieved you are back in safe hands. Get well soon. Love, Susie and James.' The message was telephoned to the helpful American who said that he would telex it right away, and if there was a reply he would call them. Don't mention it, sir, just part of the United States service. No reply was received and after a week or so the matter lost its importance, except as a bizarre end to a holiday encounter.

Around this time a matter of great importance was taking place at the printers that James owned. It was changing its way of printing, from hot metal, which, one way or another dated from the days of Caxton, to a method that used computers. The linotypes and the Ludlow casters had gone with their rattle and smell of ink and in had come dustless cubes that whispered at work. The printing shop was as clean as a clinic and the compositors wore white overalls. One room still to be neutered contained the firm's records. James's father had kept a sample of every piece of printing done by the firm, catalogues, posters, business cards, even a local newspaper that had run for a short time. The clever young man who had supervised the changeover from hot metal to white cubes said that anything that needed to be preserved could be put on microfilm, the lot if James wanted to. James looked at the shelves of decaying paper and thought it could all be scrapped. He had little sentiment for his father's days. This would be an exorcism. Perhaps he would keep a few things, nothing more. One file he took down contained the pamphlet he had done for George Watney at the time of the march on the base. How old-fashioned it looked now, with its decorated border and french rules between paragraphs. At the top of the pamphlet there was a drawing of Uncle Sam and John Bull arm in arm. He had forgotten that. Did anyone now think of Sam and John linked together, like a song and dance team? It seemed unlikely. Even those who believed in the special relationship, or whatever it was now called, distanced themselves, however slightly, from the Americans. Politicians who ate Russians for breakfast and had faces like Union Jacks felt it necessary to shake their heads from time to time over whatever the United States was doing or not doing.

James read the words in the pamphlet. They were a collection of commonplace observations. He noticed a misprint. How careless. He took a pencil from his pocket and corrected it, then he crumpled the pamphlet into a ball. It was an embarrassment. If he had been a collaborator, he had been a very banal one.

When he arrived home that evening Gerard was there. He got up from a sofa as James entered the living room and held out a hand.

'You remember Gerard, George Watney's film friend in Morocco?' Susie said, providing in one sentence all that James did know about Gerard. He had seen him at Watney's party, but not spoken to him. He took Gerard's hand.

51

'Of course. How is George?'

'Getting better.' Gerard resumed his place on the sofa and stretched out his legs. He looked as though he had been settled there a long time.

'He's been quite a hero, it seems?'

Gerard nodded slightly, and smiled briefly. He was, it seemed, of a taciturn nature, or it may be that, having given all the details of Watney's adventure to Susie, he did not think it necessary to repeat them. He seemed even younger than he had at the party, younger and paler. Perhaps he wasn't well. Perhaps he had been wounded, too.

Susie brought James the whisky that he always had at the start of the evening. She and Gerard were drinking tea. James stood in front of the fireplace, with his back to the fire.

'And how is Merle?' he said, having nothing else to say.

'I believe quite well.' Gerard leaned forward from the sofa. 'Tell me, Mr Palmer, do you usually stand in front of the fire when you come in at the end of the day?'

'I suppose I do. I'm sorry, am I taking the heat from you?'

'No, no. I'm quite warm. But fires interest me. This is the first I've seen for a long time.'

'Nothing like a coal fire.'

'Primeval,' Gerard said.

'A bit old-fashioned, but nothing wrong with that.'

'I would see it, Mr Palmer, as a kind of altar that you acknow-ledge for your safe homecoming. I hope I'm not treading on any religious beliefs.'

'No, not at all. Well, that's certainly one way of looking at it.'

Gerard seemed a rum young man. James looked towards Susie but she seemed intent on drinking her tea. James bent down and poked the fire. When he got up Susie said, 'Gerard is making a film about George Watney.'

'That's interesting. About his Morocco exploit?'

'About his life,' Gerard said.

'His whole life. That sounds like a long film.'

Gerard poured himself another cup of tea. He held the pot high, so that the tea splashed on to the polished table. He relaxed back into the sofa, seemingly oblivious of the mess he had made.

'I'll get a cloth,' Susie said, jumping up. Gerard frowned

slightly, as though his thoughts had been interrupted.

'A film about a life need not necessarily be long. It can, for example, be episodic. Do you know the work of Godard?'

James vaguely recalled a French film he had seen on television late in the evening which had sent him to sleep. 'Just as a name.'

Gerard examined this response for a few seconds. 'How honest you are, Mr Palmer. I think we're going to get on very well.'

Susie returned with a cloth. Gerard took it from her and wiped the table clean with great thoroughness.

'Thank you,' Susie said.

'I was very careless.'

Gerard was not only rum, James thought, he was unpredictable. Both qualities James found irritating. He had early-evening tiredness. It was his slump in the day. He did not want to get on well with Gerard. He wanted to take off his shoes, talk to Susie, have something to eat, watch the box or continue his conquest of *War and Peace* in which he had reached a point of no retreat.

Gerard presumably sensed that not all was well with his welcome, for he said, humbly, and looking more than ever his youthful age, 'Will you help me, Mr. Palmer?'

'If I can, of course.'

'You're one of George Watney's oldest friends. I thought you could help me with the early years.'

'I hardly know him. When I bumped into him in Agadir, that's the first time I had seen him for twenty-five years. Or more.'

'But did you know him back in the 1950s?'

'Yes, all that time ago. But I can't say he was a friend.'

'You used to go to the base to see him?'

'Oh yes.'

'Honeysucklelay?'

James smiled. 'Yes, that was its name. You know more than I do.'

'Is it still functioning?'

James shrugged. 'I suppose so. I haven't been that way for years.'

'It's far from here?'

'Not far. I just don't go that way.'

'I'd like to see it.'

'I don't suppose you can go in unless George can fix it. But no doubt you can look at it, this still being more or less a free country. Have you asked George?'

'Will you take me there?'

'You mean show you where it is?'

'Yes.'

'I can show you on the map.'

'Could you spare the time to take me?'

'Well . . .'

Susie said, 'You could pop over with him, James. It's not far.'

'It's quite important,' Gerard said.

Important. That was an odd word.

'In making a film anything can be important,' Gerard said, softening the word. 'A friend of mine made a film about a horse. He slept in the stable all the time he was making it.'

'Did he? Fancy that.' James regarded Gerard, who returned his stare evenly. James had the momentary idea that Gerard was contemplating sleeping with him. Gerard would consider any intimacy. His code of behaviour was not James's.

'Perhaps Susie will drive you over. But I don't expect there's much to see.'

The question of who would accompany Gerard, or if anyone would, was not pursued. Gerard stayed for supper. It seemed that Susie had invited him earlier. He also stayed the night. It was not quite clear to James how this happened. He remembered asking Gerard during a lull in conversation at supper where he was going to sleep that night and Gerard, seemingly taking this as an invitation to stay, had accepted; not so much accepted as agreed. James had been too polite to demur and it did not seem to have occurred to Gerard that he might be other than welcome. James suspected that anyway Gerard would have asked to stay. He had his luggage with him, so he had not booked into a hotel. He reminded James of a young man he had once talked to on a train who had travelled in numerous countries, but had never paid for his lodging. There was always a door to knock on, a phone number to call. A name, supplied by a friend or a friend of a friend, was enough. A smile and a thick skin did the rest. The young man had been a bum, James thought, although not a tramp. He was clean and not destitute. He was, James decided, a member of a new breed of young people founded on the principles of self-regard and irresistibility. A sect of spongers:

54

what a good word that was. But the young man did not think of himself as a freeloader. In return for a bed and food his hosts were rewarded with his presence. He had been an American, but Gerard was not American, at least James supposed not. James supposed Gerard was English, but it would be easy to be mistaken. The word androgynous came into James's mind, but that was to do with sex. He wondered if there was a comparable word to do with nationality.

The following day James and Gerard did not go to Honeysucklelay. Gerard said that he would like to see James's printing firm. James showed him round, although there wasn't much to see. There would have been more before the old machinery was scrapped. Gerard lolled around the place all day, sometimes talking to a compositor, sometimes just reading a magazine. He had a pub lunch with James and at the end of the working day went home with him.

'Are you getting anything out of this?' James said over supper.

'Oh yes, Mr Palmer.'

'Is this the stable treatment?'

'Pardon me?'

'You said a friend of yours slept with a horse in its stable.'

Gerard smiled. 'That was the easy part. Filming is the hardest work in the world.'

And the most tedious, James thought. 'But when does it start?'

'Pardon me?'

'The filming bit. Camera, action. That sort of thing.'

Gerard did not answer. He continued eating, as though such a remark did not require an answer.

'I mean,' James persisted, 'how far have you got with this film of George's life. The Morocco derring-do, I suppose?'

'I wasn't with him when he was wounded. And even if I had been, I doubt if I would have filmed it.'

Susie said, 'Very dangerous, I expect.'

'Puerile.'

'I don't think so at all.' James suddenly found himself vehemently defending Watney against this squirt. He felt a great surge of passion, of anger almost, against an attack by a sneak, a boy, against a member of James's own generation, even though that was about the only thing he had in common with Watney.

Gerard put down his fork – he did not seem to use a knife – and watched James during this outburst.

'That was interesting,' he said. 'I would film that. Passion is interesting. Passion is not puerile.'

'Has anyone ever told you that you're a little prick?'

'Not in precisely those words.' He smiled. He did have some charm, but he used it sparingly.

'But why make a film about George if you despise him?'

'He's one of the most interesting people I've met. But in ways he may not realise. That's what I'm going to make the film about.'

Next day they did go to Honeysucklelay, but only briefly. Gerard seemed to have got what he had come to see James for, whatever it was, and was now returning to London. James found himself almost persuading Gerard to see Honeysucklelay.

'You've come all this way. You may as well see it. George will want to know what it was like.'

On the first road-sign to Honeysucklelay they came on there had been painted the nuclear disarmament symbol. On a sign further on Norwich had been crossed out and Hiroshima written in its place.

'Vandals,' Gerard said.

When they got to Honeysucklelay James had no difficulty recognising the place, but he did so in a way that one might recognise a person from a photograph taken years earlier. The prominent features were unchanged but they had become firmer. When he had run his errands to Watney there had been a hedge along one side of the base; a hawthorn hedge, but hardly a barrier, more a marker of the base's limits. No doubt anyone could get over it, if they didn't mind a few scratches, but James could recall no one having done so. The march that had so upset Watney had halted in a field nearby. A meeting had been held, but no loudspeakers had been used at the request of a farmer who said that they might upset his cows in calf. There had been missiles at the base, very prominent ones that could be seen from the road. No doubt they had been guarded, but the hostility they attracted was chiefly in scatological references to their shape. Their official name was Thor. Someone in the arms business had had a classical education.

The Thors had gone. Whatever had replaced them was not on show. They were buried secrets. The hedge had gone, replaced by a tall wire fence, no, two fences, between which he could see a soldier walking, like a mite caught between the sheets of double glazing. The soldier was walking towards a scaffold on which was perched a hut made of breeze blocks which looked as though they had been cemented together by someone who had used a trowel for the first time, hoping to conceal his ineptitude by decorating it with some strands of barbed wire. In the hut was another soldier, with binoculars, perhaps examining from his rampart James and Gerard. Soldiers still lived in castles, but no one would give a coin to wander round this one when it was discarded. It wouldn't even give pleasure as a ruin. Left for a little while, it would return to moorland.

But these were incidentals. The obvious thing about the camp was that it was populated outside, too. A signal of smoke arose from a wood fire around which a number of people were sitting. James could see two large plastic barrels marked WATER, and there were other badges of permanency, a line of washing and a tap where two women were rinsing dishes. All the people that James could see in this settlement were women. He felt conspicuous standing there watching them, as though he had opened the door of a room where a private event was in progress.

It had started to rain.

'What do you want to to do?' James said.

'We might distribute a few tablets of soap.'

'That's unkind. Perhaps we should just say hallo.'

'Why?'

'Pass the time of day. Country manners.'

'They won't talk to you. You're man. Bad. They're women. Good.'

'Oh, come now.'

'It's that simple, baddies and goodies.'

'Surely not.'

'Surely not,' Gerard mimicked. 'Try them with your liberal good manners and you'll get a kick in the crotch. Even boy babies aren't safe here. They're killed at birth. Let's go back to the car.'

James himself felt timid, if only because he was shy of any new experience. But he did not like to give in to his shyness. He saw that there were two policemen standing by the gates of the base, just beyond the wood fire. He saw that a notice had been erected

57

by the settlement. It said PEACE CAMP. Everything did look quite peaceful. A jeep went by driven by a man in a baseball cap.

'Sure you won't want to call in at the base? Use Watney's name?'

'I think not. I'll tell George I've seen it. These places are all the same.'

As they were walking back to the car there was a shout from behind them.

'Uncle James!'

The young woman who stood before them was an advertisement for wool. She had on a jumper stitched together from woollen squares, thick stockings and a fisherman's hat, each garment a shade of red. At her throat was a badge on which was a drawing of wire-cutters. She was panting and her face was pink.

'Were you looking for me, uncle?'

'I wasn't actually, Pippa. I didn't know you were here.'

'What are you doing here, then?'

Pippa, James remembered, asked direct questions.

'This is my friend, Gerard. He makes films.'

Pippa looked at Gerard, at his precise clothes and his neutral face. 'He wants to make a film about us?'

'No, nothing like that. We were just passing.'

'Ah,' Pippa said, not very convinced. 'How's auntie?'

Gerard said, 'I'll see you back at the car.'

While he was probably still within earshot Pippa said, 'Who's the spook?'

'He really does make films.'

'And you were just passing?'

'Gerard's a friend of the chap who used to run the place. I knew him, too, many years ago. Sentimental journey.'

'A nice man like my uncle mixed up with a place like this?'

James felt a trace of annoyance at his niece's confidence, of her certainty that she was right; that anything he said about the base that was not wholly condemnatory would be wholly rejected, allowances possibly being made because he was her uncle, and ancient. There was a bit of a zealot about her. She had sensitive buttons that if touched would produce howls of dismay.

He said, 'Are you keeping warm? You look well.'

'I'm well. Women are very sensible about keeping warm. Anyway, it's very healthy in the open.'

58

Pippa had once walked across an African country on her own. Which one was it? Somewhere black. Kenya, perhaps, or Tanzania. James had forgotten. But he remembered her story: her small pack on her back, just walking because she had lost her money or it had been stolen, and spending the nights in African villages, when she could find them. James had been both appalled and enthralled. Pippa had convinced him that there was a genuinely new generation. His own children had been conformingly dull. His friends' children were dull in other ways, wearing funny clothes or listening to loud music. But Pippa was a surprise. He was pleased to see her. He had not seen her for, how long? Years. He had paused before he had recognised her.

'Would you like a cup of tea?'

James was about to say that he had to rejoin Gerard, but Gerard could wait.

'Love one.'

'Tea or coffee? We have both.'

'Tea would be fine.'

Pippa put her arm through his and led him to the fire. He watched her take a steaming kettle from the ashes and pour hot water into a china pot. The setting was unusual but the gestures were habitually domestic. A patch of ground had been marked out as an allotment and two women were digging methodically. Time to sow potatoes, James thought. Several women acknowledged him with smiles, but did not stare at him. He wasn't going to be kicked, it seemed. Gerard was wrong, or perhaps Pippa was his safe conduct pass. He remembered once being in Manchester and deciding to watch United. For some reason he didn't have a lot of money on him and saw the game from the Stretford end, where the young fans had willed on their team with ferocious intensity. United right or wrong. Anyone who shows tolerance to the enemy is a traitor. He had felt very isolated there. There had been no Pippa to vouch for his credentials.

'There you are, uncle.'

Pippa had tea in one hand and in the other a plate with something on it that James recognised from long ago. Bread pudding.

'The Hastings women brought it yesterday.'

James bit into the stomach-filler of his childhood.

'This is nostalgia day,' he said. 'My mother, your great aunt,

made a redoubtable bread pudding. No better than this, though.'
He was not hungry, but in deference to the Hastings women and
to the memory of his mother, he ate up, feeling, God help him,
like a good boy. 'Gerard said that men weren't welcome here.'

He wondered if he had touched a sensitive button, but Pippa
said, 'Perfectly welcome, but not to stay. We think they can help
in other ways, like looking after the children so that their wives
can come here.'

'It sounds like a bit of a nunnery?'

Pippa did not smile. 'A nunnery was a powerhouse of
prayer. We're a sort of powerhouse, too. A feminist one.'

James recalled a long talk he had once had with Pippa about
feminism. Not a talk, more a talking to. The materials of her
philosophy were extremely diverse, the bound feet of Chinese
women, infibulation and goodness knows what else. It was as
remote from James's understanding as a lecture on Fermat's last
theorem. He understood that she cared, and that was about all.
He did not want to be lectured again, but, tapping his meagre
resources on pacifism, he ventured, 'Is the peace camp a sort of
Gandhi-ism?'

'We believe in a kind of active passive resistance. We cut
through the wire and try to invade the base. We're nits on the
back of the military. But Gandhi was violent towards women. He
slept with young virgins to test the strength of his resistance to
temptation. But what about the women?'

James feared a new lecture emerging. 'Talking about sleep.
Where?'

Pippa slept in a home-made shelter which she called a
bender, presumably because the frame was made of bent
branches. The frame was covered with a blanket and some sheets
of white plastic. Pippa's bender was in a group of half a dozen.
James thought they looked like fungi that had suddenly swelled
up from the ground. He peered inside Pippa's. It was furnished
with a substantial sleeping bag and a rug. In a corner was a teddy
bear.

'Primitive,' he said. 'But cosy. It's how I imagine the gipsies
used to live before they got luxury caravans.'

'The travelling people,' Pippa corrected him. 'Yes, they've
helped us.'

'Why don't you get a caravan, too?'

'Oh, uncle, we're not millionaires.'

James and Susie used to take caravan holidays, and they had never disposed of their van. It was old, parked for ever by a shed in the garden, but still habitable, better than a plastic hut. The impulse came to James that he must offer it to Pippa, and then he had an equally compelling impulse that he must not. Pippa wanted to be a martyr. No, that was not it. That was the sort of thing Gerard would say. Pippa wanted to play at adventure games like a child who pleads to sleep in a tent in the garden. No, she was serious. Overbearingly confident, but serious. Sleeping in a ridiculously inadequate shelter outside the walls of the rich and powerful was a gesture. Pippa would argue powerfully for it. But it was not an argument, James thought, that he would provoke. It would be as pointless as trying to persuade a medieval anchorite to leave her cell.

He said, looking at the sky, 'I think we're in for a bit more rain.'

'I may get some sleep. I'm on the night watch. Sometimes the beast comes out at night.'

'There used to be Thors here. At least they've gone.'

'The beasts are worse. Do you know what one cruise can do?'

She looked him in the eyes. They were full of information but he did not want a seminar on cruises.

'A lot of damage, I'm sure. Pippa, I must go. Gerard is my guest. Courtesy continues despite the nuclear threat.'

'It's lovely to see you, uncle. Will you come again? Bring auntie.'

'Of course,' he said routinely. A pause. 'Would your organisation accept a contribution?'

'Money? Lovely.'

James gave her a ten-pound note. For the second time, or was it the third, he had the sense of partaking in a religious ceremony. Pippa folded the note carefully and put it in a pocket of her fisherman's hat. She gave him a kiss on each cheek. As he walked to the car he turned to wave goodbye, but she was gone. He noticed for the first time that inside the gate there was a large board which said, RAF HONEYSUCKLELAY. WELCOME. He couldn't remember that in Watney's day. Perhaps it had been introduced to soften the barbed wire, the guard towers, and even the reproachful women. A thought flashed across James's mind of the sign the Germans put over the entrances to concentration

61

camps: what was it, something about freedom through labour? But his sense of fair play, his Britishness, immediately rejected the connection. What would have happened to German dissenters who camped outside Treblinka or Dachau? They would have been killed, within hours. There would have been no applying for eviction orders at the local magistrates court.

'I was worried about you,' Gerard said when they had driven away. 'Did you see any other males there?'

'Just a teddy bear.'

'Poor thing.'

James drove Gerard to the station to get a train to London. He looked at his watch. 'Just right. Fifteen minutes, if it's on time.' A taxi manoeuvred in ahead of James's car and two American sailors got out, pulling their duffel bags after them. The sailors had pimples and were chewing something, presumably gum. They were, depending on one's point of view, either part of an army of occupation or guardians of the west. James thought they looked too sloppy to be either.

Gerard said, 'You'll be seeing George again?'

'I hope so.'

'I mean, seriously.'

'Well, no. I'm not actually planning to.'

'Supposing George needed you?'

'This sounds very mysterious. Unless you mean the wound.'

'The wound is nothing. How much has George confided in you, James?' It was the first time that Gerard had allowed himself to use the intimacy of the first name.

'Confided?' James considered the word. 'Nothing confided. We had a rather drunken session in Agadir where he said he was disappointed he hadn't shot anyone. Do you mean that?'

'George Watney is a puzzle. Sometimes I think he is no more than what he affects to be, an obsolescent piece of hardware. Sometimes I think he may turn out to be a man of destiny. Forgive the melodrama. He has this plan, you know; well obviously you don't know. If you did know you'd probably think it daft. Mostly I think it daft. Any intelligent person would think it daft, and George is certainly intelligent.'

'What is this plan?'

'I'd rather George told you, if he wants to. It would sound even dafter from my lips. Anyway, if you're interested, perhaps you'll want to see George again. I'm very fond of him. He's quite a lonely person. I'm a friend and, whatever you say, he regards you as one.'

Gerard got out of the car and took his case from the back seat. He leaned into the car and shook hands with James. 'Be seeing you,' he said.

When James got home that evening Susie was arranging some flowers that Gerard had sent with a thank-you note.

'This really was decent of him,' she said.

'Not bad, a bunch of flowers for two nights' board and lodging.'

Susie kissed him. 'You're so hard, James. He's really a rather nice young man once you get to know him.'

'I still don't know why he came.' During the day James had pondered over the reason for Gerard's visit. He hadn't done any filming, and had not been interested in Honeysucklelay. Perhaps he had come to see James because he believed that James could help Watney in some way. Gerard had said that he was fond of Watney. Perhaps Watney had turned queer. It seemed improbable, but anything could happen these days.

'Did Merle ever say anything about George and sex?'

'Quite a lot. You remember that second honeymoon business?'

'Did she ever say he might have unusual preferences?'

'You mean, was he gay?'

'Yes, that's the word.'

Susie laughed. 'I wouldn't imagine so. Tell me more.'

James frowned. 'No, no. It was just a wild thought.'

He felt uncomfortable discussing sex as though it were a subject as ordinary as the weather. This was a dated view, but he was dated. Being dated was a refuge. He felt uncomfortable about many developments over the past twenty years or so, say, since he was forty. Forty seemed to him to be a natural, and indeed healthy, age to have completed one's development. Those people who claimed to keep up with every novelty into their dotage had something wrong with them; they were as misled as rich people who had once hoped to prolong their life by a painful injection of monkey glands. Stay young, never stop learning: what an absurd injunction that was. His small knowledge of missiles was confined to the Thors at Honeysucklelay. He could understand them. They were stuck on a piece of ground and had rockets under them which took them somewhere

63

else. The things that Pippa spoke of, the beasts that crept away from their lair so that they could be fired in secret: they involved knowledge that James had not been provided with. He did not miss it.

'Who do you think I saw at Honeysucklelay?'

'Pippa, I suppose.'

Again, knowledge he did not have.

'She sent her love.'

'Silly little nuisance. She wants her bottom smacked.'

How irritating Susie could be.

'I quite admire her.'

'Better not tell Belinda. She's livid with her.' Belinda was Susie's sister.

'I gave her a tenner.'

'A tenner for the Russians?'

It was a silly conversation. Susie was being silly and James had nothing sensible to say in reply. Probably he had handed over the tenner because he was sorry for Pippa, not because he admired her. So that took the politics out of the gesture. He thought he was apolitical, although that was too grand a word for not bothering much either way. He was what the populist newspapers called a member of the silent majority, inflating the apathy of their readers into something important and British. The thought came to James that he really cared about very little. Or rather he cared only about little things. He wanted to move without too much trouble from one day to the next. That didn't seem something to reproach himself over. And yet he would never say, outright, to anyone, I don't care about anything much. So perhaps there was something to be ashamed of. Don't care was made to care. That was an ethic in his upbringing. He couldn't reject it now. But he no longer cared about it. He cared a bit about his work. Changing over had been interesting. But he cared less about the new way of printing than the old. The secrets had gone. He cared about his sons, he supposed, but they were grown up. One lived abroad and the other lived in the north, so he saw them irregularly. They were both in good but boring-sounding modern jobs that he did not understand, one a systems analyst, the other a loss adjuster. He cared about Susie, despite her stupid remarks. Or thought he did. He had pondered a lot over her wild oat in Morocco, although he had said nothing.

He was immune to the consumer society. He understood it. It offered shiny things, but he didn't want any of them. He could make quite a long list of things he didn't want, although he could afford them. They included a personal computer, television games, a second home, a cycle exerciser, private health insurance, a car telephone and a video of the sort Watney had offered him. Susie wanted a microwave oven and a home sunbed. If she wanted them enough, that is, coveted them, he wouldn't oppose her. It was no argument simply to say he didn't want them himself.

'People are what they seem,' Susie said.

'Are they?'

'You're not listening. You think you're clever and superior because I say your tenner will go to help the Russians. But I'm not stupid. Pippa's a little fool who thinks she can stop war by sleeping out and getting pneumonia. That's my opinion, and it's as good as yours.'

'I don't think you're stupid, Susie.'

'I won't be patronised. I was screwed by a strange man in Morocco. Why don't you say something about it?'

'You didn't want to talk about it.'

'But you're thinking about it. Don't brood. You're getting very broody.'

Susie wanted a quarrel. Her decision to quarrel about her infidelity, just as he had been thinking about it, did not surprise James: umpteen years of marriage had convinced him that there was a rough telepathy between people who were close. The theme of the quarrel did not matter. A quarrel had been declared, and any theme would do. Before reading *War and Peace* James had read Clausewitz, and had made the discovery, as he thought, that family quarrels were a continuation of policy by other means. Theirs had not been a quarrelsome marriage, but its very length meant that there had been a number of quarrels, and that one or two had been of historical power, building up like crises between states and settled only by prolonged negotiations.

'I don't want to quarrel with you,' James said. 'But I can't refuse you anything.'

'You are a nasty bastard sometimes. I don't want a quarrel. I just want to tell you something.'

James said nothing. Perhaps he had got the signals wrong. He waited for Susie's diplomatic note to be delivered.

'I'm leaving,' she said. 'Going away,' she amended.

Leaving. Going away. James examined the words with a diplomatist's pedantry. 'To Belinda's?' From time to time Susie went away to stay with her sister.

'Not to Belinda's, no. To Susie's.'

A confused look from James. The communiqué did not appear to be at all well drafted.

'I've taken a little place of my own.' Clarification of a sort, but of a sort that only demanded further questions.

'Let me spell it out,' Susie said. 'I am going away. I don't want to be dramatic about it. I don't want to be hostile. I accept that this is a surprise, possibly even a shock. No, there is no one else, notwithstanding the Morocco business. That may have had something to do with it, or may not have. It would probably, certainly, have happened anyway. I simply want to live on my own.'

Susie paused. A form of words that encapsulated the reasons for leaving seemed suddenly to come to her.

'I'm over the accepted age of retirement, and I want to retire from marriage.'

James felt himself smile, either from its absurdity or perhaps its aptness.

'Very well,' Susie said, 'I may come crawling back like a stupid dog, a silly bitch, and then it will be up to you to decide whether you want to have me back in the kennel. But I may not. Don't count on it. I haven't decided to go with the idea of coming back. Obviously.'

'How long has . . .' James began, and then broke off the sentence. He didn't want to say anything that might be mis-understood. He felt himself caught up with the passion of Susie's ultimatum. He felt very affectionate towards her, perhaps loved her.

'Quite a long time,' Susie said, 'but then my thoughts suddenly came together and I saw the beautiful logic of it.'

'Leaving me?'

'Don't be mawkish. You're perfectly capable of doing for yourself the duties which I have long done for you. You can make your own evening meal, or eat out. You can send your things to the laundry. You can keep the place tidy yourself or get someone to come in and do for you a couple of times a week. As for me, I have a place, which I like.'

'And can pay for it?'

'Ah, the facts of life. If need be, I can support myself. As a retired wife who has given devoted service, I believe I qualify for a pension. You can afford it, but I won't take you to an industrial tribunal.'

'Of course I'll look after you.'

'That's a bit wishy-washy, but I accept. So much for the practicalities. The impracticalities are more difficult. I have to hope that you'll be able to solve them yourself. What I mean is, I suppose you'll feel rejected. I'm not rejecting you. Children are allowed, expected, to leave home. Decent parents make it as easy as possible for them to go without whining about rejection. Why should children have all the privileges? I hope you won't grumble. I hope that we'll stay, godawful word, friends.'

'When is this going to happen?'

'I'm off tomorrow.'

They talked a little more, but not much more. James thought afterwards that it was like receiving the resignation of a long-serving and highly regarded employee. One's immediate impulse was to reject the resignation as absurd, but the very length of the employee's service, the employee's experience and judgement meant that the decision could not be rejected impulsively. If so many previous decisions had been regarded as sound, why not this one? James considered the possibility that Susie had suddenly gone off her head, but decided that, as a husband, he could not possibly judge. A consequence of living with one person over a great period of time is that anything that person did, though seemingly unusual to an uncommitted observer, came within the acceptable limits of normality to the spouse. James knew a couple where the wife's behaviour seemed to him eccentric but which her husband seemed to believe was simply endearing. The world of marriage was a laboratory of delights for the psychiatrist. What would a psychiatrist make of Susie? He would probably say that there was nothing wrong with her. James was the nutty one. That is how it worked out in television series. He was, what? Confused? Concerned, per-haps. Not so much about Susie. She had an option to return and resume her life as though nothing had happened. He faced the possibility of an enforced change in his life. Susie had spoken of retiring from marriage. But retirement was planned. When it arrived no one in the circle of the person who was retiring was particularly surprised. Really? Already? Well it comes to us all. There was no more surprise than that. Susie's departure had been sprung on him like a death in the family, but it was more surprising than that. Death is commonplace. One could hardly say that about the retirement of a wife.

Susie did leave next day. She packed the clothes she would need for the following week or so, and said that she would send for the rest, together with her more bulky possessions, including some furniture. She provided James with a list. She gave him her address and said that he would be welcome to call, but should phone her first. To begin with, he hardly noticed that she had gone. The momentum of her management of the house carried on for a few days. There was food in the kitchen, and the place became untidy only slowly. Susie had left lists about when the rubbish had to be put out for the dustmen and when the milkman called for his bill to be settled. She was not there when he returned from work, but even that was not immediately notice-able because she had often gone out for an evening. Occasionally someone asked for her on the telephone, and James said that she had gone away for a bit. James told himself that this was a miserable business, but partly he did so because he thought he should be miserable.

However, after about a week the routine of the house began to falter through lack of maintenance. One evening James found the fridge empty of anything pleasing. The freezer was full, but he had not put anything out to be defrozen. The following day, when he was down to his last clean shirt, he bundled up his dirty laundry and took it to a launderette. The cheerful Irish lady manageress took it and, for what James considered to be a remarkably small extra sum, said that she would put it in the machine and it would be ready for him to collect that evening. So she did, but when James got his laundry home he discovered that, clean though it was, it still had to be pressed. He hadn't used an iron since his time in the army. While he was ironing the phone rang. James was inclined to ignore it: the call would probably be from one of Susie's friends. But conditioning made him pick it up. It was Gerard.

'I was wondering when you were coming to see George?'

James had a clear recollection of saying that he had no plans to see him, but he did not say that. He was not displeased to hear Gerard. He belonged to more or less normal days.

'How is George?'

'George is in London now.'

'Is he better?'

'Better?'

'The wound?'

'Oh yes, tons better. Writing his memoirs.'

'Interesting.'

'I think he'd like to see you.'

'About the memoirs?'

'That, and other things. His other ideas, you remember, the ones that interested you?'

James had forgotten them, and was not sure they interested him now. But he wouldn't mind getting away for a bit, to think things out from, what? A different perspective. Yes. He didn't find George Watney's company displeasing. He didn't even mind Gerard.

'I might manage a quick trip,' he said.

'When?'

'Well, I'll have to fix up a hotel.'

'Stay with George. He has room.'

James hesitated. The chief appeal of the trip was a few days of normal living: meals cooked by someone else, ironed shirts. Two men sharing a flat, which presumably was what Watney had taken, did not sound very comfortable.

'George would really appreciate it.'

'Very well. Thank George, and say I'll be glad to accept his invitation.'

He could always move out.

'When?'

'In a day or two, if it's convenient.'

'Tomorrow?'

'All right, tomorrow.'

James was glad to abandon the house next day. He banged the front door shut as he left, as though to shut in the muddle. He had the thought that if Susie returned she would be cross; no, disgusted. But at least she would restore it to order. If she didn't come back, he would have to get someone in to take it in hand. It was a job for a specialist.

The train was fuller than he had expected. Sitting opposite James was a young man, presumably in the army as there was a soldier's number on his valise. He examined for a long time a piece of paper which looked like a pay slip, but otherwise appeared to have nothing else to read; perhaps he was in training for the monotony of his profession. Next to him was a pretty black woman who looked about thirty but when she examined her wallet James noticed that she had a student's railcard. Sitting next to James was a child writing a story entitled 'The Train Accident'. James had a corner seat and he felt chirpy as he watched the landscape going by in circles. London suggested civilised sanctuary from the trials of Norfolk. He opened *War and Peace* at page 1168 and rode with Kutuzov as his soldiers harried the retreating army of Napoleon.

At Liverpool Street station James was met by Gerard, who was wearing a jacket that looked as if it was made of green oilskin. It had the appearance of a rural jacket. In rural East Anglia he had worn a town suit. James felt warmth towards him. Gerard had a sort of predictable pattern.

Gerard was in one of his courteous moods and insisted on carrying James's suitcase to the taxi. They drove through the City and towards Euston Road. Trading cities look more comfortable than manufacturing cities, James thought.

'Is it far?'

'Regent's Park.'

'Oh yes,' James said, although the name meant no more than a name to him. He was a peasant: it was extraordinary how ignorant he was of the geography of London. 'The Zoo?'

'Pardon me?'

'It's in Regent's Park, the Zoo.'

'Never been there.'

'Funny, neither have I.'

As they passed King's Cross, James said, merely to fill the silence, 'So Merle has gone back to America?'

'I believe so.'

'Leaving George alone?'

'Not quite.'

A conversational thought occurred to James. 'Does the name

Frances mean anything to you?'

'Of course. George's first wife.'

'What became of her?'

'Still about, I believe.'

'George never mentioned her.'

'Minefield. Dangerous. Keep off.'

James was unable to pursue this promising thread of talk because the taxi had arrived at its destination.

They were outside one of the Nash terraces that stand with casual confidence overlooking the park.

'This isn't all George's,' Gerard said as he touched a bellpush. 'Just the top bit.' The entryphone emitted Watney's voice and they walked in. He was waiting for them when they got out of the lift and gave James a strong handshake accompanied by a grasp of his shoulder. It was a soldierly welcome, but the soldier had become a writer. He wore tweed trousers, a loose suede jacket and a flannel shirt. Watney, James thought, liked to be seen in the right uniform.

The top bit, as Gerard had called it, was on two vast floors. Watney said it was the servants' quarters, which it probably had been, but it had been built at a time when even servants' rooms had pretty cornices in the ceilings. Whoever had converted it into a modern flat, adding a gadgety kitchen and a well-plumbed bathroom, had kept all the gentle features. 'I could have gone for the big number,' Watney said, 'but I thought, why not live as the locals live?'

James smiled but Watney seemed to be serious. He showed James to his room. 'I guess a maid slept here, James. Hope the thought won't keep you awake at nights.'

The room was larger than James's bedroom at home. A window gave on to a stone balustrade on which there were pots of geraniums. It might have been a maid's room, James thought, or possibly a room for several maids, but more likely for a servant higher in the hierarchy, even a butler.

'You're making me very comfortable.'

'My pleasure. Anyway, if you want anything just ask Molly.'

Molly was standing in the doorway, appraising her new charge.

'This is Mr Palmer, Molly. My very good friend.'

Molly was pretty, but James's immediate thought was that she was a provider of laundry and of meals. 'Hallo, Molly.' He gave her what he hoped looked like a friendly nod. He wondered if she lived in or if the place was now too grand to be a home for servants. He wondered if Gerard had a room in the flat or was merely a visitor. Both questions were soon answered. The three men had lunch together and afterwards Gerard left, saying that he would look in the following day, or if he couldn't he would phone. Molly did live in the flat. Watney seemed surprised that James should ask.

'But treat her kindly. She's sweated labour, but I can't fill up the place with staff.'

James was wondering if Molly might complain of unkind treatment were he to ask her to iron the half a dozen shirts he had brought, clean but crumpled, from home. But when he went to his room his case had been unpacked and the shirts, miraculously, were stowed neatly pressed in a drawer. London, he felt, was returning his life to normal.

James had expected, or perhaps half expected, Watney to be recuperating from his wound; not perhaps in bed, but at least would have an arm in a sling or a bit of a hobble. Watney did have a wound, but it had not in any way crippled him. He took off his shirt to show it to James. There was a shallow scar across the top of his left shoulder. It was still pink and was decorated with a parallel line of pink dots where it had been stitched. The bullet that had hit Watney had not, he believed, come from the enemy Polisario but from a wayward shot from the besieged Moroccan truck. Watney explained at some length how this could have happened, pointing in the air with his long bony fingers to indicate the trajectories. James nodded in what he hoped looked an intelligent way, but he understood little of it. He found himself wondering how Watney, having at last seen action, felt about being hit by a friendly bullet. Watney answered without being asked. Action was action. Anyone could be caught in crossfire. He hadn't complained about the booby in the truck. At Layoun the incident had been recounted in the simple way of good military history. Watney had been recommended for a Moroccan medal. He was satisfied, and the incident had done some good for the United States in the region.

'Many useful acts on the battlefield should not be too closely investigated,' he said.

'Something for your memoirs?'

A long pause from Watney. Eventually he said, 'Writing is hard, James.'

James smiled. 'I'm sure it is.'

'No, I mean very hard. So hard. I can tell a story. I've just told you a story. You found it interesting?'

James nodded. It wasn't uninteresting.

'Right. But putting it down on paper . . . Ah.'

'Writer's block.' James murmured a phrase that seemed apposite.

'I haven't written enough to have a block.'

Watney said that he had considered taking some kind of practical course in writing before beginning his memoirs. Such a step would have been in line with his experience. Each step he had taken in his life had been preceded by a period of training. But a friend, a former colleague who was now a publisher, had assured him that such an act would be unnecessary, even unwise. Watney had something to say. So say it. To become the pupil of a probably failed writer, who would use words like syntax and discourse on the philosophy of the full stop, would needlessly harass Watney. It would be a crime, the publisher said. 'Did he say crime? He was probably pissed at the time.'

Watney, in a rare moment of hesitancy, had told the publisher that his writing would not be very stylish, but he was assured that stylishness was not required. What he should aim for was straightforward, gutsy writing. Watney had been known in the service for frank, clear and sometimes hard-hitting memos. Exactly right, the publisher had said. Think of the book as a memo, rather longer than usual.

So he had taken this flat in London instead of returning immediately to the States, where every old friend, every relative would be expected to be seen. Merle had gone ahead and was now happily looking for a house for them; and he was happily undistracted. All he needed was the words. Each day he sat at his desk. Hours later he had written two or three paragraphs, much of which had been crossed out. There were days when he thought he was making progress because he seemed to be crossing out fewer words. But the sheer labour of filling up a whole book was beginning to appal him. It would take years at this rate.

'I feel, James, like a butterfly collector unable to net a single

73

butterfly. I'm buzzing with ideas but I simply can't collect them.'

This conversation between James and George Watney was taking place in the room which Watney had furnished as an office. It had a solid desk that Dickens would have been content to use, an electric typewriter which had been presumably installed for atmosphere as Watney could not type, and an antique-looking cupboard which James knew contained drink. He and Watney were both nursing glasses of whisky. The window had a view overlooking the park. It was the ideal garret for a writer who did not have to pause to consider the quite ridiculously high rent, but it had not enabled Watney to write. Watney looked vulnerable sitting there in this silly writer's room, in his silly writer's clothes. Gerard had said that Watney was lonely, and perhaps he was. A soldier, James thought, was rarely lonely, in a physical sense. There was the loneliness of command: lonely at the top, that sort of thing, but there was never a shortage of companions. Privacy was the problem. Now Watney saw few people, Gerard, Molly the maid and now James. Even Merle had gone, or had been sent away, as part of Watney's writer period. What he should do was to cut his losses, which anyway he probably wouldn't think very high, and resume his normal life, whatever an American ex-General's life was: running a battery chicken farm, perhaps, or becoming chairman of a unit trust company. However, James said none of this. He remarked, 'Why don't you just chat into a tape-recorder?'

'And get someone to turn it into words?'

'Yes.'

'Has Gerard been talking to you about this?'

'No.'

'Because this is my idea.'

'No, he's said nothing. It's worth trying though.'

'Will you do it? The words.'

James smiled and shook his head. 'I'm a printer, not a writer.'

'Are you bargaining, James? I don't mind. I just want to know.'

'Of course not. It's not my skill. I'm no more of a writer than, well, you say you are.'

'I won't be ungenerous.'

'No, it's not that. But there shouldn't be any difficulty finding a . . .' James searched for the right word: not ghost, not hack. '. . . finding an editor.'

'I don't want an editor. I want you. You did all right on that Honeysucklelay leaflet. I still remember that.'

'That was long ago.'

'James, why are you here?'

Why was he here? Because Gerard had persuaded him to come by telling him that Watney was lonely and wanted the company of an old friend. That was one reason. Another, and perhaps more persuasive, reason was that after Susie's departure and the mess in the house he had felt like a change. Neither of these reasons now sounded particularly compelling. Gerard had also talked of some plan of Watney's. James should have pressed him about what it was. The memoirs of an old soldier were far from intriguing.

Watney apparently misinterpreted James's silence, for he said, 'A thousand a week. No, let's make it two thousand. Britain can do with the money. Generosity, James, is the socialism of America.'

James's first thought was whether Watney was talking about pounds or dollars. But in either currency it would be an extraordinary large sum; by Norfolk's standards anyway, and, he would have thought, by the standards of anyone he knew. It was the sort of money you read about in gossip columns. He was astonished by it, although he did not covet it. He had an income big enough for his needs, and a bit more. He did not have the greed that makes an outstanding businessman. All the same, Watney's offer was dazzling. He gave a little snuffly laugh. It was like winning something.

'Here's the deal,' Watney said. 'I'll dictate two or three hours a day. Just random stuff. But I'll try to keep it in some kind of sequence. You get out of that, say, five thousand words. That's twenty-five thousand words a week. We'll knock off the book in a month. How's about it?'

James said nothing.

'Try it for a week?'

James had planned to stay in London for a few days. The visit could be stretched for a week. He heard himself say, 'All right.'

Watney took his hand and squeezed his shoulder. 'You're a tough man to haggle with, James.' He went to the drinks cupboard and refilled their glasses.

'James,' he said, 'you don't mind if I have you checked out?'

A little American joke. James smiled. But Watney seemed to be serious, or else the joke was a clumsy one.

'Not in depth, of course,' he said. 'You'll hardly notice it.'

James said nothing for a moment, not because he was thinking, but because he wasn't sure what to say.

'Is this necessary?'

'No, I guess not. No, not at all. I'm talking rat shit. You'll have to bear with me, James. I keep forgetting I'm no longer a soldier.'

Watney was trying to make light of an awkward moment, but he did not have a light touch. Instead of humour he offered expletives directed against himself. Rat shit was one he favoured. People he disliked might be a bunch of jerks, and if they appeared to have changed their mind they were getting religion, possibly after having their feet held to the fire. However, those unable to see reason had their minds set in concrete. This, however, was not to be confused with getting into bed with someone. Watney was always prepared to hash things out, to have things run by him again in order to achieve happiness. There were pastel shades of feeling in such primary-coloured language. However, Watney used all such colour sparingly, perhaps aware that it lost its impact on repetition. Mostly he spoke in simple, almost formalised, English, as though he had spent his life trying to perfect the art of unambiguous communication.

★ 4 ★

Freed from what he called the tyranny of the pen, Watney produced a fluent and extensive flow of reminiscences. He had an orderly mind and used the David Copperfield system of biography, starting with his birth and working onwards. When James, in his new career as editor, began to transcribe the tape-recording he found that there were long passages that could go straight on to paper, putting in the necessary punctuation, and using the general style for capitalisation, collective nouns and other pedantries that were in operation at James's printing firm. There were two problems. One was the sheer bulk of Watney's output as he rolled out all the lumber of his life as though Mr Freud himself was listening. Freud might have made the occasional note between dozing off. James had to type out every conjunction. He could type. In his employee days he had learnt to use a Linotype, and the knowledge of the keyboard soon returned to his fingers. But it was laborious work. The other problem was that, although Watney tried to report his life in a simple sequence, he occasionally interrupted it to amplify an earlier passage, or to recall a new anecdote. He also spoke of letters and other documents that James had to find in Watney's vast files. There were also tapes that Watney had made years before, particularly early in his career. Fitting together this jigsaw not only took a great deal of time, it also meant that the type-script then needed to be retyped to produce a fair copy. Watney then read this through and made new corrections.

All these snags came up on the first day. By the third day James had made his labours much easier by acquiring a word-processor, which can reshape sentences and paragraphs as though they were made of putty. By fortuitous coincidence James knew a great deal about word-processors. They had been installed in his firm as part of the great change-over. He put the idea to Watney of buying one, prepared to argue that, although it would be costly, it would probably work out cheaper than getting a secretary. Watney didn't argue. He agreed to it as though it were no more a luxury than a wastepaper basket, which in some ways it resembled. James phoned the salesman who had sold him the equipment for his firm and the machine was delivered immediately. At the end of the third day James placed before Watney a sheaf of faultless, immaculately typed pages. As Watney gazed at his pristine masterpiece he said, 'Is this a British machine? Japanese?'

'American.'

'Ah, we do some things right.'

James had taken over Watney's office. Watney seemed happy to surrender it. He dictated into his recorder while laid back on a sofa in the living room. The time passed easily. Although the work was new to James, the routine was familiar. It was a male routine, serviced by Molly, who did all the non-male duties, concerned with food and such domestic matters, with unobtrusive efficiency. Gerard did not appear for several days. He walked in one morning when James was scrutinising the screen of his word-processor.

'You've joined the team?'

'Just helping out.' James looked up briefly, offering only the minimum of politeness. He had, he calculated, at least two hours' work ahead of him. But Gerard apparently wanted to be companionable, or had nothing else to do. He sat down.

'Anything I can do?'

'Thanks, no.'

'Is this the new technology?'

'Some of it.'

'Computers and so on?'

'That's it.'

'You old guys are full of surprises.'

James turned to look at Gerard. 'This old guy's quite busy.'

Gerard smiled pleasantly. 'Sorry. What about a cup of coffee?'

'All right. Will you tell Molly?'

'I've told her. She's bringing it in.'

Gerard settled back in the one easy chair in the room. He had a way of looking like a fixture. The coffee arrived. 'Five minutes and then I'll have to turf you out,' James said.

'The workers need their break,' Gerard said easily. 'An

exchange of grumbles between mates, some gossip about the boss.'

Gerard's assumptions did not appeal to James. He did not see himself as a mate and he did not care for the idea of having a boss. He was about to say something on these lines, but held back. Gerard's provocative style should not be encouraged.

Gerard got up and went over to the printing machine where the typed pages of Watney's memoirs were stacked. He picked up a page and started to read it.

'Any good?'

'Very passable.'

'Very passable.' Gerard repeated the words slowly as though tasting them. 'Isn't that what reviewers say about junk books when they've nothing to say?'

'Or about junk films?'

It wasn't a bad retort and Gerard acknowledged it with a little laugh.

'We workers mustn't squabble. That's doing the boss's work. Divide and subjugate.'

'I'm not a worker, except in the most general sense. I'm not your mate, Gerard, and while this is Watney's book I'm editing, I certainly don't think of him as my boss.'

Gerard nodded, as though agreeing with James. Having achieved his apparent aim of irritating James he resumed his chair and sipped his coffee. 'Forgive me, James. I get bored.'

'Perhaps if you did some work?'

'Oh, James.'

'I know all about gathering atmosphere, and sleeping in stables with the horse. But there must be a time when you actually do some filming. Or is it just a concept? The film is in the viewer's mind?'

'That's not a bad idea, James.'

'Seriously.'

'Seriously, I'm waiting for something to happen. So I become a nuisance.'

Gerard was like a pestering dog that rolled on its back when a hand was raised to it. He now regarded James with reproachful eyes.

'Don't be stupid, Gerard. You're all an act.'

James listened to his own words. That was true. Gerard was an act. But Watney was an act, too. Even Molly was an act. She was almost too accomplished as a maid, as though she was on stage in a small part, a soon-to-be famous actress at the beginning of her career. She dressed well, in well-cut uniforms which she changed according to the time of day. They had the look of expensive clothes. James had had enough experience of servants to know that they weren't accomplished and well dressed. They were sloppy and didn't much care for their jobs. Only he of the four people who used this flat was ordinary, normal. James had a twinge of yearning to be among real people again. Susie was normal. She had this silly idea of retiring from marriage, but she was mostly normal. His two sons and their families were normal, desperately normal. Pippa was normally keen to get rid of the bomb; nothing abnormal about that for a young person. Even Merle was normally interested in shopping and scandal. James wished vaguely she were here. At least he understood her.

'Do you feel trapped, James? No, I'm not trying to provoke you. I sometimes feel trapped.'

'Then untrap yourself.'

'Perhaps trap isn't the right word. George wouldn't like it, being a freedom-loving American. You won't tell him, will you? Of course not. I think I see him more as a collector. He likes a few people round to furnish the house. You know what I mean? He's collected me. I am, you'll have to take my word for it, quite a clever maker of films. I can get work. But here I am, a piece of furniture, nothing much to do, bothering you.'

'Why don't you push off then?'

'You think I should? I value your advice.'

James smiled a bit helplessly. 'I can't advise you. But if you want to get on with something else, why not do it?'

'Just go, you mean?'

'Well, tell George of course. Have a chat with him. He's a reasonable man.'

'Reasonable? You think people become generals by being reasonable?'

'I've always found him reasonable.'

'But you haven't seen him for a quarter of a century. Did he used to be reasonable?'

James found it irritating to be arguing over a word.

'Why not just chat with him?'

80

'He'll try to talk me out of going. He's very persuasive, and I'm persuadable. What he can't do by persuasion he'll try with bribery, and I'm bribable.'

James hated the word. 'He's a very generous man.'

'Oh, there's that. But what's he up to? That's the thing. That's the bribe.'

James shook his head. 'You've lost me now.'

Gerard regarded James for a few seconds and seemed about to say something. But he got up and walked to the door. 'Workers' break over. Thanks for the coffee.'

That evening, according to a routine that after only a few days had become a custom, James had dinner with Watney. Gerard was not there. Molly served the meal, and had presumably cooked it. She was wearing a grey dress that James thought might be of silk. It went well with the dining room, but was quite impractical for the kitchen. The fancy occurred to James that perhaps she changed clothes as she went from room to room. Or, more prosaically, perhaps she had an assistant who came in for the evening. The food was simple and delicious. Susie cooked well, but this food had, what?, a kind of restaurant style about it. When they had had a couple of glasses of wine each James asked Watney about Frances, the wife James had known. Watney said that they had divorced, got tired of each other. He didn't show any desire to talk about her, but the mention of her name did not set off the minefield that Gerard had spoken of. His daughter Prettiford was living in the States and had a grown-up family. Time passes. That seemed to be all that was to be said about her. They talked about Watney's memoirs, but not very much. James said he had chatted to Gerard and wondered how the film was coming along.

'You've noticed it, too?'

'I did wonder when the cameras were going to start turning,' James said and then had a qualm of conscience, as though he was sneaking.

'Don't worry about it,' Watney said. 'Gerard's a very sharp boy. I'll show you something later.'

Watney's praise for Gerard made James feel sneakier still, and a touch put down. He would liked to have erased his remark. Ridiculously, he felt he had lowered himself in Watney's estimation. It was an absurd feeling for a person of his age, the owner of his own business. Perhaps Watney was the boss, or at least thought he was. However, by the end of the meal, when they had left the table and James was sitting in an easy chair and sipping brandy, any feelings of inadequacy had passed. His relationship to Watney was what it had been on that evening after the party at Agadir. They were two old friends chatting together. The something of Gerard's that Watney had to show James was a typescript which read as follows:

CHARLESTON: A TREATMENT

At fourteen minutes past eight on the morning of August 6 a B29 bomber appears in a cloudless sky over the American city of Charleston and releases an atomic bomb, killing or injuring some 78,000 people. At least, these become, for a time, the generally accepted details. The parallel between the bombing of Charleston and the bombing on Hiroshima all those years previously seems so clear that there is a natural loony desire to make all the details match. It is quite likely that the bomb explodes at, say, 8.15 or 8.17, but the Hiroshima time was, according to history, 8.14, and reporters like their facts to fit. The time of the Charleston explosion is later fixed in the public's mind by a widely published photograph of the face of a pretty woman whose last living act is to shield her eyes from the flash. The time on her digital wristwatch is clearly 8.14. This photograph becomes an ikon of the event, in the same way that the picture of soldiers erecting a flag symbolised the United States victory in the Pacific in the Second World War, and, like it, is of doubtful provenance.

Then there is the state of the weather. The sky may be clear, as it had been over Hiroshima, but early mornings on that part of the Atlantic coast are often misty. And who actually sees the B29? Who can have known that a picture of Rita Hayworth was pasted on the bomb just before it is released, just as the Hiroshima bomb, Little Boy – or was it Fat Man? – had been similarly tastelessly decorated? The figure of casualties is purely notional. Charleston has, or up to now had, an official population of 66,000, although on a warm day in August there are a lot of visitors.

Reports of the event begin to seep out to an ever wider

audience, sweeping effortlessly to a position of unchallengeable importance as the talking point of the world. Some of the more solemn newspapers, and the more cautious television stations, if such exist, treat the more bizarre details with caution, but the central fact, the dropping of an atom bomb on an American city, secures its priority over almost any other conceivable event, and certainly over the normal chaff of the day, the state of the economy, the doings of royals and the thoughts of statesmen. It is a prodigy, not simply a surpassing calamity but an American calamity. Watching the United States deal with a disaster is an entertainment, black and appalling, but irresistibly watchable. The Soviet Union and China are boringly shy: catastrophes are state secrets. They are ashamed of them. But for Americans they are a test of confidence, a trial by ordeal to be enacted publicly, aided by the most voyeuristic information system in the world. London and Paris and Budapest are obviously moved by the fate of their fellow whites in Charleston; but Bangladeshis, watching on communal television in the middle of nowhere, are also transfixed. Their own continent has natural catastrophies more enduring, but they affect only the poor. How much more interesting to watch the rich at bay. Even the disposal of a head of state, a Kennedy, a Nixon, a routine enough event in many countries, and swiftly remedied, becomes in the United States an engrossing mystery story. What will the Americans do with Charleston?

The world is not at war. The possibility that the Russians have lobbed over a missile is swiftly and almost desperately dismissed by the Russians themselves. Within minutes, or perhaps seconds, of the explosion being detected by their satellite they protest their innocence with the indignation of naughty boys caught with stones near a broken window. The Americans already know the Russians weren't to blame; nevertheless, their denial is generally greeted with relief. A more likely explanation for the explosion is that a bomb had been dropped by a butterfingers in an American air force plane. The air force denies that any of its planes has been near Charleston, let alone one carrying a bomb. This denial is treated by the public with more scepticism than the Soviet denial had been. It is assumed that the air force would lie. But the government is satisfied that this is true, leaving official spokesmen in the quite impossible position of not having the slightest idea what caused the explosion. However, they rally, concealing their ignorance by simply being uncommunicative. Their silence allows a number of interesting, though fanciful, theories to be taken seriously. One is that the bomb came from outer space. A crashed satellite, aliens, an extraterrestrial? Take your choice. Official sources do not discourage this speculation. If, as many people are still inclined to believe, the explosion has been caused by some dreadful official blunder, an alien may be the perfect scapegoat. The fairy tales of the twentieth century are powerful. Now put your faith in Captain Kirk to get us out of this mess.

A variation of the alien theory is the natural phenomenon. A kaleidoscope of vaguely connected scientific phenomena circles the earth. Of pollution and ecology, space probes and the ozone barrier, lead in petrol and wanton damage to the Brazilian rain forest. It is a good time to be an expert.

In this period of confusion it is natural enough that most decent Americans want some reassurance from the President. But the President is in Africa. The news of the Charleston explosion is conveyed to him, seemingly with difficulty, over a crackly telephone, and naturally he decides to fly home immediately; and thankfully, it seems. The African visit has been arduous, compounded of heat and flies and indigestible food and arguments with his host, also a president, who seems to think that the purpose of the visit is to provide him with large numbers of military aircraft of such sophistication that even Americans find them almost unflyable. The President is an uncomplicated man. His first thought, on hearing the news of Charleston, is of the amazingly good judgement of Providence in placing him safely in Africa, dump that it is, rather than the States, where he would now be dead, or flying around for ever in an aerial White House deciding which Russian cities to blow up in retaliation. For the President, like most ordinary people, assumed at first that the devastation of an American city could only have been the result of Russian mischief. The exoneration of the Russians, though a relief in some ways, means that an alternative enemy has to be found, sternly denounced and dealt with. The possible candidates seem to be rather limited. However, help is at hand. From the Japanese. A story is circulating that some crazy Jap has dropped the bomb in revenge for Hiroshima.

Tora! Tora! Tora! The date is right, and a look at the atlas shows that Charleston is about the same size as Hiroshima and, like Hiroshima, is by the sea. It is even about the same latitude as Hiroshima. A single Japanese avenger is soon discounted. There has to be a number of revengeful Japanese if a bomber has been used for the raid. The bomber could have taken off from a private landing strip anywhere near Charleston, arriving undetected over the city because no one expects it. The bomb has presumably been made in Japan. No problem there. Everyone knows how clever the Japs are at copying things. There is so much weapons-grade plutonium available in the world that this is the least mysterious aspect of the event. Where is the bomber now? No doubt that will emerge. It is all suspiciously incredible.

The President does not name Japan, but neither does he not name it. He promises unremitting pursuit of the barbarians, whoever they are, and the full weight of American retribution. He says that Charleston's agony is America's agony. Indeed it is. Historically minded Americans recall that not one, but two American atom bombs fell on Japan, the second on Nagasaki on August 9. Is the terror bomber even now being refuelled and rearmed for a second attack on an American city? Which city is at risk? Look at the atlas again for American cities around the same latitude as Nagasaki. There seems to be an awful lot of them. A lot of American homes apparently have atlases, for people in these cities are leaving in large numbers. The President calls for calm and for trust in the government. Every one of these Hero Cities is being given the very finest defence that America can provide. No one, especially in the Hero Cities, has much confidence in this.

The Japanese government is understandably upset. It points out that there are no nuclear weapons in Japan whatsoever. No one takes much notice of this. Nevertheless, it offers help and its own experience in helping to clear up Charleston. This is ignored. The windows of shops selling Japanese televisions are smashed by patriotic Americans. It is reported that a Japanese pilot has been arrested in connection with the explosion. Much advice is offered on how to deal with him, some of it coming from professional torturers who promise one hundred per cent results. The arrest, however, turns out to be only a rumour.

A somewhat unhealthy interest in Charleston is being shown by the Pentagon. The place is regarded as a laboratory of warfare, of far more use than those nuclear tests that, to appease the pacifists, are held underground. They privately prepare to monitor the results of a second raid, should the unthinkable happen and the bomber get through. The pollsters are busy too, with their clipboards and questions. From being rather frightened, the United States becomes rather interested. It is extraordinary how people do adapt to crises.

James said, 'Is that all?'

'For the present.'

James shuffled the subversive sheets of paper. 'Is it a bit, well, frivolous?'

'Gerard has a black sense of humour. You've probably noticed.'

James hadn't noticed. But it wasn't important. Black humour sounded to him like bad taste. But he didn't want to have another exchange about Gerard.

'Very imaginative,' he said.

'Got you hooked, hey?'

'Well, naturally one wonders who can have dropped the bomb.'

'That's it. Who done it? Who did do it, James?'

No solution came to James's mind. He didn't much like mysteries. The denouement, where the least likely candidate turns out to be the villain, was never convincing, and the intricate explanation tiresome. His own experience of the little mysteries in everyday life was that the villain was the person you first suspected.

'My guess would be an official blunder, an accident.'

Watney closed his eyes for a moment, as though considering this for the first time.

'What about the Japs?' he said.

'A bit far fetched.'

'Wasn't Pearl Harbor far fetched? And Hiroshima itself? And the Kennedy assassination? And the Falklands war? Was Churchill far fetched? Am I far fetched, a General who has never seen action, a deficiency that I remedied only recently? For fuck's sake, do we have to rule out everything in this rat shit world because it's far fetched? I like you, James. I trust you. But I've got to tell you one thing. You've got to let your imagination free sometimes. You can't go belly up just because something is far fetched. There are more things in heaven and earth: you know the saying?'

James knew it well, but he assumed that Shakespeare had something deeper in mind than a crass film about blowing up Charleston. He did not say this. He was saved from saying anything at that moment because Molly was standing at the door. She was wearing a white coat over her dress.

'Come in, Molly.'

There was a couch in the room. Watney got up and went over to it.

James got up to go. He assumed something intimate was about to take place.

'No, stay a bit, James. The talk was just getting interesting. Molly, give Mr Palmer another brandy.'

James sat down again. His brandy glass was recharged. 'I'll leave the bottle there,' Molly said, smiling, and placing it on a side table. She looked very calm, James thought, in her various roles. He wondered again if she were an actress. He had heard that actresses often had to take odd jobs between plays.

Watney had undressed and was lying on the couch, face down. Molly knelt beside him and massaged his neck and back and the backs of his legs. Watney uttered grunts of encouragement. 'That's good. That's good. That's very good.'

Molly had with her a small leather bag of the sort that doctors used to carry. She unfastened the clasp and took out a bottle, poured a little oil on her hand and applied it to the scar on Watney's shoulder.

'How is it today, General?'

'Easing nicely, Molly. Very nicely.'

Molly took from her bag a plastic sheet. 'Lift up, General,' she said and slid the sheet neatly under his body. In her hand now she had a rubber tube with a bulb in the middle, and something like a hot water bottle at one end. James recognised the apparatus, although the memory was a distant one from a time in hospital. Watney was having an enema. Molly put a little oil on her forefinger, moistened his anus, and inserted the tube. She pumped the bulb gently.

'You know, Gandhi used to give this little service to his friends. Did you know that?'

87

Watney was suddenly speaking to James, as though he had been ungraciously ignored. Gandhi: it was the second time recently that James had heard the name. Pippa had mentioned him, or he had mentioned him to Pippa.

'No, I didn't know that.' He wondered if his voice sounded casual. What a strange evening this was. This was far fetched, far more so than the Charleston story. And yet it was happening.

'Well, that's a fact. Not much time for Gandhi, but he certainly knew a good trick.'

Molly withdrew the tube, wrapped it in a cloth and returned the apparatus to her bag. 'All right, General?'

'Certainly all right, dear. It really clears you out. How about you, James?'

James looked at his two fellow human beings; Watney, sitting up now, pulling on his underpants, smiling hospitably as though he were doing no more than offering James yet another drink; and Molly, standing, standing by, waiting attentively in case her service should be further required.

'Not for me, thanks.'

Watney laughed. 'I think Mr Palmer is a little shy. Another time, perhaps. Thanks, Molly. Can we have some more coffee? Coffee, James?'

'Coffee would be fine.'

Watney did not return to the subject of the Charleston film. They talked very little after Molly left. Watney suddenly seemed weary, and James was content to go to his room where he read a chapter of *War and Peace* before going to sleep.

The following day, when Gerard looked in on James for what he again called the workers' break, he said that he had seen the Charleston script.

'The treatment?'

'Yes.'

'There's a difference.'

Gerard explained the difference between a treatment, which was a summary, and a script, which contained all the details. James tried to listen politely, but felt his mind wandering. Often it was interesting to hear a workman talk about his trade, but James was a difficult audience to hold at that moment. When he thought about the script he thought about the peculiarities of the previous evening.

'But it's neither a treatment nor a script,' Gerard said.

'Oh.'

'Do you follow?'

'Not entirely.'

'These are some thoughts, mainly, of course, of Watney's, which I put together in the form of a treatment. As one might, well, put a picture in a frame. To see it better? Now you follow?'

'A frame in a picture?' James had a feeling that in his daydream he had missed something important that Gerard was saying. But he didn't want to ask him to repeat it. He would have felt stupid.

'I don't think it's a film I'd want to see,' he said. 'I'm a bit old-fashioned. I like happy endings.'

Gerard let out a burst of laughter, which was unusual for him.

'You're a bit of a card, James. Happy endings. George will like that.'

In the afternoon James went for a walk in Regent's Park; not so much a walk as a saunter. He liked grass, and missed his garden. He came across a nest that had fallen, or been blown, from a tree. Nature does not build to last. In the park the first snowdrops were out, but they had been warmed by the city. In Norfolk they would still be a week or two away. An airliner was gliding slowly in a circle, like the kites he had seen in Morocco. He passed a woman who was giving her duck an outing. She had it on a lead, like a dog. In the distance he heard a lion's roar from the Zoo. On the previous day, when he had also taken a stroll, he had also seen the duck and heard the lion, and he had been momentarily surprised. Now they seemed merely curiosities that happened away from home, and no more curious than Watney with his enema, Gerard with his film that apparently wasn't a film and Molly the accomplished maid. Staying at the flat was a little like being on holiday. There should be glossy postcards he could buy. He thought he would go home to Norfolk soon. Perhaps Susie had returned and had tidied up. But if she hadn't he now believed he could fare for himself, perhaps getting in a treasure a couple of times a week, perhaps not even needing one. Watney's memoirs were weeks away from completion, perhaps months, despite James's agility with the word-processor. Perhaps Gerard could take over; it would give him something to do. In any case they were Watney's problems. James had not come to London to do the memoirs. Watney had said he was lonely; or Gerard had said he was lonely. But Watney did not appear to be a hermit.

When James returned to the flat, Watney was in the office and with him were four men, all strangers, although there was something familiar about them. They had what Watney called a soldierly look, although they were wearing civilian clothes. James was glad to see them. It made Watney's claim to loneliness even more improbable. Obviously there were plenty of old buddies who dropped in to talk about battles they had never fought. James was about to withdraw, but Watney waved him in and pointed to a chair. He was in commanding mood. He introduced the four men and they nodded at James in a polite, though not effusive, way. One man was called Freddie. He was English. The names of the other three men James instantly forgot. They were American names, but new American, like the Karls and Kurts and Als that Watney had spoken scornfully of during the drunken session in Agadir.

They were talking about Charleston.

'The structure is totally enchanting,' Freddie said.

'Enchanting?' Watney demurred over a not entirely soldierly word.

'Elegant, if you prefer it,' Freddie said. 'The thinking is masterfully elegant.'

'The problem as I see it', said one of the Americans, Karl or Kurt or Al, 'is the moral one.'

'Isn't that the point?' said Al or Kurt or Karl. 'We must retain the moral advantage. I see that as our fall-back line. Breach that and we're running for cover. Can we get the churches on our side?'

'I don't see any great problem there,' Watney said. 'In the end the churches are the great realists. Christianity would not have survived by being pacifist. Isn't that so, James?'

Five heads were turned towards James for his guidance on Christianity and pacifism. On Watney's face there was an encouraging smile, a fatherly smile, urging his protégé to demonstrate his promise. James hardly thought of himself as an authority on religion. The last church he had entered was a ruin in Greece, when he and Susie had attempted a bit of sightseeing on an appallingly hot afternoon. They had been taken there on a smelly and probably sick donkey. His knowledge of British churches was even more distant. But he had to say something.

'The church has always tried to be on the winning side,' James said. 'The Inquisition, Joan of Arc, the bishops in the Spanish civil war. The chaplain in my unit was more bloodthirsty than any of us.' His ragbag from the history of Christianity drew at least a nod from one of the Americans. Encouraged, James said, 'Praise the Lord and pass the ammunition,' and this drew a laugh like a round of applause. Watney looked pleased. He said, 'James was actually in the big scrap. Dunkirk, Normandy, the desert. That right, James?'

James nodded. It would seem pedantic, if not actually discourteous, to tell Watney again that he hadn't been in the desert.

At this moment Molly entered the room with a tray containing a large pot of coffee and six cups. James counted them. She must have seen him return from his walk and enter the room. Molly missed very little. As she was pouring out, one of the Americans leaned towards James. 'You were in Normandy. Did Ike really blow that thing?'

James turned his mind from the role of the priest in secular matters to the grand strategy on the battlefield.

'It was touch and go.'

The American considered this appraisal, and was about to ask another question when Watney called for order.

'Shall we get on, gentlemen? Shall we discuss Charleston? Is Charleston our place?'

'What's it like?' Freddie asked.

'It's where the civil war started,' someone said, setting off a discussion about the town's merits which Watney interrupted. 'I think we have to forget the sentimental details,' he said. 'Let us look at it as a city that has to be sacrificed. The analogy with Hiroshima makes it the obvious candidate; and whatever it is famed for now, which doesn't seem to be much, will be nothing to its subsequent fame.'

It occurred to James that what was going on was not a chat among old buddies about a screwy film idea that Watney had become interested in. The meeting had formality. It was reaching decisions. But perhaps soldiers, old or new, were incapable of informality. They were discussing the destruction of Charleston, not as a film, but as a reality; although that was understandable. Making a film no doubt called for dedication. It would cost a very large amount of money. The film had a serious theme. It was sensible that it should be carefully discussed. Once the theme became public it would attract widespread and informed criticism. Charleston itself might be upset about being killed off, even in fiction, although, as Watney had said, it would become famous and no doubt tourism would benefit. These were matters which it was sensible to think about ahead of the event. It was odd, though, that Gerard was not at the meeting. Perhaps he had some more compelling duty elsewhere.

While James was having these random thoughts the meeting came to an end or, as Watney put it, adjourned to a date to be fixed. James found his hand shaken warmly by the visitors as they left. Freddie, the last to leave, said, 'And how is Honeysucklelay?' He smiled at James's surprise. 'I knew you didn't recognise me, Palmer. Fairbanks, Watney's oppo. No offence. We didn't see a lot of each other. You were more Watney's man. Glad you're part of the team. Strengthens the English side. No doubt we'll see more of each other.' He gave a half salute and was gone.

James turned to Watney who said, 'No time for old grievances, heh, James? Freddie is going to be useful, and we're all in this together. As for you, James, you were great. All the folks liked you. I could tell that.'

At supper that evening were Watney, James, Gerard and one of the Americans from the meeting on Charleston whose name turned out to be not Al or Karl but Gunther. He had worked for a time at the American embassy in Moscow, and his speciality was, Watney said, the psychology of the Russians. Watney from time to time called him doctor, but it was unclear to James whether he was a real doctor, or had some doctorate in an academic subject or whether Watney was simply being courteous. James's impression of Gunther was that he was a quiet, rather gentle, man. He said that the incident that had left the deepest impression on him in the Soviet Union was when he had travelled on a domestic aircraft, and the hostesses had handed out pocket chess sets to the passengers. A country whose people whiled away the time by playing chess had to be taken seriously.

'But that's their game, doctor,' Watney said.

'I know it's their game.'

'You might see a couple of Americans playing poker on a

long-haul flight. That's their game.'

'Poker can also be a taxing occupation.'

'You see,' Watney announced to James and Gerard, seemingly assuming that he had won an argument, 'you see, we are always taking the rat shit Russians seriously. We treat them as a super-power, as equals. You see it all the time in the media. The superpowers, they say, Russia and America.'

'There are many similarities between the two countries,' Gunther said.

'That's what the doctor always says.' Watney was again talking directly to James and Gerard, as though he was an interpreter for Gunther, who either spoke in a tongue that neither of them understood, or whose thinking was so rich that it needed simplification. The idea that Russia and the United States were similar did not seem to James to be particularly exotic: he was sure he had heard it expressed by talking heads on television. It seemed to him to be fairly obvious, and nothing for Watney to get excited about. Perhaps, he thought, Watney was affronted that a democracy should be compared with an authoritarian state. But this, apparently, was not his grievance.

'There are not two superpowers,' he said. 'There is one. If Russia is a superpower, America is a super superpower.'

Gunther smiled; not mockingly, but as one who had heard this before, had made a response and was not going to re-run the argument. Gerard seemed to be lost in eating his steak. Watney's suppers usually seemed to be of steak. James was also eating, but he was also thinking. He was puzzled about Watney's references to superpowers, not because Watney said that Russia was not one, but because he had had a vague idea that there were a number, China, Britain, and wasn't there somewhere in South America that was supposed to have the bomb?

'What about China?' he heard himself asking.

Watney merely grunted, and for a moment James had a feeling that he was going to be snubbed. However, Gunther intervened. 'I think George regards China as a backwater. It has a large number of people but is not otherwise important. Merely being able to make a nuclear weapon does not make a country a superpower. In this I would be inclined to agree with George.'

'I see,' James said. He decided not to mention Britain. 'I suppose though,' he said, 'it doesn't matter who is and who isn't a superpower, if a couple of bombs can blow us all up.'

Nothing was said for a few moments, and James wondered again whether he was going to be snubbed. Gunther seemed about to intervene again but Watney said, 'No, I'll bat this one, doctor.' He put down his knife and fork and sat back and regarded James. 'You're a man I like, James Palmer,' he said. 'I like you because you're honest, you've led a decent life and you've been a soldier. These are qualifications that set you above the majority of people. I apologise for not answering your earlier question. I accept that it was honestly asked, and that it was not some snivelling provocation. I have a view of the world that I believe is sensible and just, but it is not one that at present is shared by a majority. The majority are like children. You cannot be natural with children. But I would like to get the respect of the James Palmers for my view.'

James wasn't sure whether to go on eating, occasionally looking up, as one normally did during mealtime conversations, or to lay down his knife and fork and sit back, as Watney had done. He decided to stop eating. Watney had a compulsion in his voice of someone giving, what?, an oration. One did not eat through an oration.

The Watney view of the world, he said, was that it was full of hope. He rejected utterly all stupid predictions that it was coming to an end; sci-fi, planet of the apes, all that rubbish about mutants and the heritage of death to unborn generations made up by potty professors, or by people who should know better. The gloomy seers, the Orwells, the Huxleys, had already been proved wrong.

'The future, if you could visit it, would be a little like your first night in a foreign country you had not been to before. Strange, but not totally unfamiliar.'

The end of a century was often accompanied by riots inspired by superstition, and that was what was happening now. But the next century would come and go like any other. 'Life is a relay race to the end on time,' Watney said. What had to be restored in people's minds was the ordinariness of life. One of the ordinary things about life was war. Many people now said that war, a major war, was unthinkable. Unthinkable! He thought about it, frequently. It was unthinkable to contemplate a future without war. In every age there had been a foe to fight. The peaceniks said that liberal states should never declare war. They had not read their Kant.

'You'll have read Kant, James?'

James shook his head slightly. He had only just about heard of the name.

'Kant saw that liberal states would never make war on each other, however much a pain in the arse they are. This gives them the confidence to make war on the baddies.'

In his father's and his grandfather's time the baddies had been Germany, Watney said. In his time it was the Soviet Union. It was them against us. There wasn't room for both. Delenda est Carthago. It was as simple as that. America would go to war with Russia, and America, with or without the active support of its uncertain allies, would win. The winner would be a global sovereign power willing and able to enforce a monopoly of atomic weapons. The world state might not be very intellectual to begin with, a bit rubbishy at the edges, but only the United States had the means and the will to run it. It would rule indefinitely, as once Greece did, as once Rome did, spreading prosperity, enforcing justice, until it too was eventually spent. That was the ordinariness of history. James had talked about a couple of bombs destroying the world. He was to be forgiven for being a victim of the propaganda put out by the potty professors. There was a lot of it. The entire Swiss population was going underground, human embryos were being deep frozen for future use.

'But what nonsense that is, James. The professors would say that I am a mad general. But I am a soldier, trying to make as efficient as possible the resources that politicians put at my disposal. To do this I need to put the bravery back into war. The professors say that atomic war would be beastly. But war has always been without charm. Do you think that the guy in his Spitfire in the Battle of Britain, roasted on a pyre, died with poetry on his lips, or that Agincourt was anything more than a butcher's block? All the generals, all the good ones, have to be butchers. What we call bravery is the result of temporary insanity. It won't be any different in the future, except that death may possibly, mercifully, be quicker. But countries need the myths of bravery and merciful generals in order to fight a successful war. Could the Elizabethans have fought the Spaniards with such confidence had Shakespeare and his fellow writers been pacifists? Churchill had a division of the sharpest minds in the arts to manufacture propaganda against Hitler. Where is the intellectual division to throw against the Soviets? I sometimes get the impression that it would be easier to muster one here if Britain declared war on the States. Now eat up.'

James's steak was cold. He ate a potato and abandoned the meal.

'I suppose people are frightened,' he said.

'There is no need to be frightened of the Russians,' Watney said. 'Given the will, the States could subdue Russia within days, perhaps even without fighting, without letting the doberman off the chain. Just economically. It depends on the dollar. Russia will collapse like the Tsarist empire did. America could damn near smother it with sentiment. No wonder the Commies worry about the insidiousness of pop culture. I sometimes think America prefers to keep Russia intact, as a king of the world opposition, a creepy giant with which to frighten American children when they go to bed at night.'

'Or grown-up children,' Gerard said. 'Where would thriller writers be without the KGB?'

Watney grunted. 'There's that, too. But I don't want to make too much of it. Russia is no superpower, but it has to be dealt with sternly. We'd be running Russia now if we'd had a perceptive president in 1945 instead of Truman. We're still ahead, but not as much. We are clearly superior technically, we have fallen behind in morale. America needs to be leaner, fitter, more spartan. We have to exorcise our fear of the bomb. That is why I support the Charleston idea. Bomb an American city and discover that life goes on. The wound heals.' Watney patted his shoulder. 'Very quickly.'

The doctor, if he was a doctor, said that the life he was interested in right now was life extension. 'How old do you think I am, James?'

James hated this sort of game. He always got it wrong, or offended people by getting it right. Gunther, he thought, must be in his late fifties, but he said, 'Around forty-five?'

'I'm pushing sixty. I plan to live to be one hundred, at least.'

James was not sure what to say that would sound polite. He thought it pointless to tinker with things you did not understand. Most people were baffled by cars, let alone bodies.

'Plenty of exercise, that sort of thing?'

'No. I'm not into jogging, I smoke and I eat butter. You have to live in the world with its vices. I have a formula to combat them.'

'What Gun doesn't take he pours over himself,' Watney said.

'That's not fair, George.'

'Even his dog took it.' Watney was enjoying himself.

'Took?' Gerard said.

'Unfortunately, the dog died,' Gunther said. 'But it did very well for a time.'

Watney, James and Gerard laughed quite uncontrollably. It was the merriest moment of the evening. Death is always good for a joke.

After supper James wondered if Molly would come in with her enema apparatus, but she didn't. Perhaps it wasn't a daily delight for Watney, or perhaps he considered three people would be too large an audience. At any rate he had ordered another entertainment. Gerard put up a film screen, threaded a film into a projector and turned off the lights. James wondered what was coming: perhaps a blue movie? But the film was of the bombing of Hiroshima. James had seen some of the bits before, the American bomber, the mushroom cloud, the aftermath, but this evening they made an impression on him that he had not experienced before. Perhaps this was because they followed Watney's oration, perhaps it was something to do with the way Gerard had edited them together. He probably was a clever chap. It suddenly came to James why the Japanese had given in so suddenly and completely when they saw what had happened to Hiroshima and Nagasaki. The Japanese would never surrender. It was against their genetics, even. Yet on seeing these ruined cities they had given in. Not all the scars of war are unsightly. A man can lose an arm and show himself in public without causing revulsion. Damaged cities are patched up. But here there was nothing. What had happened did not belong to the evolution of warfare. The Americans had made a jump in time. It was as though someone had introduced the machine gun or poison gas during the Crusades.

However, the film show was not concerned merely with what had happened long ago. Next on the screen came a map of eastern America. James had had only a vague idea of where

Charleston was. He now saw that it was on the coast between Miami and New York. A large-scale map of Charleston filled the screen. On it were imposed circles showing the extent of the damage that would be caused by bombs of various strengths that exploded in various places. It seemed rather technical for a film that was presumably designed for a general audience. James looked around at his fellow audience. Watney and Gunther seemed absorbed. When the film came to an end Watney made noises of approval. 'That's coming along very well, Gerard.'

That seemed to be the end of the day's agenda. Gunther and Gerard left. Watney pressed James to have a goodnight drink, and as he was pouring it James said that he had to return to Norfolk.

'Trouble at home?' Watney said.

'Susie is getting restless,' James said, and could hardly believe he said it.

'Take a few days,' Watney said, as though he were granting compassionate leave. 'A week if you like. It won't affect your pay.'

'I'm sorry about the memoirs.'

'We'll catch up. Settle your problem. You've got to have a clear mind.'

It wasn't how James had planned to leave. The farewell scene with Watney that he had rehearsed while walking in the park had been final. Watney would have been a bit put out, a little cross even, but James was firm. Watney had offered more money but James said that money wasn't an issue; already Watney had been fair, even generous. But in reality Watney had not spoken his lines. He had misunderstood James, or had been too clever for him. In the face of Watney's unexpectedly sympathetic response James had faltered. It was not important. He would write to Watney from home. A better method, really. One could be more precise on paper.

In the morning, when James was packing, Gerard came into his room.

'Goodbye? So soon?'

'A little problem at home.'

'You'll be back, then?'

'Of course.'

How he did hate lying.

'Or not?'

'I've told George I'll be back.'

He had. That was not a lie.

'What, in a day or two?'

'More like a week. Perhaps longer.'

'Longer?'

'Perhaps a little longer.'

It occurred to James that Watney might have sent Gerard to nose around. One should not underestimate Watney.

'I'm distressed you're going,' Gerard said. He sat on the bed. Distressed: it seemed a strong word to use. 'I hope you do come back. You're a voice of sanity.'

'Well, it's nice to be loved.'

'I mean it. That's why George likes you around. But perhaps he doesn't deserve you.'

'What is this?' James laughed. He was embarrassed. He was glad he was leaving. It would be good to get back to Norfolk, for all its problems.

'Have you called a taxi?'

'I thought I'd get the tube.'

'Take a taxi. Spend some of your riches.'

Gerard did seem to know an awful lot.

'Perhaps you're right.'

Gerard made a phone call. Fifteen minutes later James was outside on the pavement, saying goodbye to Gerard, who insisted on shaking his hand several times.

'Shall I come to the station with you?'

'No point.'

When the taxi was a hundred yards down the road James looked back. Gerard was still standing on the pavement and he raised his arm. James had the thought that although Watney probably wasn't lonely, Gerard was.

On the train James opened his now worn copy of *War and Peace*, but it did not hold him. The story was over but Tolstoy could not let it go. Gerard on the pavement made a stronger thought in James's mind. He had said he was distressed to see James go. Gerard liked a touch of drama but, James thought, it was not wholly bogus. Gerard had said that he was the voice of sanity. Watney the previous evening had said that he was honest and decent. Sane, honest and decent. These were rather flamboyant ways, he supposed, of saying that he was ordinary. But in the circles that Watney and Gerard moved, being ordinary could be extraordinary.

James thought about being ordinary. He was law abiding, and, he supposed, law believing. He believed the government mostly came to the right decisions. It was composed of mostly intelligent people who were trying to do their best. He felt fairly secure with them. They didn't much care for the bomb, but couldn't see how they could do without it. They wouldn't have shared all of Watney's views, but would make allowances because he was a soldier. James thought Americans were mostly decent people, but slightly worrying because they might not be as cautious, because they weren't as experienced, as the British, or so the British thought. The Russians lived under a dictatorship. That was a hardship which would pass eventually. They said many worrying and stupid things, but it seemed unlikely that they would want to start a war. Pressed, James might say that he distrusted the Germans more than the Russians. German meant hard. Russian meant a bit soft and sentimental. But he wouldn't take such personal prejudices too seriously. He would attribute them to his being of the generation of the Second World War, which had liberated German-occupied Europe. No one then had spoken of liberating the Germans from the Nazis; the two were indistinguishable. If anything, it had been assumed that the Nazis had once been the liberators of Germany, allowing it to do as it wished, storming over its neighbours, stealing whatever it desired, killing whom it disliked. Liberalism had been imposed upon it by the victors, forcing it to play at democracy to con-descending applause from the French, who were unreliable but good at wrapping up gifts, and even the Italians, who were good at clothes.

James read the *Daily Express* but occasionally bought the *Daily Telegraph* because he felt he should. He watched *News at Ten* on commercial television but believed he was better informed when he listened to the BBC news on his car radio. His views made a fairly humdrum list, James thought, but they had been tested by experience. The majority of Britons would agree with them, and they were not necessarily wrong. He could understand why Watney liked to have him about, as a sounding board. He was less sure why Gerard found him a voice of sanity. He would have thought that most of what he considered of value would have been despised by Gerard. Gerard would not like to be heard supporting the government, any government. He perhaps did not vote and made a virtue of not voting. James tried to think of other credentials for Gerard, but kept thinking of activities that Gerard would not do. He would not commute, he would not tend a garden, he would not take holidays, although he might go away. He believed in not doing things. He made a strength out of unenthusiasm. He worked quite hard to stay detached. His attachment to Watney was a temporary necessity. He could not make a film about Watney by remote control. But he had surrendered some of his detachment to James. He was distressed to see James go. That was not a detached observation to make. James had been momentarily embarrassed by the word. Part of James's ordinariness was a belief that men did not show emotion to each other; it might look queer. But in retrospect he was touched. A long dormant paternal nerve had been stirred. If Gerard was worried about something he should have said so, instead of acting out this detached pose.

James considered what might be bothering Gerard. He knew little of Gerard's life, who his parents were, if they were alive, whether he was married, or had been married, or lived with anyone. It was no use speculating on any possible domestic worry; and had there been one, presumably Gerard could have gone to Watney who would have given him what he called compassionate leave to sort it out. James did now know something about Gerard's work, or lack of it. Had he been Gerard he would be worried that he had not got any film in the can, if that was the phrase. He had come all the way to Norfolk to interview James and had not even brought a camera with him. Yet he had done some work. He had written the film script, although it was unfinished. He had made the Hiroshima documentary, which James had thought accomplished, tacking on at the end that odd bit about Charleston. It was a strange production for a young, avant-garde film-maker to be mixed up with; or rather Gerard's seeming acquiescence to Watney's ideas was strange. James would have thought that Gerard's ideas about nuclear warfare were nearer those of Pippa, his anchorite niece at Honeysucklelay. Yet Gerard had declined to talk to the women there, in

101

his detached way. As James was dwelling on this puzzle the train arrived at his destination. When he got out he sniffed the air theatrically. It was rather chilly, he thought, but he was pleased to be home.

★ 5 ★

Three days after James had returned home he had a letter from Gerard. 'My dear James,' it began, a touch intimately. 'I hope you had a good journey, and that you have managed to sort out your domestic problems, whatever they may be. Things continue here much the same, although I am not sure that "the same" means to you precisely what it means to me. It was a bit of a pity that you had to leave so soon because you and George were getting on so well and I was sure that in a day or two, perhaps a little longer, he would have got around to confiding in you. I hope that I'm not in any way putting pressure on you to abandon whatever it was that took you away and rush back here; I know from my own experience the nagging nature of private worries. On the other hand, I hope you will not be absent for too long. I'm not just thinking of George's silly memoirs; not really thinking of them at all, although George clearly thinks that I should step in as punctuator and typist in chief during your absence (but each man to his last, I've said). Perhaps I should not call the memoirs silly, as I wouldn't to his face. However, I don't think from what I have read of them that they are going to be treasured by posterity. There isn't enough of the real George, the disappointed soldier, in them to be of real value. They just give a public relations view of him by himself. I hope, incidentally, that you don't think I am getting at you. Nothing could be farther from my mind. You have turned George's violence on the English language into something readable and that is no small feat. However, when the real story of your days with George comes to be told (as they say in films, although not, I hope, in my films) what will turn out to be important is that the writing of the memoirs encouraged George to trust you. All this probably sounds a bit weird, but it is a weird entourage that I find myself attached to. No doubt you noticed it, too. I did, I admit, at one time have my doubts about you. I wondered who this James

103

Palmer was, with his links to George's distant past, and why George was so anxious to bring you into his circle. But now I accept that you are, if you will forgive the word, an innocent (like me). And, looking at things from your point of view, I dare say that you thought I was one of the weirdos. Perhaps you still do, although I hope that, if you do, this letter will satisfy you that I am a true innocent.

'I met George at a party. He was interested that I made films. I was interested in his personality. That was the beginning of our friendship, nothing more. He struck me as being vaguely old-fashioned, the sort of General one reads about who rode on a tank to Berlin with an ivory-handled pistol at his hip, born out of his time, a Hamlet in uniform. I thought I could do a little film about him. No more than half an hour or so, for one of the minority channels on television. It is the sort of thing, that done right, "a little gem", attracts nice critical paragraphs in the nice papers, and wins minor awards at obscure film festivals. It's a little rung in one's career. It is still my best thought for George. However, there is also Charleston. This is to be a feature film, an epic. Watney outlined a story to me, the Bomb (which we now spell with a capital letter, like God) dropped on an American town on the anniversary of Hiroshima, and who dun it? Watney wanted to know if this would make a film. I said I would try a treatment, which you have read. You must understand that in film-making many treatments are called for, but few are chosen. Sometimes the story, when set out, simply does not look like a film. Sometimes there is no suitable star. But usually a film falls down for lack of money. Even films on so-called modest budgets need huge sums of money. Naturally, I told Watney this and he said that a substantial sum of money was available. Perhaps millions? I said. Millions, he said. He put me on a generous retainer to make the point. Sources of money in the film world are rarer than sources of rivers. You would be surprised at the explorations deep into the unknown heartland of moneydom that film people make. Banks, pension funds, widows' mites; these are just the start. So when a Watney appears, a seemingly assenting Midas, one's tendency is to hold on to him. Charleston might make a film, yes, no, maybe. But some even better idea might be found to make use of all that lovely cash. I am fascinated by America and the two dreadful crimes it is burdened with, dropping the bomb and living on stolen land. So I, the innocent, hang on. There isn't, or so far there isn't, any alternative in Watney's mind to Charleston. That is the film he wants to make. Very well. We have a whodunit, but who dun it? The revengeful Jap? The blundering air force? Something from space? Watney considered the Jap idea too obvious, an official blunder unpatriotic and the space idea childish. He was being difficult. If you rule out banality you deprive yourself of a large part of the seedcorn of moviedom. The idea he favours, which is his own, is that Charleston should be demolished by a bomb set off by the government. America would bomb itself. That is ingenious. Not totally ingenious: it follows the set pattern of whodunits in that the least likely suspect is the villain. All the same, it has appeal as a story, certainly better than the revengeful Jap, although not as plausible as the official blunder. But why on earth would the government want to bomb one of its own cities? According to Watney the explosion would be part of a programme to remove the fear of the bomb. It would go off. The nation would be terrified. Then the great rescue would take place. More of Charleston would survive than anyone would have believed. People would say that perhaps the bomb was only a horror story. A new climate of public opinion – Watney's phrase – would be created. The bomb would simply come to be regarded as another piece of ammunition, rather than something that would turn mankind into eunuchs (Watney's phrase again). Just as Hiroshima had been a turning point away from international war, so Charleston would be another turning point back. The world would again be safe for the generals.

'I am probably simplifying Watney's idea: it is the job of films to simplify. Many fairly obvious questions arise. What government, what president, would, under any circumstances, drop the bomb on an American town? It depends, according to Watney, which government. America, he says, has one public government but several private ones. Oh, well. So Watney says. But whoever dropped the bomb: would they not be condemned? Perhaps, at the beginning. But no one would be sure who did it: the Japs or the spacemen or whatever. The silly rumours would preserve the mystery. The important thing is that the bomb has been exploded with, let us assume, remarkably little damage to people and property. How is that? Because there are now many types of nuclear bomb. The Charleston one is of a kind, let us say, designed to black out communications rather than to black out people. Again, Watney's supposition, although presumably based on knowledge. A humane atom bomb? Well, we are in the realm of story-telling. So, we have Charleston, shall we say, the host to the bomb. The result turns out to be not as bad as was expected. People, some people, are saying that perhaps the bomb isn't so bad after all. We can live with it. Watney takes it a little further. He sees the Charleston episode as a contribution to the wintering of America, which has become too soft, too fond of easy living. It has got to be ready for war. For war? I think by now you know Watney's view of the inevitability of war with Russia. You'll remember the sermon over dinner before you left. Watney is a little in love with war. Love, I think, is not a bad word to describe his feelings for it. War is the elusive woman in his life, the enigmatic Mona Lisa beckoning him in his thoughts. He is, of course, as you know, perfectly willing, at interminable length, to discuss the inevitability of war on, if you like, an intellectual basis. Them or us. In the history of the world no two strong powers have been able to survive for any length of time on equal terms. Rome and Carthage, Spain and Portugal, France and England, that sort of thing. But his heart is in conquest. Imagine, marching at the head of a victorious army through Moscow to the tune of the Radetzky March. Watney's words, not mine. And, I suppose, it is what keeps a soldier going. How he adores that word, soldier, the ring of it. Most soldiers now are clerks or executives, but Watney talks of the job as though he were a yeoman holding a pike.

'I have two problems, James. One is the simple problem of making a film, assuming it comes to a film, that contains Watney's extraordinary ideas. You have read the script I have done so far. But how do I end it? Surely not with a war-happy America marching off to do in the Russians. Hardly in the mood of our time, I should think. Those who didn't find it totally alarming would laugh it off the screen. Not many prizes there. One could end it with the "hero towns", the successors to Nagasaki, waiting for the bomb to drop on them. Such an ending would be artistically acceptable, although I would be a bit worried about using the names of real towns. I don't imagine that Charleston will be very pleased to know that a bomb is going to be dropped on it, even in a movie, even if it doesn't destroy the place. Do we have the right to bomb a city, even in pretence? Do we have the right to kill even one person in pretence, without some kind of moral justification? In the old movies bad people were killed. Or if a good person were killed, there was retribution. There are no morals in films now, although there is reality. Is amorality the price we have to pay for reality? Deep thoughts. So that is one problem, or bits of a problem, all bound up with the filmscript. All of them not uninteresting and all of them, I suppose, resolvable.

'My other problem is this. Does Watney want to make a film or does he really want to drop a bomb on Charleston? Having written that sentence, I realise that this is the first time I have actually put the question to myself, unambiguously, bringing together all my worries. I read it again, and I give a little laugh. It is a ridiculous idea. But I am not ridiculous and I have this idea. It comes to me most strongly in the grind sessions (Watney's phrase) we have which start out on some point of detail in the film. Ten or fifteen minutes into it and Watney is talking as though he is discussing a real event. Yesterday I said (as I thought, lightly), "Well, this sounds authentic, anyway." Watney didn't laugh, didn't smile. "Of course it's shit authentic". I quote him verbatim. Of course. But (dare I say it, me, an artist?) it's only a movie. And then there are those weirdos. Freddie Fairbanks and the three Americans. Watney says they are advisers. But I didn't bring them in. I haven't asked them for any advice. At their sessions they jaw on without any reference to the film, just talking military things. Sometimes I sit in with the weirdos, sometimes I don't. If I don't, they don't seem to miss me; if I do, they ignore me. It is not unusual in a film to have an expert consultant, but not four, and not four who have had no previous experience in films. Anyway, Watney is there to verify any military points. So what are they up to? Just buddies that Watney likes to have around? I don't know that they aren't. I merely say that they worry me. They seemed to like the film I made about Hiroshima and Charleston, but what was it for? An exercise, Watney said. But an exercise for what? I didn't mind making it; quite enjoyed it, and Watney paid for all the library film, but it left me puzzled. Watney said to me the other day, "Extraordinary events have still to be enacted before this century

107

is done." Chilling. The last thing this century wants is any more extraordinary events.

'You may think that I am merely being foolish. If you said that, I would hear it with relief. You are not a weirdo. You are, banal though it sounds, the only person I can turn to for advice: you know Watney, you know what he is supposed to be up to, and you are reliable.

'This letter is much longer than I had intended it to be. Really what I am saying is, come back soon, James Palmer, you are needed. So, salutations from Regent's Park. I'd be grateful if you'd destroy this letter. I know this sounds melodramatic, but I do feel that I live in a somewhat melodramatic household. Best regards, Gerard.'

James was not sure what to do with the letter. Its very length argued against destroying it. Anyway, that would have been melodramatic, and was no less melodramatic for Gerard saying it was. He thought he might read it again later. He folded it and placed it with other pending letters and bills behind a clock on the living room mantelpiece.

'More coffee, uncle?' Pippa said.

Pippa had moved James's domestic life roughly back to normal. When he had returned from London the house had been as he had left it. Susie had not been at the door in a brand-new apron with a duster in her hand to announce that her escapade was over and to ask forgiveness. However, that evening Pippa had arrived, a little battle-weary from the trenches of Honey-sucklelay. She had decided to take a few days off, and had gone to her parents' house, had received a less than enthusiastic reception from her mother, had heard that James was on his own and thought she might get a more accommodating welcome there. She offered to straighten out the place in return for a bed and unlimited baths. To James it seemed a perfect deal. It had not been totally perfect. Pippa's house manners were like a child's. Behind her she left a trail of shoes, discarded underwear, used dishes, opened packets and muddled newspapers, as though someone would follow her with a large toy box to throw them into. The telephone seemed to be used more; if James phoned from work to speak to Pippa it always seemed to be engaged. Tea seemed to have been abolished and had been replaced by coffee which was available on demand. Pippa smoked, and ashtrays, banished by Susie, had returned. Nevertheless, the house was working again; life had been put back into it.

'You're not listening, uncle.'

'I am. Coffee. Perfect.' He sat down again at the breakfast table.

'Uncle, do you mind if I have a couple of friends in ce soir?'

'Peace people?'

'Very peaceable.'

'A couple? Two, that is?'

'If three turn up, I can't ask one to wait in the garden. But you can say no. It's your house.'

James found himself considering the disadvantages of allowing a party of Pippa's friends taking over the house for the evening, perhaps into the night, perhaps until next morning. Children made a mess. A lot of children made a lot of mess that sometimes developed into damage. Even his two sons, conforming as they now were, had made a mess during the adolescent parties they had given, usually when he and Susie were away. But Pippa was not a child. She was a young woman. She had assumed the role of mistress of the house, although perhaps she would not describe herself in those words, so had a temporary interest in seeing that the place remained in reasonably good order. Her friends would hardly be tearaways. Camping outside a military base, whatever its value, must be an eminently serious matter. Anyway, he did not want Pippa to feel unwelcome.

'Of course,' he said. 'That'll be perfectly all right.'

'Thanks.' Pippa got up, came round to James's side of the table and kissed him on the cheek. 'You're a good man.' The spontaneous gesture made James feel how sensible he was to have said yes. It also gave him a tumescent twinge. Pippa had a robust body and was wearing only a dressing gown. He felt a need for sexual contact soon, although not of course with Pippa; he wasn't a wicked uncle.

'In fact I wasn't planning to be in for supper this evening,' he said. 'I thought I might go and see Aunt Susie, wherever she is.'

'You're sure, sure I'm not pushing you out?'

'Quite sure, Pippa.'

'Well, if you change your mind there'll be plenty for you. I'm going to make a really super stew. A real froggie dish.'

'I'm very tempted. But I think it's about time Susie and I had a chat.'

'Give her my love.'

'If she deserves it.'

'Uncle! That's not like you.'

'No one likes to be deserted.'

'She's retired, so mummy says.'

'It's playing with words.'

'Mummy says she is thinking of retiring, too. Auntie may have started a whole new movement.'

James smiled, although he was not sure why. Perhaps because Pippa expected him to. Something would have to be done to get Susie back, but he did not see it as an insoluble problem. Probably she was already fed up with living on her own, and would have returned already but for pride. James would say he was sorry for whatever he was supposed to be sorry for. He would offer his own pride as a sacrifice. Pride did not seem to him to be un-negotiable, as Watney might say. But more pressing problems faced James today. When he got to his office, his manager, whose name was Albert Miles, said that the compositors were objecting to what they called 'prolonged exposure' to the screens of the word-processors.

'They are complaining of eyestrain?'

'That's about it, Mr Palmer.'

'Is this a reasonable complaint, do you think, Bert?'

He shrugged. 'Might be something in it, hard to tell.' He was not a man of the instant decision; not really a manager at all of the sort that won awards for shaking out and slimming down. More of a foreman who ran the place because he was more experienced than anyone else. When the new printing machinery had been installed it had been hinted to James that a younger, more thrusting, person might be brought in to manage the firm as it entered its new era. But James liked Albert Miles and did not want him thrown out with the old machinery. He also judged that the staff would have been upset by his disposal. Enough was enough. But, it seemed, the staff were upset anyway.

'Don't they watch television? That's the same.'

'These screens are brighter, and they have to get nearer to them.'

'So what's the answer?'

'They want a break, fifteen minutes off every hour.'

'Doing nothing?'

'Resting their eyes.'

James Palmer's firm was of modest size: it provided jobs for only thirty people, and that included himself and the women who worked part time in the bindery when there was a rush on. One of the reasons for buying the new machinery was that it would enable the firm to turn out more work without increasing costs.

'The feeling is very strong, Mr Palmer.'

'If we go bust, the feeling will be strong, too.'

James wondered whether he should see the four compositors, whether seeing them would undermine Miles's authority. But the compositors knew who would take a decision, and it wasn't Miles, who in most respects was one of them. James, too, felt like one of them. He had been a compositor. But he had a role to play, of the boss, the provider of pay packets, the representative of them against us. So the four came in, and extra chairs were brought in to accommodate them. The little office seemed very crowded.

'Well, what seems to be the problem, chaps?' This was the language of paternal authority that was apparently required. It seemed that an article had appeared in a printers' journal saying that staring at the screen could cause headaches, had in some cases caused headaches. It wasn't a stupid suggestion. James had long been suspicious that prolonged exposure to television was harmful, and had rationed the time he had allowed his children to watch it. But the problem that the four compositors brought into the office was not specifically eyestrain. They didn't much like the new technology, and they wanted to say so; being reasonable men, they wanted to inform their dislike with specific complaints, rather than seeming to grumble for its own sake. But they were grumbling, and James felt they were entitled to grumble. Three of the four were middle aged or a bit more, and the youngest had been with the firm for more than ten years. All their working lives they had operated Linotypes, machines as large as church organs and with intricate harmonies set in motion by the strokes of knowing fingers. The Linotype was not a machine of antiquity: go back perhaps three generations and it would be an innovation. But it was an innovation that had emerged from the experience of several centuries of printing. Gutenberg would have found it surprising, but he would have

111

understood it. The word-processor was a jump, not an evolution. You pressed a key, and something happened, but you did not understand what happened, as you did when you pressed a Linotype key and there was a fall of letters. With a Linotype, heat and simple mechanics merely replaced human muscle. The word-processor did its work with electrons and solid state mechanics at the speed of light, concepts beyond the reach of normal people. Suddenly the pictures of Hiroshima came into James's mind, the jump that broke the rules of war. The four compositors in his office had been asked to make a comparable jump. No wonder they were upset. They were suffering not from eyestrain, but from mind strain. James remembered that before the last Linotype had left the works, one of the printers, an amateur artist, had done a painting of it. Presumably it was now in his home, the memory of a lost love.

James and the four compositors and Bert Miles talked for more than an hour, a discursive conversation that to any chairman with a mind for efficiency would seem to have got nowhere. But it was a laxative. The men left the room, grunting thanks. Watney had his enemas, James thought, but he had his patience. The problem had not been solved but no problem ever was, unless it was a mathematical problem, which wasn't a problem at all, but an exercise. Natural problems, those that often came in the disguise of troubles, questions, vexations or merely irritations did not have a solution on the next page. Usually you simply tried to deprive them of nourishment until they withered.

James was conscious of the development of a new problem, a natural problem, an irritation that threatened to become a vexation. This was sex. When Susie had moved out of the house, taking her belongings, she had also removed one of James's belongings, the facility of sex on demand, or on request or for pity's sake. James could solve this problem as he planned to solve that of the upset compositors, by depriving it of nourishment. This might take time, but perhaps only a little time. He was of an age when the body is content to wither. However, this solution did not appeal to James. He was fond of sex. The fact that he still had an appetite for it, that the little white stuff continued to be manufactured and sought to travel into another body; this service seemed to him to be a symptom of health, and once shut down it seemed unlikely that it could be restarted.

Health was the sublime barrier between now and death.

Because sex in a man is a physical problem that builds up each day if it is not relieved, it had assumed a priority in James's mind that, intellectually, he told himself, it did not deserve. He had caught himself daydreaming during his talk with the compositors, although seemingly no one had noticed. The brain has an abundance of robot-like gestures and words to pilot along a conversation seemingly unattended. Not only sex, but the events in London and Gerard's plea for his early return slightly nagged at James; he would have to reply to Gerard, if only to send a postcard. The thought came to James that if he did return to London he could extinguish his lust, if that was the word, by going to a prostitute. In London, it was clear, if only from television programmes, that sex was a commodity. In the small Norfolk town James lived in, sex was not a commodity, or if it were it was not on view. There had been a sex shop which sold 'marital aids' but it had been closed down after two months because it was near a school. Some of the newsagents sold girlie magazines, but they were hardly the real thing. There might well be prostitutes there, but how did one find them? They weren't in the yellow pages of the telephone directory. Presumably, if they existed, they would solicit for custom in pubs or dance halls. But the homely pub where James usually had his lunch did not look as though a prostitute had so much as glanced through the window. There was one dance hall, a disco, in the town. James could not imagine himself there. He was a virgin husband. He had never had an affair. The permissive society had come and, if not gone, had gone stale. Skirts had risen and fallen. Breasts had become as commonplace in films as legs once were. Wives were swapped like cigarette cards, or so some newspapers said. But James had remained constant to Susie. Constant: the word suggested fidelity despite temptation, but his marriage had not presented him with any great agonies of choice. There had been women who were pretty, or personable, or both, whose company he had enjoyed. There might have been momentary flirtations, but no hopping into bed with someone because they held your stare for a couple of seconds. That would have been absurd, and anyway he did not believe that it happened among normal people, whatever contemporary legend might suggest.

These thoughts, or thoughts like them, were with James when

he went to see Susie that evening. He had phoned, as she had asked, to say that he would like to see her, and she had sounded warm and welcoming, but it felt strange, standing at the door of his wife's flat waiting to be let in; a first.

'Good evening, Mrs Palmer. I've come about your lost husband.'

He bent forward to kiss her, as he always did on returning from work. She did not draw back, but she turned her face slightly, so he kissed her on the cheek.

'You're looking well, James. I should be furious.'

'And you. You look well.'

Susie always looked well; but this evening she also looked relaxed and, possibly, James thought, younger. But he might think that because he hadn't seen her for a time; although he would have guessed the absence would have made her seem older. She was wearing what looked like a set of dungarees. He wondered if he had arrived too early and had caught Susie in the middle of cleaning, and she would excuse herself for looking such a mess, and he would deny it, but she would vanish for a little while and reappear in a dress. She did none of this. She said, 'I'm in the kitchen. Come and talk to me.'

Supper was being made, but there was no sign of any cleaning. James tried to remember what Susie normally wore in the evening, but he could not think of a single garment. It wasn't dungarees, he was sure of that, although they were perfectly clean, and in a pleasant, though probably impractical, shade of cream. She was wearing black, shiny slippers, or they might be shoes, and a string of pearls.

'You're having a good gawp, James. I'm quite flattered.'

'When are you coming home, Susie?'

'Oh, straight in, eh? No softening up. No waiting until the wine has made me pliant and yielding. You haven't changed, James.'

James had forgotten the bottle of wine he had brought, even though he was holding it in his hand. He put it on the kitchen table. He had always found it difficult to hand over the obligatory bottle of wine when invited out to dinner, and with his wife it seemed absurd.

'Open it, will you, James? I'll put some in the gravy.'

'Corkscrew?'

114

'Here you are.'

James recognised the corkscrew; at least, it seemed identical to the one he had last seen at home. He felt irritated. However, he wasn't going to have a quarrel about who owned what, certainly not over the ownership of a corkscrew.

'This isn't a bad bottle,' he said. 'Don't expect you keep much of a cellar these days.'

Susie smiled. 'Straight in again, James. Trying to find out if I'm hard up.'

'Is it a banned subject?'

'Don't be silly, James. Nothing is banned. But I don't want to be interrogated. It's not like you, anyway, to keep asking questions. Live and let live. It's something I've always loved about you.'

Susie made it sound as though their marriage had been a model of civilised behaviour, discreet over every indiscretion. It was true that James had never questioned Susie very much about how she occupied her day. Often when he got home he was too tired to do more than exchange pleasantries, or believed he was; but, in truth, Susie's life did not intrigue him. He presumed she was content with it, but from the glimpses she volunteered, her routine seemed unexceptionally dull. Of course he had not asked questions. He wondered in retrospect what they had talked about over umpteen years. This evening he did have questions, interesting questions, but Susie was declining to answer them. He wondered what there was still to say to each other without questions and answers, how they were going to pass the next couple of hours before he could reasonably go home. James suddenly felt depressed. Susie had seemed pleased that he was coming to see her, and had taken the trouble to cook what looked like a decent meal but clearly this evening was not going to be a milestone, marked by Susie confessing that she had come to her senses, and James conceding that perhaps he had lacked understanding, with them snuggling into bed for a blissful reunion.

'Talk to me, James,' Susie said when they were eating their supper.

James was tempted to say that there was little to talk about, but he did not want to quarrel. He told her of his trip to London, of helping Watney to write his memoirs, of the peculiar household in the flat in Regent's Park, with Molly the all-purpose housekeeper; of the plan to make a film about the extinction of Charleston, and of Gerard's long letter to him.

From time to time Susie murmured 'extraordinary, extraordinary,' once laughed delightedly, and several times interrupted James to tell him to eat up before his food got cold. James felt his spirits lift. Susie was a responsive audience, and it was good to be applauded.

'What a time you've had,' Susie said.

'Pretty awful really.'

'I'm terrifically envious.'

James gave a modest hero's smile. It had been an odd tale and he knew he had told it well. For the first time, while telling it, he had seen it as a whole, rather than as a series of incidents in which he had been the reluctant participant.

'What are you going to say to Gerard?'

'Say?'

'About Watney's plan to blow up Charleston.'

'He doesn't say that.'

'But he thinks Watney might?'

'He's an imaginative young man.'

'But supposing that is Watney's plan? A little bomb on an American city to show it doesn't hurt too much. It sounds plausible.'

'Plausible, I suppose so. Everything now is plausible. A disposable society prepared to dispose of itself.'

'But if Gerard has tumbled to something?'

'Let him go to the police.'

'What, the local copper?'

'You have to start somewhere.'

'I don't think Gerard would thank you for that advice.'

'It's probably too sensible for him.'

'He's depending on you for guidance.'

'Well, he shouldn't be.'

'He's a nice boy.'

'So you believe. And, in all honesty, I don't dislike him. But I have no advice to offer him. I need advice myself. How do I persuade my wife to return home? How do I persuade my printers that, unless they stop buggering about, the firm could go bust? These are everyday, insoluble, normal problems faced by an ordinary, everyday, normal chap. I can't really be expected to spend my days worrying over some problem that probably doesn't exist, and if it does exist, I don't understand it. There are governments, spies, psychiatrists, journalists to deal with this sort of thing. I have to live in the real world. Not very glamorous, I admit. But I'd rather have my wife back doing the shopping than trying to save this Charleston, if it exists, and I'm not even sure of that.'

'I'm fond of you, James, you know that?'

''And I'm fond of you. Love you.'

'I haven't moved out because I'm not fond of you, you do realise that?'

'No. No, not really.'

'Well, it doesn't matter. Give me a little time.'

'How much?'

'Ah, questions again.'

'Well, one more. Is this something to do with Merle?'

'That's easy. Nothing.'

'She's not with Watney. I thought she might have come to see you.'

'She did.'

'Ah.'

'Just a friendly visit, before leaving for America.'

'Another wife flown.'

'She's not Watney's wife, not legally. She was in the army with him. His chauffeur; his bodyguard perhaps. A tough lady.'

'Fancy that. And body companion.'

'That, too, of course.'

'How peculiar.'

'Not really. People fancy one another. The circumstances sometimes seem a bit exotic, that's all.'

'So where is the real Mrs Watney?'

Susie shrugged. 'Perhaps there isn't one. You were right about Frances, though, the wife of long ago.'

'What happened to her?'

'According to Merle she left Watney for a German, one of the eastern sort.'

'A Communist?'

'I don't imagine they all are, but it must have been a blow for poor George.'

'Defecting?'

'That's how he would see it.'

'More, please.'

'That's all I know. Or rather, all Merle told me, and only that in the spirit of vindictiveness.'

'He threw her out?'

'So it seems.'

As he was leaving, James said, 'If I was prepared to see Gerard, take him seriously, do what I could, would you return home?'

Susie did not answer for a moment and James thought that she had lost the line of his reasoning. Then she said, 'It's your problem, James. Watney's your friend, otherwise we'd know nothing at all about all this.'

'The answer's no?'

'It's a silly proposition, James, completely irrelevant. Of course the answer's no. I live in the real world, too. But I'd like you to see Gerard. I'd think well of you for it. Talk to Pippa, see what she says.'

'She wouldn't side with Gerard. They met at Honeysucklelay. Instant antipathy.'

Susie shrugged. 'They have something in common. They belong to a generation that likes to believe in doom. We don't so much. By the way, Belinda's grateful to you for taking Pippa. She asked me to say.'

'Pure selfishness on my part.'

'That's what I told her,' Susie said, but she smiled as she said it.

As he drove home James found himself whistling. The evening with Susie had been, what, buoyant? A lifting of the spirit. Perhaps even that. It had begun badly, but it had continued grandly. It had been a long time since he had enjoyed the company of a woman as he had this evening with Susie. But what had they talked about during that long passage of life they had spent together? The children, he supposed, with their interminable problems. He tried to remember if he had thanked Susie for the meal. He would phone her next day, or send her a postcard.

There was an old car outside the house with a notice on its windscreen saying, 'Licence applied for,' and a motor-cycle resting against the garden wall. It had a nuclear disarmament symbol on its petrol tank. James let himself into the house quietly but not, he thought, secretly. It was, after all, his home. As he passed the living room door he heard voices in the rhythm of discussion. He paused for a moment to listen.

'Hallo, uncle.' Pippa had emerged suddenly from the kitchen carrying a tray of steaming mugs. 'Fancy a cuppa?'

'Thanks, no, Pippa. I was just creeping in.'

But she already had the living room door open. 'Come and say hallo, anyway. We're all terribly grateful.'

James had an impression of perhaps a dozen people in the room, some in chairs, some on cushions on the floor. The fire had been lit but had burned low. The lighting was unfamiliar because napkins had been placed over the two standard lamps. It was extraordinary, he thought, how quickly the atmosphere of a room can change.

'This is my Uncle James,' Pippa announced. 'He lives here.'

There were some murmurs and grunts and someone said, 'Hallo, uncle.'

James nodded genially and said, 'Well, if you'll excuse me, Pippa. Hard day tomorrow.'

'Lovely, uncle. We won't make a noise.'

As James walked upstairs he had a sense of *déjà vu*. He struggled with an obstinate memory to identify the connection, and as he was getting into bed he remembered what it was: the meeting of the military men he had interrupted when he had returned from his walk in Regent's Park. It is in quiet rooms among quiet people that dreadful events are imagined, perhaps always have been. Before he went to sleep James read an article in a printing journal about the problem of eyestrain when using visual display units. Tomorrow, he thought, he would have another talk about it to Bert Miles.

However, Miles was not there next day, or he was not there when it was convenient for James to see him. He was also away from the works for most of the following day delivering printing orders. James did not mind greatly. The compositors, as far as he could tell, were working normally. What slightly bothered him was that Pippa asked if she could have her friends around for a second evening. James agreed, although without enthusiasm. He had nowhere to go and, deprived of his living room, had his supper in the kitchen and afterwards sat in his bedroom listening to the radio. When Pippa asked to use the house for the third night running, James demurred.

'I'd quite like to sit by my own fire tonight.'

'Of course, uncle.'

'I'm not unsympathetic, but I don't think it is up to me to provide the means by which your friends can change the course of world history.'

'Don't scoff, uncle.'

'I'm not scoffing. But they must have somewhere else to go to.'

'You are scoffing. You are fucking scoffing.'

'Pippa.'

'Oh, you piss me off. You're a fucking ostrich. There won't be any fucking world history if it's left to you, and people like you. Have your fucking fireside. You'll soon fucking fry, anyway.'

Pippa stood before him for a moment, her hands on her hips. James wondered whether she might try to hit him, and what he would do if she did. But she turned and left the room, which happened to be the living room, and tried to slam the door, but it was on a spring that prevented it closing quickly. James's instinct was to call after her, but he didn't. He wasn't sure what course of action to take. A minute or two later Pippa returned.

'Forgive me, uncle. I'm stupid. I get carried away.'

She stood close to him, her head lifted, with her lips pursed like a raspberry, waiting like a child to be kissed. She had on her dressing gown, and it seemed to be casually loose. James wondered if he was being manipulated. It seemed extraordinary. Surely, to Pippa, he would seem beyond manipulation, beyond the temptations of sex. Yet he did have an unsatisfied sexual urge, and possibly Pippa could sense it. How pleasant it would be for the palms of his hands to make a mould of her breasts. But to do so would in an instant change the rules of their relationship, in her favour. He put his hands in his pockets and lightly kissed her raspberry lips.

'Such shocking words,' he said. 'You must be growing up.'

'Now you're laughing at me.'

'You're too old to scold, and I'm too old to lust after you. Laughter is a good compromise.'

She came even closer and placed her head on his chest and he could feel the unambiguous movement of her body. But now he was in control. He took her by the shoulders, and kissed her forehead.

'Let's forget it. And now I must go to work.'

However, he did not forget the incident, neither did he try to. He found that he was not greatly surprised by Pippa's outburst. Up to then, he realised, she had been slightly too docile to be real, acting the perfect niece. It must have been a strain, and when James, who had been acting the perfect uncle, said no, a breaking point had been reached. No doubt Pippa's mother knew the moment well, which was why for the present Pippa was staying with him and not with Belinda. He wondered how long she intended to stay. She had come to the house to indulge, as she had put it, in the unimaginable luxury of hot baths, but now presumably she was scrubbed clean. The number of people prepared to besiege the ramparts of Honeysucklelay must be limited. Presumably, James thought, there was a rota system. After you had done a stretch you would be given leave, as in the army. James's recollection of his army service was that he tended to get restive for leaves, and restive to return to see what was happening when he was on leave. Pippa, however, seemed to have no inclination to move out of James's house. Over supper she said, 'I hope you're not going to throw me out, uncle. I behaved abominably.'

'Don't be silly. Forget it. I have.'

'I was carried away.'

'Of course. Quite understandable.'

'But you're just saying that. You don't really understand.'

'I try to, in my uncle-ish way.'

'The bomb, the world, it's a kind of everything . . . I'm not expressing myself at all well, and I'm supposed to be the press officer.'

James ate a few mouthfuls of his supper. It was a stew. Most of Pippa's suppers were stews. She had a gift for them.

'I think of you, Pippa, sometimes, and I hope you won't take exception to my saying this, I think of you as a kind of modern anchorite, or anchoress. You know what I'm talking about?'

'Of course.'

'I don't mean in a specifically religious way: I have no idea if you have any religion. But you have in a way withdrawn from the world as a gesture to live in your cell, even though it is a bender outside Honeysucklelay. I hope I haven't offended you.'

James took another mouthful of delicious stew. When he lifted his head Pippa was looking at him, but not in a hostile way, certainly not in a docile way. The word that came into James's mind was 'sharp'.

'Uncle, there's hope for you yet.'

'Oh, really?'

'I'm no anchorite, but your idea is really rather sweet; no, it deserves more than that. It shows a sophisticated train of thought.'

'That's good.'

'You're laughing it off, uncle. But, you see, you've told me something about yourself. Several things. You've told me that you've thought about why I'm at Honeysucklelay, why other people are there, and you've come to a conclusion. Not bad.'

James smiled, but he did not feel entirely at ease. The relationship between him and Pippa was being challenged again, quite as dangerously as it had been when she had stood close to him in the morning. Pippa had her girlishness; he could patronise that, but she was also patronising him in a markedly adult way.

'You mustn't think, Pippa, that thinking stops at thirty. Us senile ones are just as concerned as you.'

'But you aren't, uncle. All right, you are. You've proved it. But the huge mass of people, what you call the silent majority, what we call the dumb majority, the dumbies, they're not concerned.'

'There are other things. Paying your electricity bill seems more important than Armageddon.'

'But when Armageddon comes, whose side will they be on? The good or the evil? Or will they be too busy watching *Dallas*?'

'Not a bad programme, speaking as a dumbie.'

'You're not a dumbie, uncle.'

'But you thought I was.'

'Are you hurt?' Pippa got up and was clearing the table. 'I'm sorry if you were hurt.'

James did feel a little hurt. He was an intelligent person and yet was assumed by another segment of the population to be one of this horridly named group, the dumbies. It was almost racial. He wondered if Bert Miles, the compositors and the others at the print works were dumbies. Probably they were. Was Susie? Perhaps not. It was quite likely that the bomb was now one of her causes, along with retirement for wives. Gerard was not a dumbie, although neither was he an ally. He was an informed but disinterested observer. Would there be a word for him? Watney

122

was certainly not a dumbie. He was on the other side in Armageddon, whichever one that was: both he and Pippa were convinced that they were on the good side. And, like Pippa, he was trying to persuade the dumbies to support his cause. If his Charleston exercise removed some of the fear of nuclear war, it would be a defeat for Pippa and her friends for whom fear was their most powerful message. He wondered what Pippa would say if he told her of Watney's plans, and of his adventures in London. He was tempted to. He found that he wanted her attention: not admiration, she was more likely to be appalled than admiring, but for her to know that he was an individual, not just another dumbie; that he thought. The man who proposed the anchorite idea was also the repository of other disclosures undreamt by her. But he said nothing about London. Watney, if James did tell Pippa about him, would save. The talk had been a good one, as good, if not better, than the one he had had with Susie, and it could be savoured.

During the evening Pippa had given him some pamphlets. He read them in bed. Their message was a conventional one: that a nuclear war would either extinguish human life on earth or make life unbearable for the survivors. Repent or regret, James thought, the message of fundamentalist preachers since Noah. But that did not make it wrong. What was wrong was its confident sense of doom. You'll fry anyway, Pippa had said during her outburst. Hell without redemption. It seemed to James that Watney's message, the bomb we can live with, was more artful. It accepted the continuance of war, which most people, even the disarmers, believed, and it also offered, curiously, hope. The idea had the strength of seeming to face reality quite; subtle, even sophisticated, as Pippa might say.

Pippa resumed her seminar at supper the following evening, and on the evening after that. James's role was mostly as audience and he tried to think of questions. Pippa had a chatty enthusiasm for her negative theme, and gave long answers, making his questions seem more perceptive than they were. She would have made a good saleswoman, he thought, putting huge amounts of determination into selling quite difficult things, like insurance, or advertisement space in obscure publications. Pippa now seemed to have decided that her most useful present contribution to her cause was the conversion of James. He didn't mind. It was flattering to be given such attention. But he felt a sadness that at the end of her spiel he was going to have to say that he didn't want to buy the insurance, or the advertisement space, that the car wasn't really what he wanted and that he was going to hang on to the old one for a bit. He wasn't going to be a trophy to be displayed proudly at the next meeting, probably held at his house. This is James Palmer, my uncle. He's a brill person. He's really going to lay into those dumbies.

Pippa wanted enthusiasm. Had she merely wanted money, like an orthodox sales person, he would at least have access to it. But, enthusiastically, he was almost bankrupt. Could he say that he respected her views, without feeling any inclination to promote them? Probably not. This would be considered dumbie language, and would probably release a torrent of abuse, this time without the apology. Rather than that, it would be better to say that he totally disagreed with everything she said: and attack her, Watney style. Single-mindedness she would understand, and she might relish the confrontation. She would have enjoyed Watney. Momentarily, James felt an envy of him.

Pippa acknowledged in her not entirely sensitive way that James was beyond the age when you normally long to carry banners or lie down in the road to make a peaceful protest. 'You're not over the hill yet, Jamie,' she said.

Somewhere during their conversations Pippa had stopped calling him uncle. He had not commented on it. The name James was presumably too staid for the rejuvenated ally that Pippa had in mind. He would have objected to Jim, but Jamie had a quality about it that he quite fancied, solid, direct, cards on the table. Jamie Palmer could be quite a different person to James Palmer, even though he wasn't.

'Think of Bertrand Russell and Canon Collins. They were older than you.'

Neither name meant much to James, except as people who for decades had headed processions.

'I suppose if you're born to it, it's different. I don't intend to retire either, from printing that is.'

'Oh, Jamie, Jamie, you're irrepressible. You should be beaten.'

The relationship between James and Pippa had changed, despite James's wariness. The fact that they were sharing the same house was itself probably enough to account for a change.

Until now, James realised, he had hardly known his niece. He had seen her when he and Susie and their two boys had visited Belinda of a Sunday, and on Belinda's return visits. Once they had all gone on holiday together, camping in France; not very successfully, he recalled. But these were encounters long ago. Pippa had been the reluctant playmate of his own children; he remembered the reluctance. Until he had met Pippa outside Honeysucklelay with Gerard he had not seen her since her teens. Such knowledge that he had of her life as a young adult had come from Belinda, and not much of it had a mother's blessing. She had disapproved of Pippa's hike across Africa, of her anti-nuclear work, and, particularly, that she did not have a job. She had had a year or two at a university but had left without a qualification. There had been talk that she had been pregnant, but James could not remember whether it had been confirmed or whether there had been a baby. Presumably there hadn't. Pippa had never mentioned a baby.

James watched Pippa as she placed a bowl of fruit on the table. Pudding was always fresh fruit. She had a pleasant, open face straight on, but from the side it was somewhat square. She was not pretty. She had been a plain child who had grown into a plain woman. Was that fair? Pippa was physically plain, but she did not conform to the American euphemism, homely. She had animation. That was her lure, and it wasn't a bad substitute for prettiness.

'Fancy me then, Jamie?'

James heard himself saying, 'Yes.'

'That's all right. It doesn't hurt. You don't want to die never having touched another body.'

They slept together that night. James was surprised how simple it was, the transformation from being friendly, and rather formally friendly, to being loving. Perhaps, he thought, those Hollywood films, the ones they used to make, were not so wrong. The first kiss, the synonym for sex, came suddenly but inevitably.

Pippa's skin felt young. Of course, she was young, but until now James had not had the thought that a woman's skin changes, obvious though that was. Parts of Susie's skin were smooth, the secret parts. James had sometimes remarked to Susie how smooth her skin was, but it was not young. He wondered if he and Susie would ever make love again. He tried to remember when was the last time, but could not fix the precise date. That should have been a milestone, but at the time, of course, he didn't know it was the last time. One often experienced events that, at the time, you did not know were going to be regarded as momentous.

'What are you thinking about?' Pippa said.

'I was thinking of how good our love-making was.'

'Sex is easy. All you need to do is to be kind to each other.'

'Kind?' James considered the word.

'You're not very experienced in sex, Jamie. Believe me, kindness is not to be underrated. If I hadn't believed you were kind I wouldn't have let you screw me, even though you were on heat.'

'Was it obvious?'

'Very, very obvious.'

James studied the ceiling. He noticed a cobweb, no, two, hanging down like streamers, presumably abandoned, or discarded, by their owners. Eventually he said, 'I hadn't thought of myself as inexperienced.'

Pippa quickly turned on her side and put her arms around his neck. 'Oh, my darling. I didn't mean that. You were wonderful. You just haven't screwed around, that's all. I'm glad.'

'You're sure I was all right?'

'You were a hound, Jamie. A real hound.'

★ 6 ★

When James arrived home the following evening he was carrying a bunch of flowers. Pippa met him at the door. 'There's someone to see you. Gerald?'

'Gerard.'

'You make him sound like the bailiffs.'

'No, I hadn't expected him, that's all.'

'The flowers are lovely, Jamie. I'll put them in something.'

She took the bunch, kissed him on the cheek and went to the kitchen. James went into the living room. Gerard was sitting on the sofa as he had been when he had turned up on the first occasion, also unannounced, in a time that now seemed long ago.

'What brings you here, Gerard?'

'You didn't answer my letter.'

'Didn't I? I thought I sent a postcard.'

'Nothing.'

'Well, give me time. It's been very much in my mind.'

The letter was still behind the clock on the mantelpiece. He looked at the postmark on the envelope.

'Well, time does go by when you're busy.'

'You've been away more than a month, James.'

'Have I? If you say so.'

'You said a week, James.'

'I said about a week. Problems don't always fit into a timetable.'

'Are you coming back, James?'

'If I am or not, that's up to me. You talk about "back", but I am back. This is where I live. London was a visit.'

'So you're not?'

'Probably not.'

Pippa came into the room carrying a vase containing James's flowers. She carried the vase high, a parody of a houseproud wife.

'Pippa, I think you've met Gerard before. He was with me outside Honeysucklelay.'

'I thought the face was familiar. The spook.' She placed the vase on a table by the window.

'Well, we're not going to get anywhere calling each other names.'

Gerard smiled wanly, but said nothing. James noticed that he had a rash along one side of his jaw. The spots had been dusted with talcum powder, but still looked fresh and irritating.

James got up and went to the sideboard. 'Who's for drinkies?' No one answered, but no one declined. He poured two whiskies, and a lemonade for Pippa. 'Are you joining us, Pippa?'

'If I'm invited.'

Pippa sat down and so did James. He felt like the chairman at a particularly difficult meeting.

'Gerard is making a film about an old friend of mine, George Watney.'

'Who once ran Honeysucklelay?'

'That's the man. And I'm helping George with his memoirs. Gerard has come up from London to have a chat about things.'

'He sounds quite a man, this Watney. Does everyone run around after him?'

Gerard said, 'How is Susie?'

'She's very well.'

'She's out, I take it?'

'She's away at the moment.'

'I seem to have come at an awkward moment.'

James shrugged. How helpful it would be if Gerard were now to get up and go. He had had a reasonably straightforward answer from James: that he wasn't proposing to return to London. However, he knew that Gerard was not going. He was going to hang about: that was his style. He hadn't come all the way from London simply to remind James to answer his letter. He wanted James back as an ally, as someone to whom he could pour out his anxieties. James knew that he would have to give Gerard an hour or two for a talking session before he got rid of him. But it wouldn't be this evening. Pippa was here. A couple of days ago he would simply have told her to go to another room; after all, he had been barred from his own living room by her group. But now she had assumed some wifeish rights. He would speak to Gerard the following day at his office, where he had absolute control over who was there. The question was, how he should get through the evening? He decided he would take Gerard and Pippa out for dinner: there was a steak house in the town. This would avoid asking Pippa to prepare food for Gerard, whom she clearly disliked. It would also emphasise the fact that the house, with Susie absent, was unsuited for the reception of visitors. He did not want Gerard sleeping there. Pippa would be embarrassed; perhaps she wouldn't, but he certainly would. There was a hotel near the railway station, used by commercial travellers. It wasn't the Hilton, but it wasn't a sleeping bag under a hedge either.

'I thought we might have a bite out this evening, Pippa. You feel like something, Gerard?'

Pippa and Gerard made noises that indicated no more than that they had heard the invitation, but they were not dissenting.

James looked at his watch theatrically. 'Is that the time? No wonder I'm famished.'

The meal was, James reflected afterwards, tiresome. Pippa declined to eat the steak. She said it contained chemicals that had fattened the cattle artificially. She agreed to have a salad and an ice-cream. Gerard said he would like fish. He said, oddly, that he always ate fish when he was out of London. There was no fish listed on the menu. The manager was summoned and he said he could offer fish fingers, which Gerard accepted. Gerard did not want to go to the hotel. He said he would be happy to sleep on the sofa. James said wearily that it was the hotel or nothing. Gerard seemed about to challenge this ultimatum, but changed his mind and accepted it.

'We'll have a good jaw tomorrow,' James said in what he believed was a masterful way. 'Come to the office. I know you want to have another look around the plant. How's the park?'

'The park?'

'Good old Regent's Park?'

'You're a terrible actor, Jamie,' Pippa said when they were in bed that night. 'We could have had something decent to eat at home, and then you could have kicked me out and had your jaw with Gerard.'

'I'm stupid, I suppose. I didn't think you wanted to have to cook for him.'

'You're a nice Jamie-man. I could get to love you.'

James got to work early to deal with routine business, so that he could give over most of the morning to Gerard. Now that he had adjusted to his arrival he was looking forward to hearing an account of any developments in the Watney field headquarters. But Gerard did not turn up, either in the morning or the afternoon. James assumed that he had misjudged Gerard's persistence and that he had returned to London, perhaps in a huff. He was an unpredictable person, of nervy disposition, as the rash on his face would seem to indicate. However, when James arrived home in the evening Gerard was there, in the living room, talking to Pippa. As James came into the room they stopped talking, but he sensed that they were on easy terms with each other. There was no hostility. He had the feeling of being an intruder.

Pippa said, 'We've been talking about that awful man.' James guessed whom she meant, but he said, 'Awful? Is someone awful?' He went over to the sideboard to get himself a drink, but Pippa jumped up. 'Sit down, Jamie. I'll get that.' Whatever had transpired, apparently he was still a sort of master in his house.

He sat down opposite Gerard. 'What became of you?'

Gerard looked embarrassed; no, shifty, James thought.

'I think there must have been a crossed wire, James. Hope I didn't mess up your day.'

'Bugger the crossed wire,' Pippa said, handing James his whisky. 'What are we going to do about Watney?'

James sipped his drink, and felt a battalion of sturdy warriors, a piper at their head, march towards his mind to take arms against intruders. 'Is there some news of George?'

'I've been telling Pippa a little of George's plans, and, frankly, some of my misgivings. I think perhaps she takes a rather pessimistic view of his intentions.'

'Christ, he's going to blow up Charleston. Didn't you say that?'

'I didn't exactly say that, Pippa.'

'He should be locked up, or, preferably, blown up.'

'Not a very peaceable remark, Pippa,' James said.

'Don't be shitty, Jamie. The question is, what are you going to do about it?'

James deployed some more loyal soldiers, and held out his

glass to Pippa. 'Another, please.' With the fresh drink in his hand he said, 'Some kind of conversation has been going on that has upset you. I personally am quite tired. It is one of my declining list of privileges that I am entitled to be tired at this particular moment of the day. I quite enjoy it. All that I am prepared to allow to intrude on it is a little gentle conversation about nothing of consequence. That doesn't include wild stories about the blowing up of Charleston, wherever that is. We shall talk about it later, if you must. It sounds like the sort of theme that might enliven an otherwise sagging dinner conversation.'

James was being pompous, but pomposity was all he could think of at the moment. He saw Pippa and Gerard exchange glances, then Pippa got up and came over to him and kissed him on the forehead. 'Sorry. You're right. Let's talk about it later.'

Susie had been perceptive about Gerard and Pippa. Although they had little obviously in common, they were of a generation that liked to believe in doom. Gerard had decided that a conversation with Pippa about his anxieties over George Watney would get more response than one with James. The very phrase, American General, would call into Pippa's mind the image of the mushroom cloud. Generals were not human beings with families and problems and divorces and holidays and letters from the bank manager, and pricks and a taste for Mozart. To Pippa every soldierly virtue would be a vice. Resolution, pride, nerve, imagination, foresight, compassion: her thesaurus would be limited to one word, madness. Or stupidity. But Watney's view of Pippa would be scarcely more understanding. Pippa was resolute, proud, brave and thoughtful, but Watney would see her as a traitor. Or stupid. Their qualities had marched them off with their flags to opposite ends of belief. James felt a touch of envy for them both. Flags were reassuring. He wondered to what flag Gerard was drawn. He probably regarded himself as superior to flags. No, that was not entirely true. He was clever enough to see the need for flags, like citizens of the old frontier towns of Europe who kept a selection of flags in the cellar to choose from when the next army moved in. Gerard had waved Watney's flag. Making a film about a man's achievements must be a powerful form of flag waving. But now he was faltering. What if Watney were mad, or stupid, as the enemy said he was? Today he had come to look at Pippa's flag. What story had he told her?

Just the facts, probably. Pippa would have assumed the worst. She must have made a satisfying audience for Gerard, but to what end it was difficult to see. Presumably he was now more worried than ever.

'Let us examine this fable of yours,' James said towards the end of supper. 'Absurd though it is, let's dignify it with a few questions.' James felt at ease now. His early evening dip had passed. He had eaten one of Pippa's splendid stews, and she had made some coffee. He was going to have a brandy, and he was thinking of asking her for a cigarette. It was pleasant occasionally to return to bad habits.

'We're in Charleston, an American town that in some ways resembles Hiroshima. Supposing, as your filmscript suggests, it is bombed by a B29, where would anyone find such an old bus? Where would it take off from? Wouldn't it be intercepted long before it was allowed to lumber over a city?'

'That's just the myth that would grow up,' Gerard said. 'The bombs they make now are so neat, one could be carried in a little private plane, a Sunday plane.'

'In a golfing bag,' Pippa said.

'Well. . . .'

'It's true. In a golfing bag on a little trolley. It's really true, Gerard.'

'I wouldn't argue. It could certainly be taken into a town, in the boot of a car. You wouldn't need a plane at all. You'd still get the myth.'

'And where would you get the bomb?' James said.

'Watney could get one.'

'Buy it in the camp canteen?'

'Watney is an artillery man. That's his speciality. That's how he rose to General without seeing any action.'

James shook his head. 'I think this is where the story loses its plausibility. I don't accept that anyone, even a Watney, can pinch a bomb.'

'When you were in the army, James, didn't people pinch things, pistols, lorries, God knows what else?'

'I don't remember.' This was Gerard's fable. He wasn't going to make it easy for him.

'Of course they did,' Gerard said. 'It's easy to steal when there are so many of the things that no one notices the theft. The

132

typist takes home paper and envelopes. A labourer knocks off timber. A soldier knocks off a bomb. In 1945 there were only two atom bombs in the world. Now there are thousands. Bombs are army surplus.'

'And well guarded.'

'But who keeps count? Bored men in a boring job.'

'In that case why haven't others found their way into the hands of terrorists and dotty dictators?'

'I dare say they have.'

'Now they're ready to threaten the world?' James offered a smile.

'Perhaps when he got the thing the terrorist was terror-stricken, and the dictator wasn't so dotty. Also, it seems, the bomb is not that easy to set off. You don't just light a fuse and stand well back. It has to be expertly primed. This would not be a problem for Watney.'

James sipped his brandy and leaned across the table and took a cigarette from Pippa's packet.

'Very well, the script is plausible, if your answers are correct. So, really the question is, would anyone do it, Watney or anyone?'

Neither Gerard nor Pippa said anything. They were waiting for James's answer, the verdict of the oracle, the person of experience who had the credential that he had been born more than sixty years ago and was still alive. The oracle shrugged his shoulders. 'Well, we'll never know. Unless it happens, of course.'

'Is that all?' Pippa said.

'Sometimes you are never satisfied, Pippa. A sensible sum-ming-up, I should think. Let's put it to the vote. Those who believe George Watney is capable of anything please show.'

Pippa started to raise her hand, then brought it down with a thump on the table. 'I'm not being made a fool of. You're the sort of person who would have gone quietly to the gas chamber because you couldn't believe a human being could do such a thing.'

James prepared for more abuse, but it never came. Pippa bled easily but quickly healed.

He said, 'What can we do? Write to the *Daily Mirror*?'

Pippa did not smile. 'The media could be very important here.'

'Or the police? Susie turned up her nose at that.'

'Susie? You talked about it to auntie?'

'I mentioned it. Gerard wrote to me. It was something to talk about.' James tried to make the words sound casual but he knew that the flip remark, which had slipped out so easily, was now going to re-charge the argument that he thought he was steering into extinction.

'So even you're worried, Jamie?'

James frowned. What a nasty prodding manner Pippa had.

'Naturally I've been concerned that you're worried.'

'But, Jamie, I didn't know anything about this until today.'

'That's right. That's my point.'

If you are losing an argument, confusion is an ally.

'Now let's get this straight, Jamie. . . .' James gave formal attention to Pippa as she explained the obvious, but his mind was adjusting to the new fact that had slipped under its guard. It was possible; not probable, not even possible. Was there a diminutive of possible? James could not think of the word. To say it was just possible would be too strong, although near possibility would be too weak. 'Barely possible' would be quite near. On a scale of one to ten, the possibility was perhaps one half of one, or less. The measurement was not important. A self-revelation was an event. Pippa would say it would change your life: that was a phrase she often used. It wouldn't do that, but it could shake you. A phantom had shown itself.

James interrupted whatever Pippa was saying. 'Very well, Pippa. You seem more agitated about this than anyone. I'm prepared to hear any suggestions, as long as they're sensible.'

Gerard said, 'May I make a suggestion?'

'Why not? You started all this.'

'What I propose, James, is that you return to London, just for a day or two, if you like. Watney is, after all, expecting you. He'll be glad to see you back.'

'And?'

'Well, sound him out.'

'Question him?'

'Probe a bit.'

'You want me to say, "George, I'm a bit worried. Are you going to drop a bomb on Charleston?" '

'Not just like that.'

134

'Is there any other way?'

'He might confide in you. You've been a soldier. That makes you special. You got pissed together in Morocco.'

'In the end it comes down to putting this absurd question.'

'Lots of questions seem absurd before they are put. You dither in your mind whether to ask your first girl whether she will sleep with you. It seems absurd that you should venture to ask. If the question is absurd, let Watney say so. Let's all laugh with him.'

'Would you believe him?'

'I would trust your judgement. If you were satisfied that this was all fantasy, so would I be.'

'And so would I,' Pippa said. 'I think it's a bloody good idea.'

Two eager faces studied James. Gerard, James was again reminded, was a clever young man. He had thought through his tactics to this moment. When he had arrived at the house the previous day he had quickly assessed the new situation: Susie gone and Pippa in her place as companion and lover. He had used his charm and craftiness to befriend Pippa and tell her about the fearsome Watney. Now she, too, wanted him to return to London. They said they would trust his judgement, but they would do so only if it confirmed their own beliefs. They wanted to do something, and he was the instrument for the something. He did not want to be their envoy, unless . . . Unless what? Unless he also felt a need for reassurance.

'I'll think about it.'

'For how long?' Pippa said.

'Not very long.'

Gerard said, 'I'd better be getting along to that wretched hotel.'

'Why don't you sleep on the sofa tonight?' James said. 'You're very welcome.'

James had hoped that by morning he would have a clearer idea of what to do about Watney, but he didn't. Sleeping on something can merely make it look more shapeless. Watney was not mentioned by Pippa or Gerard at breakfast, and James went to work glad to enter the ordinary world where there was nothing to trouble him except the possibility of going broke. However, during the morning he had a phone call which, instinctively, or more probably because he had not stopped thinking about Watney, he knew was going to be from the non-ordinary world.

'Is that Mr Palmer, please?'

135

'Yes.'

'Mr James Palmer?'

'Yes, of course. That's Molly, isn't it? How are you, Molly?'

'I'm extremely well, Mr Palmer.'

James wondered what uniform the versatile Molly was wearing this morning. He thought of her in a little black dress with a white collar. She would make a good secretary, personal assistant. Perhaps that in essence was her job.

'And how is the General?' He may as well be brave. No doubt Watney was trying to get hold of him.

'General Watney asked me to apologise to you for not being able to speak to you personally, but he wonders if you could join him this evening at Honeysucklelay?'

'Honeysucklelay?'

'Have I got the name right, Mr Palmer?'

'Oh, perfectly right. What's he doing up here, Molly?'

'General Watney is driving up today. He requests, if convenient, for you to be there by seven o'clock.'

'It's possible. Yes, of course I can be there. Did the General say anything else.'

'End of message, Mr Palmer.'

'Well, thank you, Molly. It was good to speak to you again.'

'You're very welcome, Mr Palmer.'

After the call James sat back in his chair. He became aware that he was breathing heavily. The message had temporarily blocked the day. He wondered whether he should tell Pippa and Gerard of the summons, but he decided not to. They would ask questions that he could not possibly answer and would assume that he was keeping secrets from them. He phoned home and said that he would be late, possibly very late.

'All right, darling. Another woman?'

Pippa could be very mawkish.

'No time, unfortunately. Just work.'

He could be mawkish, too. 'What's the spook up to?'

'Gerry and I are thinking of having a picnic. It's a lovely day. Look out of your window.'

After the call James did walk across to his window. The view was of a road, but it was of a sunny road and cars were casting shadows. The northern summer was at last arriving, wearily, as though it had been asked to make too long a journey. James went back to his desk, and made the effort to return to the problems of the day. Pippa might convince herself that he was the key to saving the world, but he knew that the central reality of his life was that he was the key to the safety of his firm and the families who depended on it.

He had a pub lunch and worked solidly through the afternoon and into the early evening. At the end of his stint he felt he was winning; not tired at all, quite relaxed.

He arrived at Honeysucklelay just before seven. He could smell cooking coming from the camp fires outside the base: the evening meal, a stew probably. Perhaps that was how Pippa nurtured her talent. The clerk at the guardhouse was sharp-eyed but friendly. He spoke English and wore a British uniform. Honeysucklelay was still, as James had remembered it, formally a Royal Air Force base.

'You'll find General Watney at the lecture, sir. Park your car here, if you will. The hall is about thirty yards down on the left. You'll see a notice.'

The hall was like a village hall that had been bought from a catalogue, with exposed Meccano-like beams and bolts. About a hundred people, perhaps more, were sitting in rows on canvas chairs. There was a small table at one end, with two chairs and a carafe of water. Watney was in the front row, talking animatedly to someone. James stood uncertainly for a moment, wondering if he should march straight up to Watney, who did not appear to have seen him. However, two men mounted the platform. One sat down, the other tinkled the carafe with a pen for order. James took a seat near the back.

The man who tinkled the carafe was the chairman, or whatever the military title was. He spoke briefly, simply introducing the other man, whose name James did not catch. He sat down, someone clapped, alone, and the other man got up. He was French, of the tall sort, James thought, tall and rather conventionally distinguished. He probably had a de or a d' in his name. He was in uniform, cut, no doubt, in this year's style. He spoke excellent English with a slight French glaze.

He said his theme was thinking the unthinkable, or the new reality about nuclear weapons. He said that many people, even quite intelligent and supposedly informed people, thought of nuclear warfare as bombing cities, as Hiroshima had been

137

bombed. This was nonsense. If you bombed a city you could not occupy it, even if you were victorious. It also encouraged your adversary to bomb your cities. It was no way to conduct a war. In a war an army should fight an army, seeking to incapacitate each other. Fortunately, because of the growing accuracy of missiles, it was possible to attack solely military objects with great accuracy, using low-yield warheads that produced little fallout. War could become the honourable profession it had been up to the beginning of this century, fought between uniformed forces. Civilians would not be involved, and cities would be unscathed, except by accident.

James examined his fellow listeners. He was relieved to see that he was not the only person in civilian clothes. There were two others near him, although they had a soldierly look. Watney was wearing a uniform, the first time James had seen him in one. Even at the presentation in Agadir he had worn a suit. The premises, with their look of having been erected in an afternoon, had a warlike atmosphere about them, and for all he knew they may have been put up in the war. He didn't remember them from his old visits to Honeysucklelay, but he hadn't seen much of the place. He certainly remembered places like this, but they had been mainly the settings for forces' concerts, and lectures by screwy professors who talked about the aims of peace, who sometimes got the bird, because the only aim that mattered was getting out of the army. No one looked like giving this Frenchman the bird. Perhaps peacetime lectures had more gravitas than wartime ones.

The Frenchman was saying that the Soviets had got in first with low-yield, highly accurate weapons. They had tumbled to the fact that big blasts in Europe would shower the Soviet Union with fallout, because the prevailing wind blew from west to east. They were scrapping most of their monster weapons and were replacing them with decent little ones which were targeted on four hundred European airfields, radars and ammunition dumps, most of which were soft. 'Every target is on the surface, gentlemen.'

'Shame,' someone said.

Shortly afterwards the Frenchman sat down, rising briefly to nod in acknowledgement of the applause. He replied to a number of questions, which, James thought, were mostly put by experts wanting to show off. None challenged the Frenchman's argument.

Immediately the meeting was adjourned, Watney came over to James. Presumably he had seen him arrive after all. 'James, it was really good of you to come.' He gripped James's hand between his two strong General's hands. He asked how he was, how Susie was and whether he was getting his domestic troubles sorted out. James made uncomplicated replies. Watney's welcome seemed sincere and unreproachful. He made no mention that James had overstayed his leave. 'We're having a little supper, James. I'm hoping that you'll join us.'

There were four at supper, James, Watney, the Frenchman and Freddie Fairbanks, who had apparently been at the lecture, although James had not seen him. From the table-talk James gathered that Watney had come to Honeysucklelay for another of his retirement presentations, and Fairbanks, who had also served at the base, had come for the nostalgia.

'So when is the presentation?' James said.

'Here's a funny thing,' Watney said. 'There ain't gonna be one.'

'My fault entirely,' the Frenchman said.

'That's not so,' Watney said. 'And I tell you this, I'm not sorry. I've given away more presents than I've kept. Isn't that so, James?'

James did remember being offered the video that Watney had been given at Agadir, so he said yes. The Frenchman did not explain why he had come between Watney and his latest gift, but it seemed the presentation had clashed with a seminar at the base, of which the Frenchman's lecture had been a contribution. The complications of Watney's presentation were not in the forefront of James's mind at the moment. What was pressing him was that here he was, face to face with Watney, in a position to claim his entire attention, and with Pippa's and Gerard's gauche question in his mind, 'Are you going to bomb Charleston?' He thought of their nagging voices if he returned home to say, yes, he had seen Watney, but the subject had not been discussed. He could lie and say that he had put the question and Watney had vehemently denied it, but he was not confident that he could invent a sufficiently convincing form of words for Watney's denial that would shut up Pippa and Gerard, particularly Pippa. The presence of Fairbanks and the Frenchman happily put off the appalling moment, which surely must be conducted in private. But before the evening was done the question would have to be put. Fortunately, the supper was being fuelled with plenty of alcohol, and that should help. They had started with an Alsace wine, and now the steward was pouring out what looked like a good claret. At any rate, the Frenchman was sniffing it thoroughly and his nose was not turning up.

Watney was offering what sounded like a belated vote of thanks to the Frenchman for his lecture. 'What I liked about it', Watney said, 'was its solid sanity. Take the fear out of the bomb. Give war back to the professionals. The frogs are right. What did you think, Freddie?'

'An illumination,' Fairbanks said. 'Most impressive.'

There was a pause. James suddenly felt it his duty to fill it. 'In Normandy,' he said, 'we started off with the thought: let metal do it rather than the flesh. But we got only to Berlin by doing it with flesh. In the most recent big war Vietnamese flesh beat American metal. If there is another world war most of the metal won't work. It either won't work at all, or it will blow up in the wrong places. Your notion of precision seems to me . . .' James paused. The phrase on his lips was 'bloody stupid,' but he temporised with 'very optimistic'.

Silence.

Watney said, addressing the Frenchman, 'James went all through the last show, Dunkirk, the desert, D-Day.'

The Frenchman took a sip of his wine and pursed his lips as though he had located some quality in it that was not totally to his liking. James waited for a riposte, something brilliantly rude. Seemingly he had not objected to being called a frog, perhaps putting it down to American crudeness or comradeship, or perhaps Watney had said it so often that it now had no effect. But he would not like to be challenged on his subject by a mere foot soldier, and a British one at that. James caught Fairbanks's eye, and thought he detected a concord. He, too, had fought in the war.

'I have no comment to make,' the Frenchman said.

'That's a pity,' Watney waded in. 'I thought we'd have some creative discussion there. Flesh and metal, I like that. In the Western Sahara there's not much they don't know about flesh and metal.'

140

While he was talking about his Morocco exploit the pudding arrived, and a sweet white wine. The Frenchman drank his wine and ate a little of the pudding, then got up: he had to get back to the seminar, which was continuing. He offered Watney and Fairbanks a small bow, James a brief nod.

'I think he didn't like me,' James said when he had gone.

'I shouldn't worry,' Fairbanks said. 'The French never take defeat well.'

'What about the Brits, Freddie?' Watney said. 'How do they take it?'

'We've had so little experience. I'd have thought the Americans were more the authority there.'

It was a childish exchange, but there was an edge to it. James wondered what held Watney and Fairbanks together, despite their apathy for each other. He would ask Gerard about it.

The steward offered James some brandy. He accepted. He fancied a brandy. But he knew that more alcohol would take the edge off his wits. He either had to say his piece now, or let it slide.

'Can I bring up a slightly controversial matter?' he heard himself saying.

'You've upset France, you may as well take a punch at America as well.'

'You may think what I'm going to say is absurd, George, but in the interests of what used to be known in my army as man management, I think I ought to say it.'

'Is this about young Gerard?'

'It is, George.'

'He thinks I'm going to put a bomb under Charleston?'

'He's anxious, that's all. Obviously, I've said it's absurd. But I said I'd put it to you. Now, with half a bottle of wine in me, I have.'

'What do you think, Freddie? Do you think I'm going to drop a bomb on Charleston?'

'I wouldn't put it past you, George. That's why I'm coming to Charleston, to keep an eye on you.' He gave James a wink, deliberately obvious enough to be observed by Watney.

'And you'll be coming with us, too, won't you, James?'

The wine muffled James's surprise. 'I haven't really thought about it.'

'I'm counting on you, James. You're one of the team, reliable, solid. Gerard relies on you, you know that? He's a nervous, very imaginative person. Most of the time he's a pain in the arse, but I happen to think he's a genius. So there's that. Would you find it too onerous minding a genius for a few weeks? You could do with a change. I know that Susie has moved out on you and that you are shacked up with a dopey broad from the peace camp. Well, fine, but don't make her your life's companion. Plenty of grateful women in the States. And think of the trip as a business pro-position. Your firm has just re-tooled. You can do with all the work you can get. I promise you all the printing you can handle from the film. You'll be surprised how much there is. It could turn the corner for you.'

'You seem to know a lot about my affairs, George.'

'I had you checked out. I asked if I could. You don't mind?'

'No, I suppose not.'

'Of course not. You did well. Alpha. Only Presidents do better than that, and not all of them.'

Watney walked with James to his car. James had made the gesture of offering Watney a bed for the night, but, as James had guessed, Watney had accommodation at the camp. 'Real snug.' He insisted on showing it to James, who thought it looked a little spartan, although did not say so. In the corner of the room was a golf bag, on wheels, a golfing trolley. James felt a little shiver, but it looked perfectly innocent. Its only distinctive feature was that it was new.

'You a golfer, James?'

'No.'

'They gave me something useful for a change. No ceremony, but I won the prize. Ha, ha. A fine game, golf. Invented in England.'

'In Scotland, I believe.'

'Clever chaps the Brits. Not likeable, but clever.'

As he drove home James thought about how he would relate the evening's events to Pippa and Gerard. He would tell them the truth, of course. That is, his own truth. He would give them a careful account, but an account was not a recording. He was not sure that he would wish them to hear a recording of the moments of his confrontation with Watney; he might squirm a little if he could hear it himself. He was a bit deferential, even apologetic.

Nevertheless, he had put the question, and Watney had answered it. They were making a film about Charleston, nothing more. Not a very pleasant film, by the sound of it, but just a film. James tried to recall the exact words of Watney's avowal, but could not. But, anyway, that was the sense. Short of getting Watney to sign a testament before fifteen High Court judges he could do nothing more. Pippa and Gerard would be surprised, impressed, that he had seen Watney. It was only the previous day that they had put the pressure on. It would be tempting to keep the meeting a secret for a little while. Let them nag a little, become impatient, angry, demand to know when he was going to see Watney. And he would answer, quietly, coolly, 'I've already seen him.' But that was fantasy, although agreeable fantasy. He would tell them as soon as he got home.

Pippa and Gerard were watching television. Pippa got up and kissed James when he came in, and offered him supper, which he declined. She wanted to return to her programme, and he did not dissuade her. He consulted a newspaper and saw that she was watching a film, and that it had another hour to run. He made yawning gestures and went upstairs to bed. He read, but soon went to sleep. He was aware of Pippa getting into bed and her cool body drawing warmth from his, but he did not awake. Next morning almost his first words to her were, 'I saw Watney last night and he convinced me that there's nothing to these worries of Gerard.' The information he had gathered was extracted from him in bits, by Pippa in bed and while she was dressing, and by Pippa and Gerard over breakfast. Much of it was repetitive. There was no drama, no well-spun narrative to a transfixed audience, and seemingly no surprise.

'What do you think, Gerry?' Pippa said towards the end of breakfast.

'James has done what we asked him to. Let's be fair.'

That was the nearest either of them came to acknowledging the success of James's expedition.

'What did you expect, Pippa? Would you have been happier if I had come back with evidence that Watney had a bomb in his pocket?'

'I don't know, Jamie. I'd just like to think about it.'

'Please do. As far as Sherlock Palmer is concerned, the case is closed.'

143

James went to work, not in a huff, but not buoyant either. The day had started badly. Gerard called in during the morning. He was returning to London. 'I just want to say, James, I appreciate all you've done.'

James did not feel grateful. 'You've given me a lot of trouble, Gerard.'

Gerard accepted the scolding. 'I take it you're not coming back to London?'

'Probably not.'

'You may do, then?'

'Watney wants me to come to Charleston. I have to give him an answer. It will probably be no.'

'I see a patch of blue sky. Would it make any difference, James, if I said that my own decision about going to Charleston might depend on whether you came, too?'

'Not the slightest. I'm sick of being pressured. But if you feel like that, don't go. That would put a stop to the whole silly business.'

'Watney would find another director. There's plenty about, and without my moral scruples trailing around, getting in everyone's way. George's life would be easier with another Fairbanks.'

'A little unkind, Gerard. And I'd have thought untrue.'

'I know he once sided with a demo at the base. Watney still whines about it. But it was probably just to needle Watney. Anyway, that was long ago. Freddie is too hard up to have scruples now.'

'I had no idea.'

'Hasn't he tried to touch you for money?'

'No.'

'A treat to come.'

'That's very sad.'

'Very foolish. I steer clear of snorting.'

Gerard smiled briefly at the blank expression on James's face. 'You really are an innocent, James. Snorting is sniffing cocaine. Freddie is a snort. I don't think I'm giving away any secrets. I thought everyone in Regent's Park knew.'

'Not me. Is he, what, an addict?'

'The snorters say there is no dependency. That's why it is so trendy. I've never seen him coked up, but then you can be an alcoholic without getting drunk. I'll stick to my joints. You have heard of joints, marijuana?'

James ignored the sarcasm and nodded. 'But you make it sound so casual, like someone saying, "I'm a beer man, myself." '

'You a beer man, James?'

James did not answer the question, if it was a question. He did not want to get into a debate with Gerard about the merits of various social drugs. Fairbanks's need for money explained why he worked for Watney, who presumably paid him well. It did not explain why Watney should want his company.

'George once told me he considered Fairbanks a traitor.'

'That's just Watney rhetoric. Watney's foreign policy is that he dislikes foreigners, the British among them. He mentions the British a lot because he has actually worked with some of them. He also shares the fashionable American view that the British are clever, so he has recruited a number of British to his entourage. A marginal advantage is that, of the subject peoples, the British speak the best English, an easily understood dialect of the American language.'

'Now who's exaggerating?'

'Not very much.'

Gerard left without a promise from James that he would see him again, but no absolute denial either. At lunchtime James went to his bank to draw out the modest sum he allowed himself each week. He asked to see his statement and was surprised, although not totally surprised, to see that Watney was continuing to pay him an exorbitant wage, even though he was no longer doing his memoirs, in fact doing nothing at all for him. James's personal economy had been one of painfully slow growth. His father had underpaid him, meeting his grumbles with promises for tomorrow. Now that tomorrow was here James found that his new paymasters, his firm's clients, were equally begrudging. The sight of the large Watney credits on his bank statement, paid in promptly, and not under duress, struck James as exotic. He would return the money, of course. But not just yet. He would enjoy a spurious, temporary feeling of affluence. Watney did owe him that.

James looked forward to the evening. Gerard would have gone. Life would be almost normal. Pippa would have had a day to digest his report on Watney, and would accept that he had done his best. There was a strong element of realism in Pippa. However, Pippa did not welcome him with the warmth he had hoped for, although neither was she hostile. James did not ask her what was wrong, darling, as he might have done with Susie: that conjugal inquiry belonged to the depths of marriage. He assumed that eventually she would say, or that it would become evident. And eventually she did disclose her thoughts. She said that she had been to the local police station and said that she wanted to report a crime. Could she see an inspector, or, failing that, a sergeant? The constable said that certainly she could, but could she tell him the nature of the crime? She said that the crime had not yet taken place. The constable was not deterred. He said that the prevention of crime was an important part of police work. What crime was she seeking to prevent? Pippa said that it was a crime against humanity. The constable asked her to please take a seat, and he would speak to his superior. He returned a few minutes later and asked her if she would make a written statement. Could she not see his superior? No, madam, but his superior would see the statement. That was the normal procedure. Pippa wrote her statement, signed it, and took a copy for herself. The constable read it through, said that it seemed quite clear and thanked her for calling in. If they wished to make further inquiries, he assumed they could contact her at this address? They could.

'It was your idea,' Pippa said.

'It wasn't an idea. I was trying to illustrate an absurdity. Show me the statement.'

The statement named Watney and Honeysucklelay and a plan to set off a bomb in Charleston, South Carolina.

'I kept your name out of it, Jamie.'

'But not my address.'

'It's my address, too. They have to have an address.'

'I can't see what you hope to accomplish. They must have thought you were daft.'

'Oh, they thought I was a nutter all right, one of those nutters who are trying to stop nuclear war. But at least someone knows outside Watney and his circle, even if it's only the constable in his cycle clips, who wasn't a bad chap.'

'So you didn't believe me?'

146

'Of course I believe what you told me: Watney said this, and Watney said that. But I don't believe what you believe. Your ordinary decency gets in the way of your reason.'

Next day Pippa left to return to her bender outside Honeysucklelay. She did not go in a huff. James judged that the parting was rather tender. She did not say she would miss him, but she said she would miss the hot baths, and she hugged him as she said so. She gave no reason for going except that she had been away from the camp longer than she had intended, and her friends would think she had deserted them. It was a complete reason, pointless to argue against. James wondered if he could have kept her, or at least delayed her departure, if he had behaved differently, more cunningly, pretending to be more persuaded to her views, to be more distrusting of Watney. But he hadn't, and he couldn't have, and anyway Pippa would have seen through the deception. Instead of being a decent simpleton in her eyes, he would have been a dishonest one.

She said that if the nice constable called, James should tell him to cycle over to Honeysucklelay, where she would try to seduce him. James did get a call as a result of Pippa's visit to the police station, but not from the constable. He was telephoned by a man with a cultured voice who said his name was Watkins and asked if he could make an appointment to see James.

'Of course. When?'

'Would Saturday morning be convenient, sir?'

'I don't see why not.'

'At ten o'clock?'

'Fine.'

'Can we make it ten-thirty?'

'Ten or ten-thirty. I'll be there.'

'This would be at your office, sir?'

'At home.'

'Excellent.' Watkins seemed pleased that James would be at home.

★ 7 ★

Watkins, James judged, was about his own age; possibly a little younger, but certainly of James's generation. He apologised for calling on James on a Saturday morning when he was probably busy.

'Not at all. Best time for me, really.'

'Is that true? I believe it is. I am glad. It suited me, you see. I have an aunt living hereabouts. I thought I'd make a weekend of it, breathe the good air, do a bit of walking. Lucky for me that your little query landed in my tray, and lucky for me that you've been so obliging.'

James visualised Watkins's desk with its tray in one corner into which were deposited little queries which Watkins sorted through, seeking the most interesting, or the least dull, and here was one from a place that was familiar. Make a weekend of it, get out of London, see his aunt, who can't have many teeth left now, charge for a bit of overtime and a bit of mileage. Well, why not? It was only public money.

'You are, what, from the police, Mr Watkins?'

Watkins had shown him a plastic card with his name and photograph glazed inside, but James had merely glanced at it. The fact that he knew about Pippa's visit to the police station was, he supposed, Watkins's real credential.

'The police, in a general sense, Mr Palmer. I always say police over the phone because intelligence sounds sinister, spies and all that kind of thing. People get upset. I know now that this wouldn't apply to you, but you were just a name on a piece of paper. You follow?'

'Of course. What do you want to know?'

'Not very much, tell you the truth. But better go through the motions.' Watkins had with him a leather bag, black with a gold insignia: ER II. He undid the straps and James caught a glimpse of cloth, perhaps of pyjamas for his sojourn with his aunt.

148

Watkins pushed them deeper into the bag and withdrew a folder.

'Now then, let's see.'

Watkins, James thought, was a type, and he was true to it. That was a surprise, although it should not be as types were presumably the normal consequence of breeding. He had a sharp, rather weathered face and was lean. He had kept his figure in better shape than James had. He could be cast as the Briton in an espionage film of the 1940s. The only doubt the director might have was that he could look too obvious. James liked him, or perhaps he simply didn't dislike him. Types were reassuring. You felt you understood them, although it was naive to think that you did. In the 1940s you knew what side British agents were on. But the fashion had changed. Now they were frail and often unhinged people who worked for the Russians or wanted to work for the Russians but were turned down. They had gained firsts in history and buggery at Cambridge. If Watkins were a double agent, would he be twice as interested in Pippa's story, selling the results of his investigation to the Russians as well as providing the information to his employer, like a hopeful freelance journalist who flogs the same story to as many papers as will take it? However, Watkins did not seem terribly interested in the story at all.

'Now, here we are. You are the girl's uncle. Is that right?'

'Quite right.'

It was possible, of course, even likely, that Watkins was seeking to lull James into a feeling of false security, to establish a bond of trust, as a result of which James would confide his secrets. James had little to confide, but Watkins would not know that.

'And the girl, let me call her Philippa, I'm sure you do; she has been living here with you?'

'Staying here, yes.'

'But is not here now?'

'No.'

'Can you tell me where she is now? Or am I prying too much?'

'At this moment, I dare say, she's outside an American base washing up her breakfast things.'

'She favours nuclear disarmament, I take it?'

'Yes, she does favour that.'

It was also possible that Watkins was stupid. Spy trials gave the impression that the secret service was staffed with silly people. There probably was something pathetic about anyone who found themselves in the secret service. They might simply be retarded, never having matured beyond schoolboy fantasies fed by thriller writers, living in a world of dead letter-boxes and safe houses and foreigners whose tongue was English with a bit of an accent. Or they might have drifted in, perhaps after a spell in the army, because they couldn't get a proper job. James hoped that Watkins wasn't stupid. Watkins's view of Watney and his plans, if he had a view, and if he were prepared to share it with James, would be, what? Interesting? Important? Certainly interesting. James had not been greatly perturbed that Pippa had gone to the police station with her story. It had been an eccentric thing to do, but she had wanted to share the burden she felt she was bearing alone: let the official world worry about it, it's their job. In depositing her own burden she had also deposited James's burden, too; his own tiny burden, his own absurd shadow of a doubt. The constable had passed Pippa's statement on to his superior, who had taken one look at it and had been inclined to throw it in the waste-basket. But better be sure: odd events touch even rural police stations; Libyan terrorists, Sri Lankan separatists. He had passed it on, by way of some creaky conduit in re-used manila envelopes until it had arrived in Watkins's tray as a little query. It might be the pass to a free weekend away, but nevertheless Watkins had a duty to deal with the query seriously; and he should have the courtesy to tell James whether he considered it should be taken seriously. James suddenly felt righteous about it. He thought he was prepared to press Watkins on it. Watkins could provide a sounding from the official world about Watney. James was entitled to know, if only in return for the co-operation he was offering Watkins.

'You are married, Mr Palmer?'

'Oh yes.'

'And your wife: she is here?'

'She's away at the moment.'

'On holiday?'

'Not exactly. But away.'

'I see.'

Watkins's method of interrogation seemed very individual. He was behaving like someone from the social security office rather

150

than an ace from Curzon Street. Perhaps he was stupid, but he could be being clever. James found it difficult to imagine Watkins being other than stupid or clever. An average ability did not seem to accord with his idea of spyland.

'And Philippa, does she have any domestic problems?'

'Doesn't get on with her mother. The usual thing.'

'No boyfriend trouble?'

'None that I know of.'

James knew nothing of Pippa's previous affairs, though undoubtedly she had had some, perhaps many. He supposed he had been her most recent boyfriend, an old boyfriend.

'Watney, now; is he sexually active, would you say?'

'I believe so. I assume so. I hope so.'

'But you don't know so?'

'How would I know?'

'He seems an outgoing man. Might have talked. Let's go round to the local knocking shop, sort of thing. No?'

James thought of Watney on the couch receiving an enema from Molly, but that was no concern of Watkins.

'I'd say he had normal sexual needs, for his age.'

'What about his relationship with Gerard?'

'You mean a homosexual relationship?'

'Yes.'

'It would be news to me.'

'But not impossible?'

'Only in the sense that nothing is impossible. Tell me, Mr Watkins, isn't this all a bit,' James was going to say 'far-fetched' but he softened it to 'remote?'

'We in the service are a Freudian lot, Mr Palmer. Look for the sex. If only everyone was a eunuch, eh, Palmer?'

'Not much fun.'

'You see, you agree with me.'

Watkins was definitely not in the 1940s mould. It seemed unlikely that Carruthers had studied Freud.

'But at a practical level,' James said, 'at a practical level, this business of,' even now he could hardly bring himself to say it, but this presumably was what Watkins was here for, 'this business of blowing up Charleston. What's your view of that?'

'Practical?' Watkins spoke the word as if it were an intrusion, a trivial diversion from his line of inquiry. 'This fantasy?'

'You mean there's nothing to it?' This then was the official word, the distilled essence of those into whose hands the security of the island race was entrusted.

'There is something to everything. The idea of the explosion is obviously sexual, not very subtle though. It will probably make a highly successful film. What does it tell us about Watney, though? Is that what you mean?'

James allowed himself a smile, although he did not allow it to reach his lips. So the consequence of Pippa's statement was that Watney was under some sort of suspicion, not as the potential assassin of Charleston, but as a deviant. Watney was the little query. Pippa would be amused by that.

'You're not seriously worried about George Watney?'

'No, I think not seriously.'

'He's a,' James hunted for the exact word, 'a patriot.'

'Does he talk much about politics?'

'Oh, come off it, Mr Watkins. George is the definitive cold warrior. Doubt him, and you may as well doubt the President of the United States.'

James was aware that he was not helping Watney's cause by defending him so fiercely. He had read enough thrillers to know that in spyland not even presidents are immune from suspicion. Chinese agents planted brainwashing substances in their bodies when they weren't looking.

'Look here, Mr Watkins. George Watney has had a long and honourable career and has now reached retirement. I have known him all my life,' an exaggeration, but never mind, 'and I have an affection for him. I don't want him hurt. I know you have your duty to do, but I say this to you. Don't put some question mark against his name to be fed into a computer, some black mark, grey mark, to be there for the rest of his life, and after. Anyone can be sullied like this.' He was cross with Pippa now. She was a stupid little bitch.

'The Yanks don't go easy on our chaps.' Watkins looked sulky.

'You don't look like a revengeful man.'

'You don't know what I am, Palmer, and I have very little idea of what you are. In the service there is an assumption of guilt unless proved otherwise. I won't say innocent. No one is innocent, but there are shades of guilt, very guilty down to good faith and merely foolish.'

152

'None of this would apply to Watney,' James said.

'Then why is there a query about him?'

'Because Pippa went into the police station, I suppose. But she wasn't complaining about Watney's lack of patriotism. Rather the opposite.'

'A query can start anywhere. It can be luck, like finding a penny on the ground.'

James was confused. He felt himself caught in the sort of frantic logic you might meet if you idly picked a book from a library shelf and found yourself reading an argument which explained why you weren't really there. He wanted to put Watkins back on the shelf.

'What about a cup of coffee, Mr Watkins?'

Watkins followed James into the kitchen and looked out of the window.

'Is that a boat I see before me?'

In the back garden, by the caravan James had thought of giving to Pippa, was a plywood dinghy. Like the caravan, it was a toy that belonged to a bygone era of the family.

'Was once. You a sailor, Mr Watkins?'

'I fish, and sometimes I fish from a boat, so I suppose that makes me a sort of sailor.'

James put a spoon of coffee into two cups, added hot water and powdered milk. He handed one cup to Watkins, opened the back door and led the way into the garden. If Watkins wanted to talk about fishing and boats, that suited him. The garden was beginning to look scruffy. James had always assumed that he did most of the gardening, but Susie's contribution was obviously being missed. Pippa had never touched the garden, despite her open-air skills.

'Do you have a garden, Mr Watkins?'

Watkins was by the boat and had lifted a corner of the canvas cover.

'A Mirror, isn't it? An early one, too, number six hundred and eighty, my goodness, quite vintage. I once had an Enterprise, kept it on the beach. Some vandals pushed it off one night. Never saw it again.'

James suddenly had an impulse to give the dinghy to Watkins. It only took up space in the garden. But would it seem like bribery, and not much of a bribe at that, an old boat for Watney's reputation? It would not be wise. And yet Watkins clearly coveted it. Watney would certainly have given it to him by now; a generous man, Watney.

'Actually it's for sale, if you know of anyone who might want it, that and the caravan.'

'For sale, you say?'

'That and the caravan.'

'Not a van man myself, but I could be interested in the Mirror. How much?'

An expression came on to Watkins's face that James had not noticed before. Cunning. During the whole of the questioning back in the house Watkins had not once seemed to have looked cunning.

'How much, Palmer?'

'Shall we say a fiver?'

It was a stupid thing to say. Better to have given it away, as he was first minded to. A concealed bribe was even more foolish than a simple bribe. James waited for Watkins's reaction.

'A fiver? Five pounds?'

'Yes.'

'I might find a home for it at five pounds.'

Perhaps he had misjudged Watkins again. Bargain hunters had their own code. They bought Rembrandts for a song from old ladies, and Mirrors for a fiver from old fools.

'Is it just the hull, Palmer, or are there any bits?'

There was a full inventory of bits that James found in his shed, a mast, rigging, sails, centreboard and rudder and four life-jackets. He carried them out and laid them by the hull. They made an impressive pile.

'You're sure you want to get rid of it?' The bargain hunter had a touch of conscience.

'You'll be doing me a favour,' James said. 'I need the space.'

'I know the feeling, Palmer. Right then, may as well get loaded up, get it out of your way.'

Watkins had a large car with a wooden body of a type that used to be known as a station wagon. Perhaps another bargain, James thought. He helped Watkins lift the boat and its accessories on to the roof rack and secure it with rope.

When this was done the new owner of the boat stood back, seemingly assessing the load.

154

'Well, that's that then.' He did not move. James wondered whether he was summoning up sufficient gall to say that he now wanted to ask him some more questions about poor Watney. But he said, 'Fancy a sail, then?'

'Not today, I think.'

'I mean it, Palmer. Lovely day. Try her out at Muddy Creek.'

James smiled. 'Not for me. I haven't sailed for years. Anyway, it probably leaks. It needs a bit of work to make it water-tight.'

'Bet she doesn't. Come on, Palmer, be a sport. Hand over the craft in a decent way.'

Be a sport. It was an expression James could not remember hearing since his schooldays. Watkins had an expression on his face of schoolboy eagerness.

'If you want to make a fool of yourself, I'll help you put the thing together. But I'm not coming out.'

'Good man. Bring a few biscuits and a couple of apples.'

Muddy Creek was about twenty miles away. It was the nearest bit of sailing water. It had a more specific name, but to everyone who made use of it it was simply Muddy Creek, or the Creek. James had often been there with his family. He was not displeased about going there now. He had little to do that day. He had had a vague thought of taking some provisions to Pippa, but that could wait until tomorrow, if he went at all.

Watkins was whistling as he drove. James thought he recognised the tune.

'Jessie Matthews?'

'Well done. A bonus point if you know the title.'

' "Dancing on the Ceiling"? Something like that.'

Watkins broke into song. He had a pleasant, light baritone voice and he sang the distant, bittersweet words with feeling.

'What became of her?' James said.

'Dead now.'

'Wasn't she Mrs Dale?'

'That was after the war. She's dead now.'

They spoke of other entertainers who were dead, Tommy Handley, Gillie Potter. It was an exclusive requiem, James thought. You had to be of an age to remember the names. They would mean nothing to Gerard or to Pippa. Watney would be of the right age, but they would mean nothing to him either. It wasn't unpleasant to have the company of someone to whom

Itma had instant meaning, without having to translate as though it dated back to Agamemnon.

Muddy Creek had changed since James had last seen it. The local council had built a car park and a small wooden pier and had put up a notice forbidding camping and bathing. James contemplated these changes with his suspicions at the ready, as though they had been made behind his back. But the changes did not seem to have been made without thought. The Creek was now much less muddy, and that was an improvement. The car park was of the trust-you system: you bought a ticket from a meter and displayed it on your windscreen. Watkins made no move to buy a ticket, although it was his outing, and his car.

'Shall I get a ticket, then?' James said.

'If you want to, old chap. Think it's necessary?'

When James got back to the car Watkins had already loosened the fastenings on the roof rack and had unloaded the mast. James helped him down with the hull and removed the cover. The white paint had gone dull and there was a blister where James had repaired a hole made when one of his children had steered into a rock. But he thought the boat was probably watertight. Watkins held the mast on its step while James arranged the shrouds. He felt conspicuous: there were a few people about and he imagined them watching two middle-aged men playing with a small boat. But at least Watkins was helping. A memory came back to James of rigging the boat while his two sons played some game, or just sat about watching, looking bored.

A bottle-screw was missing. It was a small item, but the mast wouldn't stay up without it. James remembered it had been missing when he had last put the boat away. Bottle-screws often went missing. However, Watkins found some wire in the toolbox of his car and used it to secure the shroud. He seemed pleased that there had been a problem and that he had solved it.

They carried the boat to the water. It seemed heavier than James had remembered, but it floated alongside the pier as comfortably as a swan. Watkins had put on a lifejacket and held out one to James. 'Come on, be a sport.'

The boat did look inviting, its red sail beckoning. James got in. He took the tiller and told Watkins to look after the jib. The wind was blowing directly into the Creek, its least desirable direction for a sailor. But James turned the boat enough for the sails to fill and then tacked quietly into more open water. He heard the noise of the water curling under the bow. It was like bringing something to life.

After about fifteen minutes James offered the tiller to Watkins. This meant they had to exchange positions. James brought the boat to a standstill into the wind before they did so, and the Mirror is a difficult boat to turn over. Nevertheless, this was accomplished, by a sudden gust of wind, over-confidence or clumsiness, or a combination of all three. James felt the two or three seconds of helplessness as the boat heeled beyond its recoverable balance, and then he was in the water. Neither he nor Watkins was in danger. James found he was still within his depth. He righted the boat, and the two men clambered back in. But both were totally soaked. When they got back to the pier James was feeling cold. He also felt foolish, although the incident did not seem to have attracted any attention. He wanted to go home, to get warm. He supposed he would have to take Watkins back with him. However, Watkins proposed that they should dry off at his aunt's. Her house was nearer than James's.

'We'll hardly be welcome like this.'

'She's a sporty soul. She'll see the funny side of it.'

They dismantled the boat and returned it to the top of Watkins's car. As they drove away Watkins turned on the heater. James no longer felt cold, but he felt clammily warm and could smell the sulphurous creek mud drying out on his clothing. They discussed how the boat could have overturned, but the event was already history, and fallible.

Watkins's aunt did not seem amused, but neither did she seem very surprised. She scolded them gently. Physically, she did not seem much older than Watkins: presumably there had been a gap in the family somewhere. But she assumed unquestionable command. 'You've been very naughty boys,' she said. She watched them as they removed their clothes, which she gathered up in a bundle. She gave them each a blanket and a bowl of hot soup. James was not cold and the soup was not particularly tasty, but he drank it. How quickly one surrendered one's authority.

'That was very good,' he said.

'A little more, James?'

'No, that was just right. Saved my life.'

157

She produced a bottle of something that smelt of camphor and rubbed it on Watkins's chest. 'Wilfred has weak lungs,' she said. Wilfred Watkins, the Intelligence Man. He sounded like a character in Happy Families.

'A spot for you, James?' she said.

'Thanks, no. My lungs are pretty good.'

'Wilfred was turned down for the forces. Weren't you, Wilf?' Watkins looked discomfited, but it was difficult to tell whether the discomfort was caused by his aunt's revelations or her massage of his chest, which was now a deep pink.

'Were you in the forces, James?'

James said that he had been. She asked when and where, and he told her. She said she had been in the ATS. It turned out that they may have served, briefly, in the same place together. When she had finished rubbing Watkins to her satisfaction she left the room for a short time and returned with a battledress that had belonged to her late husband. It fitted James as well as any battledress fits. The material was rough to the skin without underclothing, but it was better than a blanket.

'I know you'll take good care of it, James.'

'I will indeed. I'm highly honoured.'

'Now, what are we going to do about you, Wilfred?' She looked at Watkins with the weak lungs that had kept him out of the forces. She produced a dressing gown that may or may not have belonged to her husband. It was certainly of civilian make.

It was now about one-thirty. Watkins's aunt apologised for being late with lunch but said that she could not do everything. Lunch was soup again, and sausages, tomatoes and chips. During lunch the aunt spoke of the good old army days, and how the young now envied them, trying to look important in their bomber jackets and stone-washed jeans. Watkins said little. However, when lunch was over and the aunt had cleared the table and said she would bring them a nice cup of tea, Watkins said, 'I'll try not to be too hard on Watney.'

'Oh, really?'

Watkins was presumably trying to regain the authority that he had been losing since falling into the water. James felt a twinge of pity for him, in his dressing gown and pink chest, but pity invites the jackboot.

'That's up to you,' James said.

'Very well, be tough.' The interrogator was feeling his strength again, even in a dressing gown.

'What I mean is, you have your duty to do.'

The boot had been withdrawn. There was no point in upsetting Watkins. 'Anyway, I dare say Watney's record will speak for itself.'

'The truth is', Watkins said, 'no one's going to get worried about Watney. Had he been a German that would have been another matter.'

'Are you boys arguing?' The aunt had returned with three cups of tea.

'We are talking about the Germans, aunt,' Watkins said.

The aunt said that she would never trust the Germans. If it came to the crunch she preferred the Russians to the Germans, not that she liked them much. As for the French and the Italians they were unreliable. James thought with a jolt that these simple sentiments weren't far from his own.

'And the Americans?'

'Nothing against them. They were a bit late, but they helped us out.'

'The Americans and the Russians have this in common,' Watkins said suddenly, 'they are soft. Big soft Nellies, barging about, getting in people's way, but with no inclination to fight each other. It's the little countries, Britain, Germany, trying to become big countries, that make war. Russia and America have their great inland empires to govern. Why should they want more?'

Great inland empires was not a bad phrase, James thought. The aunt was nodding, presumably with approval. The civilian was entitled to his view.

'But what if someone pushes the button?' James said.

'Oh, come now, old chap. Remember your Tolstoy, the march of events? Don't tell me we have a little Carlyle-ite in our midst who believes the destinies of nations are decided by leaders?'

James shook his head, hoping to look non-committal. Tolstoy's contempt for Napoleon had seemed to him the least convincing part of *War and Peace*. He had not read Carlyle, but perhaps he should.

'A more pressing problem is my own destiny. I have to get home.'

James waited for Watkins to offer to drive him there. Watkins did make an offer in a tentative way, but it was instantly vetoed by his aunt who asked him if he wanted to catch pneumonia. Watkins suggested that James take the car and he would come over by bus the following day and pick it up. James was not sure that he wanted to see Watkins again next day. He decided it would be simpler if he caught a taxi.

'It'll cost you.'

James shrugged. He waited for Watkins to offer to chip in, but he didn't. Half an hour later he stepped into an oldish, but seemingly reliable taxi, wearing his battledress and carrying his still-damp clothes in a bundle. As the taxi drove away he remembered that Watkins had not paid him for the boat.

In the evening James went to see Susie. He did not telephone in advance. If she was not there or if she turned him away at the door he would return home. He totally disliked the idea of making an appointment to see his wife. She was in but said she would be going out later. She did not say where and James, although curious, did not ask, although he could not imagine where Susie could be going on a Saturday night. The flat seemed more settled, although James could not say why. Perhaps it was because it was no longer unfamiliar to him. Susie excused herself to go to the bedroom where she was doing something to her hair. When she came back to the living room James had poured himself a whisky. He momentarily wondered if he should have first asked permission, but he said nothing, and neither did Susie. She poured herself a drink and sat down opposite him.

'Social or business?' she said.

James did have a specific reason for calling, but he felt irritated that Susie assumed there was one.

'Just thought I'd see how you are getting on.'

'Fine, as you can see.' She waved vaguely at the room. 'And you?'

'Fine.' James had a lot he would like to tell Susie, of Gerard's visit, his own meeting with Watney at Honeysucklelay, Pippa's return to the barricades, and the two men in a boat that morning. It was extraordinary how much there was to say to Susie since she had left home. But he did not want to hurry through these adventures. He had visualised a long evening of agreeable chat to an increasingly appreciative audience. That was clearly not going to happen. He would put his question and let it go at that.

'I wondered if you fancied a trip to America?'

'With you?'

'Of course.'

'You're offering me a holiday?'

'Not exactly, although there would be a bit of a holiday with it. Watney's making this film in Charleston. He's offered me the printing contract.'

'What a temptation for a girl. Miami Beach, all expenses paid.'

'Not Miami, but the beaches of South Carolina are probably just as warm.'

'When?'

'Next month, perhaps a bit later. But I'd fit in with your plans.' It seemed unlikely that Susie would have any special plans, but he wanted to sound accommodating.

'Can I think about it?'

'Not too long.'

'I may not want to end my retirement just yet. It's a bit early for a comeback.'

'Have separate rooms if you like.'

'I wasn't thinking of that. Separate routines might be more difficult. You'd want me to be with you all the time?'

'Up to you. You'd find a pal. Like Morocco. For all I know Merle may be there.'

'What about the danger?'

'That was all Gerard's imagination.'

'You sound very sure.'

'In the end I suppose I believe in common sense.'

'Does Gerard believe in it?'

James shrugged.

'And Pippa?'

'Pippa is Pippa.'

'Is that why she left you?'

'She's gone back to Honeysucklelay, if that's what you mean.'

'Not quite what I mean. I know you've been screwing her.'

James did not answer, although not because he did not have an answer.

'But two months dead, nay, not two months. I know how Hamlet felt.'

James could feel within him the stirrings of anger. It was unfair

161

of Susie to be irrational. She had been the first to break faith, with her affair in Morocco. Then she had abandoned him. He was the one who had been wronged, and was probably still being wronged. He did not know who she saw in her new life. She was going out this evening, and with whom? Yet she was pleading that she had been hurt.

'Let's not quarrel, Susie. I didn't change our lives.'

'Do you love her?'

'I'm not sure exactly what love is.'

'To be loved is a woman's dearest fantasy. Have you told her you love her?'

'No.'

'Just a fuck?'

'Not that either.'

'Did you enjoy it?'

'Very much.'

'Make you feel young again?'

'That's the cliché.'

'Do you still love me?'

'Whatever there was between us is still there.'

'Do you want to fuck me?'

'Come to America and see.'

'Living apart is a sort of travel. You distance yourself from your familiar setting and discover things about it. I've thought a lot about you.'

'Not very pleasant thoughts, it seems.'

'Now you're fishing. Pleasantness doesn't come into it. I think I love you, but, whether I do or not, I approve of you. I see you as a decent man who has given up almost the whole of his life to working hard for other people.'

'Doesn't sound very exciting.'

'Probably that's why I didn't notice it. You know the widows who say their husband was the finest man who ever lived, that sort of thing, and people have to nod sympathetically and agree? Well, I know how they feel. I've seen the widow's view without you having to die.'

'Come home, Susie. Come home now.'

'No. Who knows what discoveries I still might make?'

'But you'll come to America?'

'You said I could think about it. Don't push things. Anyway, you haven't had such a bad time since I've been away. You've found that if you look helpless enough some woman will look after you.'

'Not at the moment.'

'So that's why you want me back?'

The bell rang.

'That'll be Belinda,' Susie said.

James got up to greet his sister-in-law, if she was willing to be greeted. She was: she offered a cheek for a kiss.

'How are you, Bel?'

Bel was fine.

'And Tom?'

Her husband was fine, too. James did not ask about her daughter. If she was disinclined to mention Pippa, that suited him.

'Belinda is thinking of applying for early retirement, too,' Susie said.

A split-up by Belinda and Tom would not surprise James. It would be far less surprising than Susie's departure had been. He could not imagine Belinda, even in her deepest widowhood, saying that Tom had been the finest husband who had ever lived.

'I'm sorry if things aren't going well,' he said. 'Well, this place will be going soon, when Susie comes home.'

'I didn't say that,' Susie said, sharply. 'This is my home.'

'Well, you can both have it then. A sisterhood.'

Belinda looked from James to Susie. 'Doesn't sound like the big reconciliation scene.'

Susie and Belinda were going to see a film. Susie half-heartedly invited James to accompany them, and James obligingly declined.

'I'll only end up paying,' he said. He thought Susie seemed grateful that he had kept his good humour. It would be something to remember when she was a widow. All the same, driving home, James did not feel comforted by his talk with Susie. It had started awkwardly, had become very awkward, then suddenly had seemed to go very well, and, with the arrival of Belinda, had become awkward again. He had spoken to Susie; that was contact, that was something, but it wasn't much. James had a sense of being on a long walk in countryside which was not quite familiar enough to convince him that he was going anywhere, and he was feeling a little tired. Perhaps the sensible thing would be to try to retrace his steps and go back to where he started. Ah, the lure of metaphor. But he couldn't go back to Agadir and not meet Watney, and Susie not meet Merle, whom James continued to blame for Susie's waywardness. He could not unlearn Watney's plans for Charleston or unmake love to Pippa. He wished Pippa were at home waiting for him; and not because the dishes would be washed and there would be something delicious on the table, although these would be pleasant events; but he would miss having sex with Pippa. Susie had asked him if Pippa had provided just a fuck and his answer, truthfully, had been no. Pippa had given herself to him: that had been the central pleasure. He wished he had told Pippa that, but perhaps she would regard it as a sentiment of the aged.

During the next week or two he was drawn to the idea of going to see Pippa at Honeysucklelay and asking her to return. Once he drove to within a mile or so of the base, but he turned back because he could not see himself arguing with Pippa, or trying to persuade her, in the middle of a field. It would be better to wait. Fatigue, the battle against the climate, the primitive plumbing, would, he reasoned, persuade Pippa to get away from the place for a bit, as she had before, and then, he was entitled to presume, she would come to stay with him. James did not have the same longing to see Susie, and this vaguely troubled him, but he told himself that she probably preferred not to be bothered.

James's thoughts about his women, new and old, were interrupted when he had a telephone call from Gerard with a message from Watney. He was to be ready to travel to the States the following week.

'A week today exactly, in fact,' Gerard said. 'Should be long enough to throw a few things in a case.' Then, apparently sensing, even over the telephone, that his words were not being received with enthusiasm, he said, 'Watney's words. I'm just obeying orders.'

'What's all the hurry?'

'I don't think it is a hurry, James. I seem to have been on this project since I was wearing nappies. The script is ready, the team is ready, it's high summer in Charleston, which is what we want, and Watney's aircraft is warming up on the tarmac ready for its bombing run, so why not go?'

'I certainly can't drop everything and go next week. If Watney has bought my ticket, that's stupid of him. He should have checked with me first.'

'It's not a matter of tickets, James. George really has his own plane, his own private jet, or has hired one. Pretty stylish, hey?'

'I suppose so.'

'He says it's cheaper with all the load we're carrying.'

'What load?'

'Well, there's Watney and Molly, Fairbanks, me, you, the psychiatrist chap and two other advisers, and I'm taking my cameraman and a recordist, the minimum crew really, but I'll be recruiting the rest of the unit over there. How many's that?'

'A lot. No film stars?'

James was intending a joke, but Gerard answered literally. 'Again, I'm recruiting over there. There won't be any stars. I'm aiming for a dramatised documentary, lots of vérité; where there are people I want them to be real people.'

'Well, this real person can't make it in a week. I'll have to follow by steamer, or something.'

'You are coming, James?'

'I've said I'm coming, and that's enough.'

'You hadn't actually, not to me.'

'Well, take it that I am.'

'George is going to be upset you won't be with us. What shall I tell him?'

'Tell him,' James looked at his diary, 'tell him I'll be with you in a month.'

'He won't like that.'

'I can't see why not. I'm going to do the printing. Until there's a film, there can't be much to print about it.'

'Well, I'll tell him, but he won't like it.'

Less than an hour later Watney phoned James. 'I hear you don't want to join our little party?'

'I can't make it to your plane, George, but I'll be with you in a month.'

'The fun will be over.'

'Surely you won't have any work for me straight away?'

'I need you now, James. To handle the words. Advance publicity, press releases, you know the sort of thing. What's the problem? Susie?'

'Well, I'd like to persuade her to come.'

'If she won't, forget her. She'll love you all the more when you return.'

Simple advice. Perhaps he was right.

'There's also the', James offered a word which he hoped would find a response with Watney, 'logistics of the thing. Visas, for example.'

'Use your old one. American visas never lapse, unless you join the Russians.'

'I've never had one.'

'Never been to the States?' Watney's voice expressed surprise for the first time. 'But no problem there. I'll get you one in an hour.'

James said nothing for a moment. He was aware that his objectives were beginning to sound like obstructions.

'Look, Palmer, you have problems, and we can all find problems. But coming out a month late is not going to be any use to me, or to you. I'd like, very much, for you to be with the rest of the team on my plane next week. But if you can't I want you out not more than a week later. Come by Concorde and get an air-taxi down to Charleston. What do you say?'

'All right.'

'All right, what?'

'I'll follow you out within a week.'

James put down the phone uncertain why he had capitulated to Watney's insistent manner, uncertain why, having done so, he had not simply agreed to go on his plane, and uncertain why he was going to America at all. He wished he could talk things over with someone who would listen and say rational things in return. Susie, Pippa, even Gerard or Watkins. Watney was fortunate to have an entourage. James would occasionally like to have one of his own. Instead, he was abandoned in the court of his own mind. His initial reaction to the summons to the States was easy to understand; he was by nature a delayer. Trips, which in the past had meant holidays, had invariably been preceded by long periods of contemplation. It was reasonable, too, that he could not leave his business without being sure it was going to be looked after. But there was also something about Watney's arrangements that put him off. He didn't want to fly in a private jet; it would be like going off on a long journey in the back of someone's car. He and Susie had once had a holiday like that, and it had not been a good one. He didn't fancy going on Concorde either, and taking an air-taxi, whatever that was. He needed to approach America slowly, and even circumspectly, to feel he had a growing sense of where he was going. James was glad that he had not told Watney he would take the Concorde, he had merely listened. He was going to America in order to get business for his firm. Stated thus, that seemed straightforward; yet it was the strangest piece of business that he had been offered; he did not know precisely what printing was required, the quantity needed, when it was wanted, even whether his machinery could handle it. It was quite unbusinesslike, although he had no doubt he would be paid. Watney was the most credit-worthy customer he had acquired. There was also the lure of visiting the United States. Palmer's forebears would have approved of his pilgrimage to a new holy land. Of Britain's former colonies, America is the one that has done best.

He decided on a departure date ten days ahead: ten days seemed to be about the minimum time needed to prepare for a rush trip. At lunch he called in at the travel agents where he had booked previous holidays, and was shocked at the prices asked for an air ticket to Charleston. Had he not seen fares to America advertised at a half, even a third, of what the agent was seeking? They were very special fares, the agent said. They didn't apply to trips taken at short notice. What about – James used the phrase hesitantly – bucket-shop fares? He had read a newspaper article which said that planes crossing the Atlantic were half empty, and the airlines sold spare tickets to bucket-shops at bargain prices. The agent said he did not know of any bucket-shops in the town, or anywhere else for that matter. But would James care to go to some other place? What about Bangkok? It might be possible to squeeze him in at the last moment. James said he had to go to the United States. The agent said that James could try getting a stand-by ticket. This meant waiting at the airport in case a proper passenger didn't turn up, but you usually got on in a day or two. To Charleston? No, there were no direct flights to Charleston, but you got across the Atlantic. James came away saying that he would think about it. Perhaps he would take Watney's private express after all, or perhaps he wouldn't go.

When he got back to the works he was met at the entrance by Bert Miles who said, 'Ronald is dead.'

For several moments James could think of no one he knew called Ronald. Then he said, 'Ronnie Carpenter?'

'I tried to find you, Mr Palmer. I sent word to the pub, but you weren't there.'

James shook his head. It seemed trivial to say that he had been seeking a cheap airline ticket when Ronnie, now dignified with his unshortened name, lay dying. He took Miles into his office. 'Are you all right, Bert? Want a pick-me-up?'

With a glass of whisky in his hand Miles explained the simple facts of Ronnie's death. He had been taken ill while eating a sandwich. The ambulance was sent for and arrived within ten minutes. By then Ronnie was dead, of a heart-attack the ambulance men said. They had done their professional exercises, massaged his heart, given him oxygen, but he was a corpse by then. 'They took him to St Anne's. Frank went with him.'

'How very sad.'

Ronnie had been in his forties and looked younger, played football and sometimes jogged to work. In a fair world people would die in turn, but young men like Ronnie were moved to the head of the queue while the senile held back. But a less pious thought that came to James was that Ronnie was one of the four compositors who had been upset over the new machinery.

'It wasn't his first attack, you know, Mr Palmer.'

'No, I didn't know that.' He hoped that Miles did not pick up his sense of relief. 'Shouldn't I have been told?'

'I heard of it only by chance, Mr Palmer. People keep these things quiet.'

'I suppose so. What should I do, Bert? I'd better see Mrs Carpenter. Has she been told?'

'His mother. He wasn't married. Frank's seeing her. He's a sort of friend.'

'I should call, though. Shouldn't I?' At least comforting an elderly mother would be less difficult than speaking to a distraught wife.

'Leave it to Frank for today, Mr Palmer. Go to the funeral. She'll appreciate that.'

'Of course. Of course I'll do that. And the chaps? Should we pack up for today?'

'I'd suggest a day off later, in Ronald's memory. A Friday. Make it a long weekend. My guess is that everyone would just as soon work out their shift today.'

'All right. There's Ronnie's workload until we replace him.'

'If you think we should, Mr Palmer. Respect for the dead, but what the men were really worried about was that there wouldn't be enough work for all of them.'

James looked at Bert and pursed his lips. He did not trust himself to say anything that would not sound either glib or callous.

As Bert Miles was going out of the door the phone rang. James thought it would be Frank or some other caller connected with Ronnie's death, but it was the travel agent. 'Would Orlando do you, Mr Palmer?'

James signalled to Bert not to wait and found an atlas. Orlando was in Florida, about three hundred miles from Charleston. It was certainly the right bit of America, but how would he get to Charleston? 'You could get a local flight, Mr Palmer. Or take a Greyhound bus. Great fun.' The agent told James the price of the Orlando excursion. It seemed a bargain after the earlier fares James had been quoted. There seemed no reason not to accept.

'That'll be a reservation for two seats, Mr Palmer?'

'One or two. I'll let you know tomorrow.'

It was for one. When James phoned Susie she said she had thought carefully about going with him, but had decided not to. She did not offer any new reason for not going and he did not press her. She said she would look in at the house from time to time while he was away, and he said he was grateful for that. He told her about Ronnie, but the name meant nothing to her, and, no, she did not want to go to the funeral.

He ordered a wreath from a florist's which had a notice in its window, 'We cannot guarantee to deliver flowers on time, except for funerals,' and he contributed to the collection for a wreath which the staff were sending. Bert Miles had organised this; James thought he must be a better organiser than he had previously believed. He also arranged for Ronnie to be cremated early in the day, so that those colleagues who wished to attend could go there straight from home.

The crematorium was in a pleasant little park and was disguised as a church. It had flowers and a feeling of emptiness, and slow music was coming from somewhere. James counted nine members of the staff in the pews. They stood as the coffin was carried in by four undertakers, or rather one undertaker, a smallish man with black hair, brushed down and shining, and his three assistants. They placed the coffin in front of the altar and withdrew very quietly.

The man who took the service was dressed like a clergyman, and presumably was one. James found himself wondering whether he was employed by the crematorium, doing nothing but funerals, perhaps a dozen a day, Monday to Friday, with his weekends free, or whether there was a rota of clergy from real churches, where they also did christenings and marriages, which were presumably more pleasant. James was inclined to think that this clergyman was a specialist. He handled the service well, assuming, reasonably, that none of his congregation was familiar with the rules of worship. He spoke in simple, explanatory sentences. Please sit. Please kneel or sit for prayer. And now, the prayer that Christ himself taught us. And, to conclude, a passage from Revelation, the last book of the Bible. James thought he saw the clergyman push a button in his pulpit. At any rate, the coffin started to move and vanished through a curtain into eternity.

Outside, James met Ronnie's mother. He had been slightly anxious that she would show resentment towards him, believing James to be the cause of Ronnie's fatal worries; but, as Bert Miles had predicted, she seemed grateful that he had come to the service, which she had found spiritual. That was the word she used. It wasn't one normally in her vocabulary, James thought, so it reinforced his view that the clergyman knew his stuff. Would he come back for a cup of tea? Of course he would.

Ronnie's mother, and, until a few days previously, Ronnie, lived in a semi-detached house on an estate. James knew that Ronnie had lived in the country and had vaguely imagined him in a cottage. But this was suburbia, no, sub-suburbia, if there was such a thing, with no centre, no shops that he could see, just houses that looked as though they had been made as rudimentary as possible by the disabled, with not even a chimney. This was one of the newest pieces of architecture in the world; those who had gained the authority to plan and approve it had first had to study how people lived over several millenniums, in

Athens, Rome, Bath. It was very puzzling.

Ronnie's mother had done her best to defy the cell-like nature of the rooms with furniture so large that it was difficult to see how some of the pieces had been manoeuvred through the doors. She showed James Ronnie's room. Three walls had shelves packed with books. 'He had the finest library in England,' she said. 'Five thousand books, all catalogued.'

'Extraordinary,' James said, and he meant it. Ronnie was turning out to be a more interesting person in death than he had known him in life.

'Do you think there are books in heaven, Mr Palmer?'

'I can't imagine an existence without books, can you, Mrs Carpenter?'

Perhaps, then, James thought, but he thought only to himself, there was no heaven. Books questioned things, and in heaven, being perfect, there would be no need for questions. Theology, he suspected, had little to do with faith; it was nearer politics than religion. Moreover, you could cripple your mind thinking about it. He felt he had had enough of matters of death and the beyond, and wanted to get back into the world of simple imperfection. He left soon after, giving Ronnie's mother a kiss on the cheek and saying that he would come to see her again. On the way back to the office he had a haircut and it made him feel that he had added a few days to his life.

Two days later James was on the aircraft to Orlando. He sat next to a woman with two children. They were her grandchildren and she was taking them to Disney World, which was next door to Orlando. She thought that children should be given the experience of seeing other countries.

'I expect you know North America well, Mr Palmer?'

'Never been there before.'

'There you are then.'

There seemed to be a lot of children on the plane, presumably all on a rather extravagant treat. Many of them were asleep, or queueing for a lavatory or being sick or, James thought, otherwise showing they were bored with the long drive.

Orlando, James's first landfall in America, seemed a pleasant tropical town that deserved better than being a doorway to Mickey Mouse. He took a taxi to the hotel where the travel agent had booked a room for him. Many of the guests seemed old, or

171

very old, who had retired even from being retired, just about getting enough heat from the sun to wake up each morning. Poor Ronnie's funeral seemed lively in comparison. It wasn't the picture of the country that James had been expecting, more of a waiting room on the banks of the Styx, but he told himself that he must discard a lifetime of American rumour.

Next day he took a coach to Charleston. He thought the journey would take about the same time as a trip he had once taken from London to Carlisle. He had left London after breakfast and arrived in time for tea. The American trip, he thought, might well be quicker, as no doubt American drivers liked to hustle along as they did in the films. It took longer. The coach went less fast and there were more frequent stops. James had a double seat to himself for most of the journey, but near to Charleston a man sat beside him who wanted to talk. James did not mind. He had not talked to anyone lately. The American asked James where he had come from and where he was going to and what he did. James told him. The American said that he was a salesman, but that he was a printer, too. Printing was his hobby: high-class work with handset type.

'All the stuff I threw out,' James said.

'That really haunts me. All those Caslons and Bodonis in England.'

He spoke as though they were Rembrandts. Perhaps they were, James thought. Junk does get rediscovered as masterpieces.

'So what did you do, Jim? You sold it?'

'That last time I saw any of it, it was in the yard waiting for the dustman.'

'So it's still for sale?'

'If you were in England I'd happily let you take the lot away. Unfortunately, you aren't.'

'Isn't that terrible?'

'Terrible.'

'I think of England encrusted with all these good things.'

'Have you been there?'

'No.'

'I thought of America as fast. But you have a speed limit lower than ours.'

'Are you disappointed in us, Jim?'

172

'No, I apologise. I've just arrived.'

'I don't blame you. You're a cultured man. What will survive of American culture? A few notes of Louis Armstrong, one book by Hemingway, one by Scott Fitzgerald, the film *Casablanca*; of the fine arts, nothing. Pollock, Rothko, Clyfford Still, all art dealers' hype. Our art form is the creation of tattiness.'

James wondered what the American sold for a living. Not tourism presumably.

'What's Charleston like?'

'How do you imagine it, Jim?'

In London James had once looked through a booklet on Charleston that Gerard had shown him.

'Rather pretty, gracious.'

'Southern belles twirling parasols, Jim? Scarlett O'Hara? Nigras humming spirituals?'

'Not exactly.'

'America, Jim, is a country of ghost towns which were briefly generators of great wealth and were then discarded because their products are no longer wanted or can be made more efficiently elsewhere. Detroit is rusting faster than the cars it makes. Hollywood is a pile of films seen on television. Charleston lucked out when its plantation industry could no longer use slaves, but it missed becoming a ghost town when it discovered that ghosts have a commercial value. It has old houses, the oldest theatre, the oldest submarine and, by golly, I believe the oldest tarts.' The American laughed loudly at his joke. 'It needed one extra thing to bring in the money. The air-conditioner opened up the South, just as the railroad opened up the West.'

'You sell air-conditioners?'

'I sell air-conditioners. You'll thank them when you've been in Charleston for a couple of days. Where are you staying, Jim?'

James took out an envelope on which he had written the name of a hotel. 'The Francisco de Miranda.'

The American looked impressed. 'You British printers must be in the money.'

James was embarrassed. The extravagant Watney again. 'Just for a day or two,' he said. 'Meeting up with a few friends.'

'Well, if you fancy a homely drink with a humble American, give me a call.' He presented James with his business card. It was printed in worn gothic type that was quite difficult to read.

★ 8 ★

The Francisco de Miranda was, James's friend had assured him, only two blocks from the bus station. But James was feeling weary and did not know how long a block was. He took a taxi, and was glad he did. The hotel doorman looked as though he was used to guests arriving in taxis, if not limousines, rather than on foot. James gave his name to a clerk at the reception counter and said that a reservation had been made. Seemingly it hadn't. James offered Watney's name. This produced a response. The clerk made a phone call, and an apology for keeping James waiting, and a minute or two later Merle appeared before him.

'Well, who have we here?'

Merle, though surprised, was welcoming. She shook James's hand warmly, but did not offer her cheek.

'Sure we were expecting you, but not so soon. When did you get in?'

'Just arrived.'

'And where's Susie?' Merle looked around the hotel lobby as though Susie might have been mislaid.

'She couldn't manage it.'

'That's awful. Not coming at all?'

'No.'

'Well, that's the way things go round here. There's a sort of consistency anyway.'

Merle went to the reception counter and spoke to the clerk. When she returned she said, 'I've had to fit you in as best I can. You won't be on the same floor as us, not immediately anyway. George won't like it, but there are many things he doesn't like, including me. All right with you, James?'

'Perfectly.'

'What a soothing man you are.'

174

Merle raised a hand, a boy appeared, picked up James's case and led him to a lift. 'Give me a call when you get cleaned up,' she shouted after him.

James's room was as large as a flat. You slept at one end and spent the rest of your life at the other, sitting, watching television, drinking or even reading. You had to provide your own book but there was plenty of drink in the fridge. James thought he would be comfortable here. If this was making do, he wondered what Watney's quarters were like. He took a shower, and washed his parts in the bidet, and wondered who had invented it: it seemed too practical for the French. He unpacked and put on some fresh clothes that did not seem too crumpled. He called Merle. 'All clean now,' he said.

They met five minutes later in the hotel restaurant.

'You must be famished,' Merle said. 'I never eat a thing on a plane. Not a crumb. I can imagine what that Concorde stuff must have been like.'

James decided not to disagree. If Merle was critical of Concorde food what would be her observations about the catering on the Orlando special? Actually, he had enjoyed it, but he was now quite hungry. It was around ten in Charleston, so it was either late afternoon really or the middle of the night, he wasn't sure which. Either way, he hadn't eaten for a long time. He looked at the menu. It was long, but it seemed to amount to steak or fish. He chose steak.

'What's happened to everyone?'

'What everyone?'

'Well, George and Co.'

'George is at another of his silly farewells. Gerard, I'm not sure; somewhere moaning, no doubt. I do hate a moaner. Freddie Fairbanks is in clink on a drugs rap. Got caught with the stuff at the airport. George will get him out tomorrow, he thinks. But what a stupid thing to do.'

'Happy days. So George is upset?'

'He leaves other people to get upset. Would you believe that he ran an army when he can't keep a dozen people happy? Thank God you're here, James. We need a cool mind about the place.'

Two muffled bangs gently rattled the windows of the restaurant.

175

'Thunder?' James suggested.

'They say they're sonic booms. I think there's an earthquake on the way.'

A memory of Agadir came to James. 'You mustn't worry about earthquakes.'

'You think I'm neurotic about them. But they had one here in 1886.'

James's steak was very large. The size of it modified his appetite. Merle had ordered only a bowl of soup. James wondered if she was dieting, then the thought came to him that she had probably eaten earlier but had elected to keep him company. He was touched. He had disliked Merle for reasons that he could not now remember and now he liked her for reasons that were obscure. She asked about Susie and he told her that she had left him, giving the reasons as far as he understood them. There was no point in being discreet: for all he knew, Susie might have told Merle of their separation.

'Retirement? I like that. I must tell that to my group.'

'You're a feminist?'

'I like feminism for its absurdity.' Merle laughed. 'And because George hates it.'

James suddenly felt weary. Merle told him to go to bed.

'Shouldn't I see George?'

'I'll tell him you've touched down safe and sound. He'll be pleased.'

There were two large beds in James's room. Both had canopies, presumably to remind you when you awoke that you were in the South, and one of the canopies had a web woven by a southern spider. He chose the left-hand bed. He always slept on the left side at home. He slept well, but awoke early. It seemed unlikely that Watney or any of his entourage would be about, but he did not want to go to sleep again. He washed, dressed and went down to the hotel coffee shop and had breakfast, and walked out into the street for his first glimpse of Charleston as a resident. The sun was bright but not yet hot. It had rained in the night and there were puddles in the gutters that suddenly flashed in the sun. This particular street seemed to have a lot of shops selling souvenirs of the civil war. James searched his mind for remnants of American history. The war was not that long ago. It was not in the memory of anyone now living, but their fathers might remember it, certainly their grandfathers. It was the last war to have physically touched America. All the rest had been foreign wars. James looked at the guns in a shop window. They looked surprisingly modern. You could be arrested in Britain for carrying one. James suddenly had the thought of the South as a vanquished nation, as humbled as Germany had been, though not so quick to recover. A notice in the shop window advertised tours of historic Charleston, including a visit to North America's oldest aircraft carrier, submarine and destroyer. James had only half believed the man on the bus and was slightly irritated that he was seeing the place through his eyes. The town was a museum, but a pretty one. Perhaps even the sub had camellias growing from its conning tower.

Watney and Merle were in the coffee shop when James returned to the hotel. Watney got up and came forward as soon as he saw James, and took his hand and gripped his shoulder. 'Merle has told me how you dropped everything to get here. I won't forget this, James. Sit down, have some breakfast. Been out sniffing the Charleston air? Isn't it a fine place?'

'I've already eaten, George. But I'd love a cup of coffee.'

The table contained the remains of an extravagant meal. James regarded it benignly. He felt more in the presence of America here than he had outside. Food, he thought, is the distillation of a culture. You take into your body a more vivid impression of a people than you do by viewing old buildings.

'We have much work to do,' Watney announced, 'but first we must rescue the prisoner.' He proposed that James should accompany him to the lawyer who was arranging bail for Fairbanks. 'It must only be a formality, but it might be an idea to have one of his countrymen along.'

The lawyer had offices in a period house with a porch and white columns that would have looked well on a plantation. He had white side-whiskers and spoke with a southern accent. He looked, and talked, more like a judge than a lawyer, James thought. Bail for Fairbanks could, the lawyer believed, be arranged, but it would not be a simple formality. Carrying drugs was regarded in this city as a serious crime. This wasn't New York with its babylonian habits. Fortunately for Fairbanks the amount of cocaine found on him supported his story that it was for his own use; had he been a pusher, bail would have been out of the

177

question. 'Out of the question, suh,' he said to Watney, although seemingly including James.

Watney did not look pleased. 'I was told that you were the best lawyer here. Just give me some law.'

'I am a lawyer, suh, but I am not a fixer. Bail is not just a matter of money. Who will be responsible for Mr Fairbanks's good behaviour before his case comes to trial?'

'I will, naturally. Freddie Fairbanks is an old comrade of mine.'

'And you are living where, suh?' The lawyer looked at a piece of paper before him. Watney spoke the impressive name of the hotel, but the lawyer did not seem impressed.

'Any fixed address?'

'We are fixed there for a while.'

'But you don't have a permanent address within the state of South Carolina?'

'I am a General in the United States Army. Doesn't that count any more?'

'I am sure it does, suh. I want to present the best case to the court for your friend. Courts do not much care for hotel addresses, especially in the case of an alien.'

'All I'm asking for is a bit of common sense. Is this thing set in concrete? Fairbanks is no cokey-Joe. This is all off base.' Watney was getting angry and moving into jargon. 'I wonder what my British friend here is going to think about', he paused, 'southern justice.'

The lawyer looked at James and then looked away. James seemed to remember that the British had supported the South, but perhaps not enough.

'Naturally, suh, I shall do my persuasive best for Mr Fairbanks.'

The interview seemed to be coming to a close. James heard himself saying, 'Is it a matter of finding a local person of good reputation to say he will keep an eye on Mr Fairbanks?'

'Exactly so, suh.'

James took from his pocket the visiting card given to him by the American in the bus. 'He's a salesman. Air-conditioners.'

'A perfectly respectable calling, Mr Palmer.'

'Shall I try him then?'

'I'd be more than grateful if you did.' He pushed a telephone across his desk to James.

James immediately recognised the persuasive American voice. 'Mr Churchill, this is James Palmer. The printer from England. You remember? Mr Churchill, I have a little problem, well a big problem, and I wonder if you could help me out. Say no, and I won't be offended. This is it, briefly. A friend of mine has been arrested and naturally I want to bail him out. No problem over the surety, but there needs to be a local person to, well, not vouch for him because you don't know him, but to agree to look out for him. I promise you he'll be no trouble. That's very good of you, Mr Churchill. Just a moment, I'll check.'

James put his hand over the mouthpiece and said to the lawyer, 'What does he have to do?'

'Tell him to come to this office. There'll be a couple of forms to sign.'

James and Watney waited in another room for Mr Churchill to arrive. James was in the slight daze of someone who has done something extraordinary, the outsider who has just won the Derby; he wasn't used to being a hero. Watney showed his admiration by saying rather less than usual. He did offer to give the salesman an order for air-conditioners, but James told him to say nothing at all about money. 'He likes Britain, and he happens to like me. We were lucky.'

The rescuing of Fairbanks took much of the morning. James, Watney, Churchill and the lawyer went to the court, where the lawyer made his plea. Then they went to the police station where Fairbanks was being held, and Fairbanks was introduced to his benefactor. James was worried about what should be done with Churchill, but the salesman, having done his bit for England, graciously excused himself, saying he had to see a client. When James got back to the hotel he phoned his manager, Albert Miles, generally to ask him how things were going, but specifically to tell him to collect all the old type that had not been disposed of and to hold on to it, yes, even the stuff on the rubbish tip. It was possible that Mr Churchill's help might be needed again, and it would be unrealistic to continue to rely solely on Anglo-American friendship.

'This is a very clear line, Mr Palmer,' Miles said. 'You could be just down the road.'

James treated the observation casually but he, too, was a little in awe with the process that delivered your voice with such ease to another continent. In a vague way he had thought of the long-distance telephone as an instrument used by special people that ordinary people had access to only at Christmas when they spoke to their relatives in Australia. James felt like a peasant sometimes, come into the big city to gawp and gape.

One of the rooms of the suite that Watney had taken at the hotel was being used as an office. The word-processor that James had bought to write Watney's memoirs was there. Out of curiosity James looked through its files. Nothing seemed to have been added to the memoirs since James had left the Regent's Park flat, but there was a lot of material about Charleston, presumably to do with Gerard's film. Watney asked James to write a handout on the film for the local press.

'What do you want me to say?'

'I know I can leave that to you, James.'

Despite Watney's apparent confidence in James's ability to do nearly anything, James did not regard himself as a spinner of words. He spent several hours writing the handout. Assembling the facts of the film in a simple, yet attractive, way, was, he found, an exhausting task. However, he felt when he presented his draft to Watney that he had done good work.

Watney read it, put it down and shook his head. 'It reads well, Palmer, but we are giving too much away.' He took a pencil and crossed through about threequarters of James's words. 'Work along those lines, Palmer. We're making a film about the fine city of Charleston. That's all they need to know at the moment. Keep it simple. Hash it out with Gerard. He knows the score.'

Gerard was out but he returned to the hotel in the early evening. He had heard of James's arrival but this was the first time they had seen each other since England. 'I thought you wouldn't come, but I'm glad you did. Ever so glad.' He used the childish expression with feeling.

James showed him the handout with Watney's deletions.

'I see what he means,' Gerard said. 'Don't want to stir up the natives.'

'Isn't that the idea? The bomb that won't hurt?'

'Everyone is frightened of bombs. Tell them we're making a film about the bombing of Charleston and a lot of people are going to be upset. We know how the story goes. The relief that will follow the fear. They don't.'

180

'Shouldn't we explain it a bit? It doesn't sound a difficult idea to follow.'

'You could say that. There is an argument for getting the burghers on our side. They might love being bombed: it could be a big boost for tourism. But there is an argument for being secretive and sly, for getting our location shots and leaving. The problems are likely to be fewer.'

'I think, somehow, they should be told.'

'Ah, the moral issue. Watney and I chewed that one over, and we decided that the budget can't run to it.' He saw James's face and said, 'Yes, I'm just being silly-cynical, but if you wanted to argue about morals you should have been there at the time instead of sloping off. No, I'm sorry. But what I can say is that it's really no business of Charleston's what we do. Charleston provides the scenery and will gets its credit. The film is about the United States, the world, the whole damn thing.'

James re-wrote his handout. It now said very little. He was appalled by its feebleness. Still, he made some copies, put them into envelopes, got the addresses of the local media from the phone book and dispatched his modest intelligence by way of a messenger provided by the hotel. Next day, rather to his surprise, he saw that his story had been used more or less as he had written it. A local radio station phoned him for more information and he put the reporter on to Gerard who willingly gave an interview, saying very little about the film but delivering his views on the use of the hand-held camera, Charleston and the future of the American woman. James showed Watney the clippings and played him a recording of Gerard's interview. Watney said he should have a medal; and James felt satisfied, even self-satisfied, at his baptism into public relations.

'Is that all there is to it?' he said to Gerard.

'That's all.'

'And people make a living doing that?'

Gerard laughed. 'You really are a charming innocent, James.'

James wanted to try another handout, saying a little more, but not much more, but Gerard advised against it. 'You've done what Watney wants, established our public credentials for being in Charleston. Let it rest at that for the moment. Your trouble, James, is that you expect to work all the time.'

'Isn't that what I'm here for?'

'You've already earned your keep, getting Fairbanks off the hook. All you need do at the moment is be available. People like to have you around. You're reassuring, you make things work. Otherwise fill your day with what pleases you. See the sights, watch the box, go on the beach, find a woman, if that's your bag. Structure your day, as they say here.'

The other members of Watney's party seemed to have structured their day; that is, they appeared to be busy, although it was difficult to tell what work they did. Watney's day seemed to be a series of conferences, mostly with Fairbanks and the American advisers, occasionally with Gerard, and very occasionally and only briefly with James. The advisers had their own conferences. Gerard and his cameraman and recordist were out for much of the day, presumably looking at locations, but only looking: James had not yet seen them carrying equipment. James had seen Molly only once. Gerard had told him that Merle had banished her to another hotel on the day the Watney party had arrived from England. There was a girl called Caroline who did secretarial work for Watney, although presumably she had not taken over all of Molly's duties.

As part of the structure of his day James started to go through what had been written of Watney's memoirs. Watney approved of this, or at least did not disapprove, but showed no inclination at present to add to them. James fancied going on the beach. Like many who live in the ungenerous climate of northern Europe, James associated the south with warm seas. However, he did not want to go to the beach alone. He thought of asking Molly; perhaps she would be grateful for company after being expelled from the hotel. But he was a little in awe of her, and he told himself that Merle might object, and he did not want to be the cause of a row. But what about Merle? 'Do you fancy a swim, Merle?' he said. Of course she did: she went swimming regularly. She had built it into the structure of her day. She had rented a chalet on Folly Beach. They would go there that afternoon; better call the hotel reception now to order his bicycle; the best ones soon went. James said he hadn't ridden a bicycle since he was a child. Merle insisted that he try, and to his surprise he found he could keep his balance. He gained confidence when he observed other overweight and over-age people trying to regain a distant skill. Wobbling about on bicycles was apparently part of

Charleston's gracious charm. Merle said he would be an expert by the time they got to the beach.

'How far is it then?'

'About an hour, if you pedal hard.'

James did not want to pedal hard. They took a taxi, and Merle called him a softie.

The last beach that James had been on was at Agadir, where numerous breasts of numerous sizes had been offered to the sun. On Folly Beach the swimsuits were brief, and bra straps were loosened so that oil could be kneaded into the skin. But no woman removed her bra entirely. Merle seemed happier to be on a beach where she did not have to copy European decadence.

'I'm open-minded about these things,' she said, 'but it's just not the custom here.'

'I didn't say anything, Merle.'

'I know you Europeans. You think we Americans are all provincial.'

'I like the provinces.'

'You see, you do think that.'

'This is silly, Merle.'

'There's a bit of topless on the islands, if you fancy a boat trip.'

'It's great here. This is really a fine beach.'

It wasn't, James thought, all that great. It didn't look as though it had been cleaned lately. The sea was not cold but neither was it warm. Perhaps the Atlantic was never warm. James jumped through the rollers that approached the beach bubbly and bright, like an advertisement for a detergent, and then sat down in the shallows, feeling the undertow pulling the sand from under him. He watched a group of youths carrying surfboards. They had finely shaped bodies; the bodies of mermen, for there was something fantastic in the way they had been developed, beyond their natural shapes, into objects to be paraded for inspection in public or in front of the mirror. As they passed James he listened to the mermen's voices: 'C'mon, you guys'; 'I got it'; 'Yea'; 'Defend your pal.' The illusion died. He wished they were mute, or spoke in another language, or that he was unable to understand American.

James walked back up the beach to where he and Merle were camped. Merle was not a mermaid. There was nothing obviously fantastic about her. She was lying prostrate in the sun with little black muffs over her eyes. She was getting red but not, it seemed, brown. He felt a concern for her: his mother had often warned him about too much sun, and not all wisdom gained in childhood is discarded.

'Why don't you move into the shade for a bit?'

'I'm blissfully supine, James, thank you.'

'Shall I dab a bit of lotion on you?'

'That's a truly gentlemanly offer.'

He dabbed to begin with, then he rubbed, then he rubbed with a steady rhythm. It was not unlike waxing a car, he thought, a car that the surrealists might have thought of, made of skin. He worked the lotion into the wide expanses of Merle's body and into the joins and crevices. What he was doing was both impersonal, driven by a wish to be thorough, and personal. It was pleasant to be given a temporary licence to touch the parts of a woman's body normally forbidden by convention. The strokes he was applying were only a formality away from caresses. He wondered what would be Merle's response if he proposed that they made love; not here but under the canopy back at the hotel; and not necessarily today, but soon, when it was possible. She would perhaps not be displeased, but she would not assent, not to a simple proposition. Pippa had slept with him for rational reasons, reasons that a man could understand. Merle would seek a declaration of love. James was unsure that he would want to say he loved her, even under the pressure of physical desire which, during the past day or two, he had felt becoming noticeable. When the desire was expelled would there be enough feeling left to continue to play at intimacies with Merle, planning new assignations, creating a secret world, secret, anyway, from Watney, who, whatever his own betrayals, would regard his near-wife Merle as his own property? He had felt that kind of bond with Pippa but she, for all the obvious differences between them, had seemed to be of his own tribe. James suddenly had a desire to write to Pippa and tell her of his adventures. She would understand why he had come by way of Orlando and Greyhound coach, instead of by Concorde. Merle, he suspected, would merely think him odd, or mean.

James had come to the end of the tube of suntan lotion.

'That's it,' he said.

Merle sat up and removed the muffs from her eyes. 'I think I fell asleep.' She looked at her anointed body. 'My, you did a good job there.' She gave him a kiss, but it was sisterly rather than passionate. Perhaps he was the one who had been fantasising. He felt a sense of relief. Merle made a better friend than she would be a lover.

'Are you swimming?' James said.

'Is it cold?'

'Invigorating.'

'Thanks for the warning.'

'Who's a softie now?'

They packed up and walked to a taxi rank. On the way Merle took his arm.

Watney had invited his entire company to dinner. Usually each person made their own arrangements for eating. Some stayed in, some went out. James always ate in the hotel and dined with whoever was in the dining room that he knew, or, if there was no one, alone. This evening Watney had booked a private room at the hotel for their meal and he had let it be known that he had something important to say.

Most of those at the dinner seemed to have acknowledged its importance by wearing the best clothes that their suitcases could offer. James, who had discarded his tie on arriving in the South, put it back on for the evening. Watney wore a white linen suit pressed to military standards and had a General's star in his lapel. There were eleven for dinner, sitting at an oblong table. Watney and Merle sat at each end, and Watney told the others to arrange themselves as they wished. The psychiatrist sat on Watney's right, psychologically a strong position, no doubt, James thought. Molly sat on Watney's left. James guessed that this was upsetting to Merle, but she said nothing: she was not acknowledging Molly's presence. The two American advisers sat next to each other, and next to the psychiatrist. James had noticed that the three tended to hang together like barbershop singers. James had Gerard on his right and Fairbanks on his left. The cameraman and the recordist were Merle's companions at the other end of the table. Watney said that he had personally chosen the food. There was a saying that you couldn't get a decent hot-dog in Charleston without knowing someone. He knew someone, and he hoped they liked hot-dogs. He was in an engaging mood, and his self-enjoyment of his jokes rather than

185

their content seemed to infect everyone at the table. The food was soup, steak and ice-cream; not a gourmet's delight, James thought, but Watney was complimented on the menu by the company, James among them. The wine was French, and presumably expensive, rather than Californian, and this, too, drew applause, although it was no better than the plonk that James bought at his local supermarket. The two waiters were on the border of surliness, but the psychiatrist remarked on their efficiency. Watney said that efficiency was a quality that Americans had brought to waiting. He couldn't stand European waiters. You knew from their servility that they would never amount to anything other than waiting. As a digestive the diners were offered port or brandy. James chose port. Fairbanks shook a little white powder on to the back of his hand and sniffed it through a straw made of a rolled-up dollar bill. No one other than James seemed to notice, or, if they did, they said nothing. James took a cigar when the box came round. So did Molly and, perhaps because she did, so did Merle. Gerard talked to James about the difficulties of filming in Charleston. The place occupied a low-lying peninsula and was not overlooked by a hill from which it would be possible to take a panoramic shot. Watney overheard his grumbles and said that there should be no problem: hire a plane, a helicopter, a stepladder.

'Too artificial,' Gerard said. 'Anyway, the aerial shot is one of the clichés of cinema.'

Watney took the rebuke with undiminished good humour. 'You see what happens', he announced to the rest of the table, 'when you try to help an artist. No, seriously for a moment, I'm sure it is a problem, but we can't change the location now. But I'm equally sure that Gerard will find a way round it that will take our breath away. As it happens, this brings me rather neatly on to what I want to talk to you about this evening. I feel that we're all a little close to the star of our production. Charleston is a lovely city but perhaps we should distance ourselves from it for a little while. April may be the cruellest month in England, but August beats it in Charleston. It's a sweat and it's getting sweatier. It's not the best atmosphere in which to think. We had our little problem with one of our company when we arrived. Thanks to James we were able to get over that hurdle, but it took something out of us. James, through no fault of his own, was not able to travel over at the same time as we did; he now has to room down on another floor. Molly is sleeping at another hotel. It's no one's fault, but a few problems in human relations have perhaps been compounded by living in a steambath. Now Gerard is having problems with his camera angles. For all I know there may be other problems. If there are, for God's sake don't tell me. Tell them to Merle.' He gave Merle a beaming smile which may have helped to compensate for the implied reprimand over Molly. 'I think we're going to do what the British did in India when the summer got a little too much for a fighting man. They took to the hills. I'm suggesting that we move out of Charleston for a bit and go up country. Not far. But enough for us to distance ourselves from the scene of action. Generals and journalists usually get it about right.' This time he beamed at James.

The psychiatrist said, 'Praise be for an understanding commander.'

Watney looked around the table and was rewarded with murmurs of assent.

'Say when,' said Fairbanks.

'Tomorrow, if that suits everyone. I've fixed us up with a little place a bit to the north of here. I think you'll like it. I'll keep one room at the hotel here as a base for Gerard and anyone else who needs to come back here. Early start. Wagons roll at nine-thirty.'

If Watney's plan was inconvenient to anyone, he, or she, did not say. James had been momentarily surprised that Watney was moving out, and the reasons he gave seemed slight. Yet he made the move seem necessary, even inevitable. James found himself unbothered by the plan. The force of events had somehow, even mysteriously, carried him from his living room in Norfolk to this table in America, among a curious company. Why not move to the next square and see what happened then? It would be another bit of the country to experience, and it certainly was humid in Charleston. When the port bottle came near to him he topped up his glass.

Another person had arrived in the room. He was dressed as a cowboy, though a prosperous one, a businessman of the range, and he carried a guitar. Someone, perhaps one of the Americans, apparently recognised him and mentioned a name, Yank something; no, Hank. He had a clear and easy voice and he sang of sweethearts, blue skies and of the country that he loved, uttering the uncomplicated themes with a sincerity that, James thought vaguely, would border on the embarrassing were not his perception now in an alcoholic mist. James's neighbours at the table were regarding the singer with the same expressions that James assumed he had on his own face: of surprise at the intrusion, but not unwelcoming. At least you did not have to keep a conversation going. Watney, however, was being more demonstrative. He thumped on the table in time with the music, and he silently mouthed the songs. When the recital had finished Watney said, 'I've known Hank for many years, and when I heard he was in Charleston I pleaded with him, and pleading doesn't come easily to me, I pleaded with him to come along tonight. Hank, being Hank, didn't hesitate, and, don't forget, he has already given one two-hour performance tonight, or was it three hours, Hank? If anyone were to ask me what America means to me, and no one has, but I'll tell you: if anyone were to ask me, I'd say Hank singing his good songs to a few friends is a scene that takes a lot of beating. My secret weapon against Soviet oppression would be a hundred million tapes of Hank singing his songs. The trouble is, the peasants wouldn't have the machines to play them. They'd probably think they were something new to eat. Hank, thanks for coming tonight.'

Watney had obtained a small bus to transport his entourage to its new home, a modest form of transport by his standards, but it was shiny new. The interior smelt of varnish. The bus travelled north along a coastal road, and, some three hours later, shortly after crossing into the next state, North Carolina, it turned into a drive, at the end of which was a house set, diffidently, James thought, into the side of a hill. Inside, the house was large and full of light, a stately home, but the first that James had been in that was so modern that it did not appear to have been discarded by a past generation. A buffet lunch had been prepared, and the members of the party stood or sat with their plates and forks, like guests at a reception, talking about the house. Watney said that it had once belonged to Errol Flynn, or so the agent had said who had rented it to him. The view they could see from the windows was of Cape Fear. The local tourist interests were campaigning to have it renamed Cape Hope. James and some of the others laughed, but Watney did not seem to have intended a joke. He thought it a reasonable request as no doubt some tourists were put off by the name, which presumably had been given to the cape by the crews of sailing ships. It was healthy to reject the nightmares of the past.

Merle said that there were several cabins in the grounds and asked James if he would like one: he could work there quietly. James was not sure what work he was supposed to do, and a cabin did not sound very gracious. But it turned out to be a pleasant, though compact, building containing a bedroom, bathroom and a terrace. James unpacked his modest belongings and put them away. He was not sure what to do now. He looked out of the window at the sea that sailors feared. It certainly looked unpleasant, but he thought the scene could become monotonous. He suspected that he was going to miss Charleston. Before leaving he had bought a copy of Carlyle's *The French Revolution*, so he had something substantial to read. He had not noticed any books in the house. Perhaps Errol Flynn had not been a keen reader.

There was something lurking at the edge of his mind. Reading, printing. It had something to do with crossing into another state. Mr Churchill. Yes. It occurred to James that legal permission should have been sought for Freddie Fairbanks to be taken off to North Carolina. The United States had some kind of funny laws about boundaries. He went to the house to speak to Watney, but couldn't find him. He found Fairbanks, who was talking to Gerard, and put the matter to him. Fairbanks said that if he was out of the range of the Charleston bobbies, that must be a good thing. Gerard did not appear to be interested.

James phoned Churchill and said that he and Fairbanks had come up the coast a bit for a breather. Churchill said he envied them. The point was, James said, Fairbanks was now in a different state, and he didn't want Churchill to think he had run away. Churchill said that of course he trusted James, and it was good of him to call. Was there any chance of James being back in Charleston the following day, because did he know there was an exhibition of printing in the town? James did not know, but he wasn't planning to return so soon. That was a pity, because there was going to be some really early stuff on show. But here was an idea. Why didn't James slide down, take in the exhibition, and, while he was there, enjoy the hospitality of the Churchill household? He'd be welcome to stay the night. James thought, why not? He didn't particularly want to see the exhibition, but it would be something to do, and he was beginning to like Mr Churchill. There was just the question of transport to Charleston. No problem, Churchill said. Take a taxi to Wilmington and get the bus. After he had hung up James remembered that he had meant to tell Churchill that he was saving some old type for him. Still, that would be a pleasant surprise for him tomorrow.

The day passed noticeably slowly. In the afternoon James went for a walk towards the cape. He took his swimming trunks with him but he saw nowhere to bathe for anyone not wishing to end his life in a nasty manner. No doubt there were safe beaches. He would ask one of the staff at the house. He had noticed a pool in the grounds but it was not filled. Errol Flynn wouldn't have stood for that. He had supper with the cameraman and the recordist. Watney, Gerard and the others were not in the dining room. The cameraman thought they may have eaten earlier. The recordist thought they had gone to Wilmington. As James was leaving the house to go to his cabin Merle appeared.

'James, can I stay with you tonight?'

'What about George?'

'Oh, you know.' A pause. 'Invite me for a drink, anyway. I need company.'

'Of course.'

Then she was gone.

The interview was so unexpected and so brief that James was not sure what he had committed himself to. He tried to recall Merle's exact words. She had asked to stay with him, not specifically to sleep with him, but presumably that was what she had meant. He had then asked about Watney. His inquiry could have been light-hearted. James's lips took on a light-hearted look. But it was stupid to pretend. He had reacted rather obviously. What about the husband? 'You know,' Merle had replied. Molly, no doubt.

In the cabin James poured himself a drink and opened the Carlyle. He read a few pages, then decided that his concentration was gone. He switched on the television. There was a programme from a place called Fun City, which was having a beauty contest. The participants in the event, the women, the judges and the audience, did seem to be having fun, in an innocent sense. The ingredients were obviously sexual, the display of

190

undressed women to clothed men, yet the sex had somehow been removed, as life is removed from wheat before it becomes cornflakes. Was that it, eunuchism? That might be taking it too seriously, for there was also something about the event of children at play, copying the mannerisms of their parents.

There was a knock on the door and Merle came in. She glanced at the television and said, 'Getting in the mood, James?'

'Just dipping into American culture.'

'That's what you say. You Europeans.' She poured herself a gin and sat beside James to watch the show.

James found it difficult to think of himself as a European, in the sense that Merle meant, for presumably she was not referring to the frail new Europe of political commerce but the old Europe of tribal wars enacted to the music of Mozart. Anyone from that territory carried with him a trace of decadence, even if he were a printer from Norfolk. It was a little badge of wickedness. James did not find it unpleasant to wear it. He wondered what Merle would expect of him. Perhaps just company: a drink, a little grumble about Watney and then off back to her own room in the house. He would not press her to stay, for there might be a virgin morality in her that would be too late to try to sully now. But if she was here to be screwed, as Pippa might say, he would not discourage her. His own newly found sexuality would be appeased. Watney might be offended but that would be Merle's problem. Even if she told Watney of her infidelity, which she probably would, he would probably say nothing to James. He would consider it bad man-management to do so. Anyway, he, too, probably thought of James as a European, so there must be at least a few corpuscles of Don Juan in his blood. What a continuously useful myth sex was. In his search for the charms of literature, James had spent a holiday reading about the Blooms-bury group and had decided that their endurance beyond their time was because of their determinedly unorthodox sexuality, Strachey's, Virginia Woolf's, Carrington's, all homosexuals, and Garnett's, a heterosexual but still at it into his dotage. And their contemporaries, Norman Douglas, trying pretty well every-thing, and Lawrence and his Lady Chatterley. Of course, they were talented, and some were innovators, but that could be said about many now forgotten writers. It was their aroma of the abnormal that kept them alive, sending relays of new readers to

191

their books, sometimes with disappointing results. Another thought: would feminism, with its dry and hopeless message, be so persistently in the news without its tinge of lesbianism?

'I thought she'd win it,' Merle said.

The winner of the Fun City beauty contest looked about four-teen, although presumably she was older. Her body had only a suggestion of womanly bumps. She told the compère that she was studying hydraulics and that she planned to be a mining engineer. Lolita, if she ever existed, did not live in Fun City.

James poured himself another drink and offered one to Merle. She shook her head. There was now baseball on the television. James could have searched through the abundance of channels for something else, but he switched the set off. It was decision time.

'Are you staying with me, Merle?' He heard the nervousness that had come into his voice.

'I want to. You don't have to make love to me. I'll settle for a cuddle.'

'But I won't.' It was an arch remark, but something had to be said.

Merle's body was not totally unfamiliar to James. He had seen her swim, and she did so with an energy that he admired and knew he could never match. James liked to feel the water cradle him; Merle used it like an exercise mat. Now, in bed, when she came into his arms he immediately sensed the muscle in her shoulders, but she did not grip him tightly. Instead, she waited, like a new dancing partner expecting to be led. Her skin was coarse, at least not smooth. Pippa's had been smooth. He could not now recall the feel of Susie's skin. There was much that he no longer remembered about Susie. He supposed divorce must be like that. A wife turned into an ordinary person, and it was difficult to believe that she was once the object of your desire, your closest friend, the confidante of all the secrets you were prepared to allow out into the light of day. Now you judged her like any other woman, perhaps not even particularly interest-ing. And that, presumably, was how she regarded you.

'What good skin you have, Merle.'

'Not so good now.'

'Very good.'

Something that Pippa had taught James was to talk as he

made love. He did not find the talk came easily, for what was there to say? But he had persevered and he had found that little compliments, even little lies, were acceptable. They would be gently refused, and then reaffirmed and then accepted if only by silence.

He felt her take his penis in her hands. 'You have a good one.'

A slight shadow of annoyance crossed his mind. He did consider he had a good one, but what if Merle was using his own trick of conversation? He declined to cast doubt on his penis. All he would allow himself to say was, 'It's been a good friend.'

'It's very good.'

'Better than George's?' That was a naive thing to say, not at all European. But he had said it, and now he awaited the reply with curiosity. Supposing she said that George was a failure as a lover, that for all his outward masculinity, his drive, his sense of purpose, he was unable to achieve an erection? That would be sad, and yet it would be exciting, enobling James's own sexual gifts. Saying that a man was not much good in bed was a woman's weapon and was often used brutally. Merle could be brutal.

'No, I can't say that, but yours is very good.'

James's climax was strong. There was a lot of semen to be discharged, and Merle's strength seemed also to be present in her vagina. Merle did not have an orgasm, but she said that she had enjoyed making love and now felt relaxed. James slept well. When he awoke Merle was looking at him. He put out his arm and she slid across the bed to him. He had an erection and thought that it would be pleasant to make love again, but he decided not to. He was going to Charleston to see Mr Churchill and the printing exhibition, and it would be sensible to conserve his energy. He thought Merle would find a way of coming to him again, perhaps this evening, or tomorrow, if he decided to stay the night in Charleston.

'I'm going on a little trip today,' he said.

Merle said nothing or she may have said, 'Oh.' Her head was deep under a blanket.

'I may be back today, but probably not until tomorrow. Will you be all right?'

A noise from Merle, no more than an acknowledgement.

'A taxi to Wilmington, then the bus to Charleston. Does that sound right to you?'

Merle's head came up from under the blanket. 'Charleston? What are you talking about, Charleston?'

It was the first time he had seen Merle's face without make-up. He thought that you saw a woman completely naked only when you awoke with her in the morning. She looked older, but more likeable, more vulnerable. She had been crying. James hugged her and kissed her on the forehead.

'What's wrong, Merle?'

'What's wrong? Charleston?' Merle was now sitting up in bed. 'Have you completely flipped?'

The mind may be slow to accept what it does not want to believe, arranging attractive diversions, sometimes simple blockages, but when the truth can no longer be reasonably avoided the normal mind surrenders without fuss. How obvious it seems in retrospect.

The digital clock by the bed said the time was just after eight-thirty on August 6.

'I suppose it went off to the minute?'

'I think I heard the bang.'

'So far away?'

'Perhaps I imagined it. There's no difference.'

James got out of bed and switched on the television. There were half a dozen channels with news programmes, but none of them seemed to have anything about Charleston.

'Turn it off,' Merle said. 'You'll soon be sick of hearing about it. Come back to bed. I want to be comforted.'

James returned to the bed. As soon as he put his arm around Merle she began to cry, deep primeval bayings that she tried to control and only made sound worse. Her tears leaked on to James's chest. He said nothing. There was nothing to say. Conventional words conventionally regarded as being of comfort would sound absurd as Merle was presumably in distress for something beyond everyday comprehension, probably something she did not herself understand. When she was quiet James said, 'Who knew?'

'I thought everyone did.'

'Gerard?'

'I suppose so. Everyone had a duty, George said.'

'That could have meant anything.'

'It doesn't matter now.'

194

'Where are they now?'

'I don't know.'

'In hiding?'

'Don't be stupid. Why would they hide?' Merle was regaining her strength. She got out of bed, put on her bra and knickers and went into the bathroom. When she came out she had put on the armour of the day. James shaved and dressed and they walked up to the house together. Molly was the only person from Watney's entourage that they saw. Merle ignored her. The agony she had felt had not seemingly established a bond with Molly. James nodded and smiled in her direction. He wondered if she knew. Perhaps not, although Molly gave the impression of knowing everything.

The dining room had its normal morning calm. The curtains were as usual partly drawn to keep it cool, and through their division James could see the breakers collapsing as usual off Cape Fear. The young Cuban who served the meals greeted them pleasantly. Had he seen General Watney this morning? No, señor, he had not. James had two fried eggs, turned over, and ham. Merle had cereal and passion fruit juice. They said little to each other over breakfast. James ventured the observation that perhaps nothing had happened, or surely the house would be buzzing by now. Merle merely shrugged. He asked her if she had any thoughts about what they should do and she said, 'If George has given you no instructions, do nothing. He knows what he's doing.' Merle seemed to have become slightly hostile towards him. She excused herself, and James returned to his cabin and switched on the television. An aerial view of Charleston was on the screen, presumably taken from a helicopter. James recognised the long slim peninsula that accommodated the central settlements which had expanded across the Ashley and Cooper Rivers as Charleston had put on weight. James could see no damage because this, a woman's voice explained, was an old film made for the Charleston chamber of commerce. No film of the Charleston explosion was yet available. The voice didn't quite match the story, James thought, and he wondered why the station was not using one of the male apocalyptic voices that American television specialised in. Perhaps the woman was the only commentator available. James tried other channels. One was showing the weather, and two had advertisements. He returned to the first one. A man's face appeared on the screen. He said, 'Thank you, Dorothy.' He summarised what was known of the explosion, which wasn't much. It did appear to have a nuclear origin, and if this were so one of the effects would be to black out communications for a time. Although Charleston was known for its historical associations, he said, there were important defence installations in the area, particularly of a naval character. Polaris missiles were stored there. It was also of interest that an early nuclear merchant ship, the *Savannah*, was kept in a museum in Charleston. He was not, of course, saying that any of these was in any way connected with the explosion.

There was a knock on the door and a black maid came in. She said she was changing the towels. James asked her if she had heard about Charleston.

'I hear about it. I don't know about it. Man up at the house says it's the Ruskies.'

'I'm sure it isn't. Quite definitely, not the Russians.'

'You say one thing, he say another.'

'If it was the Russians we'd be at war, wouldn't we?'

'I guess so, sir. You want an extra towel?'

'I suppose so. Do I?'

The maid laughed. 'You should know if you want an extra towel or not. Anyway, I give you one.'

As she was leaving James said, 'Aren't you worried, if there was a war?'

'Oh yes, sir.' She smiled. 'Have yourself a good day, sir.'

James followed her outside and unfolded a chair on the porch. It was too nice a day to watch television, even if the programme was about the end of the world. Involuntarily, he looked at the sky. It looked blue and harmless. He wondered how long it would take for a radioactive cloud to blow from Charleston. Would it look like an ordinary cloud, propelled along by the wind, or would it be invisible and have something to do with magnetism? Watney had once spoken of a soft bomb that would frighten everyone but would not do any harm, or not much harm. Did James believe him? He believed, or did not disbelieve, everything he had been told or had read about the bomb and felt totally ignorant about it. It was, he reminded himself, like religion: he did not know. Pippa knew and so did Watney. One was wrong, or both were.

James read for an hour the soothing problems of the nineteenth century. Then he heard a car, or cars, crunching up the drive to the house. He put down his book and wondered whether to investigate. The telephone rang.

'Hallo, boy. Coming up to join the party?' Watney sounded in buoyant mood.

Outside the house were three Land-Rovers. Inside, Watney was talking to a group which included Gerard and Fairbanks and several people James had not seen before. Watney was wearing battledress. He detached himself from the group immediately he saw James, shook his hand warmly and thumped him on the shoulder. 'I'm sorry you had to miss the fun, James. Not everyone can see action. Thanks for taking good care of Merle. She didn't give you too much trouble?'

James shook his head. He could see Merle on the other side of the room, and wondered what she had told Watney. Not everything, presumably.

'What's happened, George?'

'I'm keeping all information on a need-to-know basis at the moment, but you've seen the television?'

'The early announcements.'

'It's going well. A couple of Jap flyers have been arrested in Colombia. Christ knows what lucky chance brought them there. Tora, tora, eh, James?'

'But Charleston? What's happened there?'

'Need-to-know, James. For your protection, as well as ours. All I'll say is that we achieved happiness. Come and say hallo to the team. You're among heroes.'

James wanted to talk to only one person, Gerard, and him privately. But for the rest of the morning, and the afternoon, Gerard avoided talking to James, either by staying in a group where he could not be got at or by not being there. James eavesdropped on what conversations he could between members of Watney's team but there were very few references to Charleston, presumably deliberately. The television in the living area of the house was left on all day but as far as James could tell little information was coming out of Charleston. The screen was mainly occupied by experts of one sort or another speculating on what might have happened.

In the evening Gerard came to see James in his cabin.

197

'At last,' James said. 'Is it my bad breath?' He brought out a bottle from the fridge.

Gerard refused a drink. 'I can't stay long. Just an errand, really. Watney wants your passport.'

'What is this, prison?'

'Better let him have it. He's more fidgety than he looks. We are stuck here, anyway.'

'Has he got your passport?'

Gerard made a shrugging gesture which could have been yes or no. 'Don't make things more difficult than they already are, James. I've got to have it. Hand it over.'

James went to a drawer, took his passport from an envelope and gave it to Gerard.

'Thanks.' He turned to the door.

'No concession for a co-operative prisoner?'

Gerard looked at his watch. 'I'll have a quick one with you. Five minutes. But don't try to pump me. I don't know all that much anyway.' He sat down and took a glass from James.

'What I want to know isn't classified.'

'It's done now. No point in talking about it. Let's hope it works all right.'

'Is there an all right?'

'James, the moralising is over. We've had months of that. We, you, let it go ahead. Can't be undone now. Look, James, I don't want to talk about it. I'm quite tired, and I'm slightly nauseated by your act of little Mr Innocent. But I don't want to argue. Everyone has to live with this thing in his own way.'

'I couldn't believe it could happen.'

Gerard finished his drink and got up. He grasped James's hand. 'Sorry if I was rude. You're a good man. Just a bit light on the imagination, that's all.'

'What's going to happen to us?'

'Nothing, probably. Trust Watney. He's quite an organiser. Why don't you come up to the house and join the company for a nightcap? It's better when you're with a few people. Brood and you brood alone.'

'Perhaps I will, later.'

When Gerard had gone James lay on the bed. It was brooding time. He would like a cigarette. How curious it was that cigarettes had been outlawed; perhaps, like dieting, it was a decoy to draw away alarm from other matters. He suddenly felt cross that cigarettes had been defamed, that their contribution to human endurance had been suppressed. He had seen men in battle breath their last smoky breath. No one had said then that smoking was bad for your health, ha, ha. He had read somewhere, at some time, that smoking was only a substitute for the breast. Only! What could be more agreeable than to imagine that you had a firm nipple between your lips. The lips craved the re-enactment of early comforts. He had noticed how many men now drank straight from the bottle. Someone could make a fortune by designing a beer bottle with a teat, although it wouldn't be called that. James opened a drawer in a cabinet at the side of the bed, and found a cigar, a souvenir of the farewell supper at Charleston. It wasn't a cigarette but it was something to hold. He thought of Merle and Molly with cigars between their lips. He had since kissed Merle's lips and much else besides. He supposed he could have had Molly, too. Watney had virtually offered her to him at the establishment in Regent's Park. It would have been interesting to have had sex with an expert, for presumably Molly was an expert in sex as she appeared to be in her other duties. But infidelity with Molly would have been unimaginable, as it would at that time have been with any other woman. He wondered if she had had sex with any other person in Watney's entourage, Gerard perhaps. Gerard's sex needs, if he had any, were unknown to James, but it did not seem improbable that Watney had provided an all-inclusive service over which he had control. Everything that Watney had done could now be seen as leading to Charleston. Gerard was justified in being irritated with James; he had even written a letter to James forecasting much of what had happened. All the clues were there. All that prevented James reading them was a normal sense of disbelief. Gerard had said that he lacked imagination. That was unfair. The judgement he had made was the same as that of any other reasonable person in his place. Partly it had been based on what he had known of Watney, whom he regarded as a rational person. Well, no doubt he was rational, but the rationality had led to an act that James had not foreseen, or could not bring himself to foresee. Now, to say the least, he should try to guess right. He imagined himself in some danger. The dangers were quite unknown, but some at least could be guessed at. There was the danger from the American authorities, whoever they might be. They would seek culprits for whatever had happened in Charleston, and James could well be considered to be one. It was all very well for Gerard, or was it Watney?, to say that the United States had a public government but several private ones. It was the public one that worried James.

There was also the danger from Watney and his colleagues. James, it was clear, was not trusted. He had been told nothing and his passport had been taken away. Watney was friendly enough, very friendly, but James was an outsider, who had not been among the party that had come from England in Watney's private plane. Perhaps the distrust had started there. James had been useful. He had got the publicity for the film on Charleston which had provided a reason for the party to be there, and had got Fairbanks out of trouble. Now his usefulness was presumably over. He might well be considered to be a nuisance. Watney still seemed to regard him as some kind of journalist, absurd as that was. No longer useful, a menace even. Disposed of. The words of melodrama came into James's thoughts. But what could be more melodramatic than what had already happened? Trust Watney, Gerard had said. It did not seem good advice. Gerard might despise his imagination, but it was sufficiently powerful to tell him that he should leave Cape Fear as soon as possible.

He had no passport, but he still had some items that a fugitive in a foreign land might value. He had some money and an air ticket from Orlando. A more thorough captor would have insisted on his surrendering these. Perhaps Watney was too tired to consider them. Perhaps the passport surrender had been meant only as a little warning. But perhaps tomorrow the money and the ticket would be demanded. All the more reason for moving soon. What a lucky chance it was that James had not taken the Concorde and air-taxi. James had told no one about Orlando, chiefly out of shyness. Need-to-know could work for him as well. The problem was how to get away from this isolated place. Once he could get to a town, Wilmington say, there would be plenty of transport. He could simply call a cab to take him there. There was a phone in his room and a directory. The simplest solution was usually the best, or so he had heard some-where. But the consequences of simple failure were alarming, and, at the very least, it seemed likely that Watney's security

200

precautions would include monitoring outgoing phone calls. It occurred to James that not all the people in the house were potential enemies. The staff were presumably neutral. The Cuban waiter or the black maid might have a vehicle that he could borrow; everyone had a car in America. Or he might simply take one of the vehicles parked outside the house, if its ignition key had not been removed. Or a bicycle: he now wished he had tested his endurance by cycling to Folly Beach. Or he might try to hitch, if there was any transport on the road near the house, which was so little used that small plants grew through cracks in the surface.

James quite quickly dismissed all these possibilities. Each relied too much on luck. He decided he would walk. He was not an athlete. He was over sixty and overweight. But neither was he a cripple. As a result of his activity lately, he was probably as fit as he was ever likely to be. He could probably manage a few hours at an easy pace without collapsing, say five hours at two miles an hour. That gave him a range of ten miles, perhaps a bit more. Ten miles away from Watney was a pleasing prospect.

The time now was just after eleven. James considered going to the house, as Gerard had suggested, to have a drink, to allay suspicion that he was going to do a bunk. But that idea had a touch of cleverness that did not appeal to him. Besides, Watney might so charm him that he would decide to stay. James undressed, got into bed and dozed. One of life's favours is that it asks you to manage only one day at a time.

He got up at two, showered and shaved. He dressed in trousers, shirt and pullover and selected his most comfortable shoes. He carried no luggage. He regretted abandoning the Carlyle, but lightness was lightness. He was at the moment under Carlyle's spell. Tolstoy had persuaded him that wars happened because they happened, and that individuals did nothing either to cause them or prevent them. It was a comforting conclusion but it was now being challenged by Carlyle's conviction that great men decided the course of history. James wondered which writer Watney favoured. He would be suspicious of both, one being Russian and the other British, but he would probably lean towards Carlyle the romantic. James put the book in his bedside drawer, and locked it. Whoever went to the trouble of forcing the drawer would be unlikely to throw away the book immediately.

James opened the cabin door quietly and stared out. It was not impossible that a guard had been set. He could see no one. He switched off the light and pulled the door closed. Goodbye.

During his strolls in the grounds of the house James had noticed a path which led downwards in the direction of the Cape Fear River. It was this path that he took. A map would have been precious, but a sense of direction would have to do instead. On reaching the river James hoped that he would find a path or a road which he would follow upstream until he came across a hamlet. It was not an unreasonable plan. This area was part of early America, and there must have been communities along this river since the days of Raleigh.

James found his community, but it was unlikely that Raleigh had been there first. It was not much more than a shack but it advertised food and drink, and bait for anglers. It was closed, but there was fresh rubbish in the dustbin, so presumably it had been open the previous day, and presumably would be open today. James sat at one of the tables in the forecourt and dozed. About an hour later a car arrived driven by a black woman. She greeted her first customer of the day affably but, James thought, with curiosity. That was understandable enough: his journey from the house had been a hard hike. His trousers were dirty and had a tear in them and he had a scratch on his face. His appearance and his English accent needed an explanation. He said that he was touring and his vehicle had broken down. This seemed to be acceptable to the woman. A walker might have aroused suspicion; a disabled driver did not. James ordered bacon and eggs and coffee and while it was being prepared washed his scratch. The woman watched him as he ate his breakfast and asked him where his vehicle was. James said he wasn't sure and pointed in the general direction from where he had come. Was it in bad shape? James said he knew nothing about cars, but there had been a loud bang. The woman said that one of her customers was a mechanic and he usually looked by during the morning. James said the car could wait: the hire company would have to get it picked up. Right now he wanted to get to Wilmington.

'Wilmin'ten?' The woman made it sound as though it was as distant as New York. She mentioned some other places, none of which James had heard of, but which presumably were nearer.

James said any would be very acceptable. Could he get a cab? No problem, the woman said. Her brother ran a cab and would be happy to take him. When would that be? An hour or two, sometime this morning at the latest.

James looked at his watch, although he knew what the time was. It was unlikely that his departure would have been discovered yet. He probably still had a few hours' grace, but time was not on his side.

'Any chance of going sooner, like in the next half hour or so?'

'You in trouble, man?'

'A few difficulties.'

The woman contemplated him for a moment. 'You look respectable. I'll put you on your way.'

During the drive the woman said that she liked the English. 'England goes down, we all go down.' James asked her if she had many English visitors. She said he was the first Englishman she had ever talked to. James thought that her instinct to like the English was no more illogical than Watney's to dislike them.

'What do I owe you?' he said before he got out of the car.

'Nothing, I guess. Call it southern hospitality. Drop me a postcard from England.'

'I must give you something.' In his wallet he found a five pound note. 'How about a souvenir?'

'Thank you, man.' She opened out the note. It was crisp. James had got it from a bank vending machine.

'A clean place, England.'

'Parts of it.'

The town the woman had brought him to was not large but it had shops and a hotel. James was tempted to book into the hotel and travel on the following day but decided that the woman who had been his benefactor could be an agent of disaster if her story of the Englishman in trouble spread quickly. Coincidence was neutral. He bought trousers, a shirt and a hold-all, and changed in the wash-room of the bus station. He was now returned to the fold of the conventional tourist, in clean clothes and with luggage. The news-stand displayed a number of papers, all of which had large headlines about Charleston, somehow shouting their inadequacy to proclaim the degree of the catastrophe. The papers seemed to be selling briskly. There was a pleasure in learning of others' misfortunes. He did not buy one. Merle had said he would get sick of the subject, and he was already. He bought a copy of *The Economist*. He liked its cheerful mottos. He took the next bus out of the station because it was going south and changed twice before he got to Orlando. Being without a passport proved to be a snag rather than a problem. He told the passport official simply that he had lost it. The official looked at James's driving licence, consulted his superior, and passed him through. It was, he said, the guys who were trying to get in that they worried about.

On the plane James experienced the sense of pleasure that he always felt when coming home, from holidays in Greece and Morocco, with Susie, to the ordinary north, where the sun was merely warm and speech was wholly intelligible, and where there were letters waiting and there was grass to be mown. There was more than that, naturally, in view of his experiences. He seemed to have been away a long time, not, of course, as long as he had been away during his first time abroad, in the war. But returning home now was a little like it had been then, a bit like that.

I apologise to Charleston for bombing it, even in the imagination. It seems a decent enough town and no one would wish it other than continued prosperity. Perhaps 'apologise' is not the correct word, for it may imply that an error has inadvertently been made by the author for which he is now seeking indulgence. This would not be true. Had I changed my mind there would have been a simple remedy, for story-tellers can, and often do, rewrite the course of events before they are sealed in publication. I would not wish to change the setting of the story.

It might be thought that it would be simple enough to give Charleston an imaginary name, or to forget Charleston and invent a town which would be unrecognisable as a real place and which, at the author's whim, could be given features that would have some cunning parallel to Hiroshima. But if Charleston remained anonymous, should not, in fairness, Hiroshima be allowed anonymity also? Hiroshima is now a thriving industrial city, concerned, like the rest of Japan, with productivity, labour relations and with persuading the world that the luxuries it produces are necessities. How weary its civil leaders must be that it continues to be regarded as a grave-marker. Japan itself might equally make an argument for its right to privacy, as might the United States, Russia or Britain. How dare you use our name, particularly in a discourteous sense, without applying for permission, which would, in any case, never be given?

Charleston, a real city, is central to the story. Charleston and Wilmington are the two towns in North America which seem to have some resemblance to Hiroshima. Wilmington is a little nearer in latitude but Charleston is nearer in character. So Charleston was chosen. The choice of Hiroshima as the recipient of the first atom bomb in 1945 was based on reasons no less arbitrary.